COLDIRON

By F. M. Parker

COLDIRON
NIGHTHAWK
SKINNER

COLDIRON

F. M. Parker

DOUBLEDAY & COMPANY, INC.

GARDEN CITY, NEW YORK

1984

W

219835

Library of Congress Cataloging in Publication Data
Parker, F. M.
    Coldiron.
    I. Title
PS3566.A678C6   1984   813'.54
        ISBN: 0-385-19168-5
Library of Congress Catalog Card Number 83–20554

COLDIRON

The Making of the Land
A Prologue

The land was vast with tall mountains, deep valleys and swiftly flowing streams. It had been formed in some ancient, primeval time when an unimaginably powerful force had lifted up the bottom of an ocean, arching the sedimentary rock layers miles into the sky. The topmost craggy peaks were made of stone, composed of the shells and bones of animals that could only live in deep salty brine.

The high crowns of the mountains brushed the heavens, their jagged spires piercing the clouds that rushed by, ripping open their stomachs to let the rain and snow pour down. On the higher elevations it was very cold and the snow never fully melted from one year to the next, accumulating into small glaciers. To slip slowly, like frigid tears, down the face of the mountain.

Colder still the world became and glaciers were birthed even on the low plains. Over tens of thousands of years, they grew together, merging into one colossal glacier over a mile thick and so broad as to cover more than half the continent. The white mantle of ice, its solid water crystals turned plastic by its own immeasurable crushing tons, flowed outward slow and cold to smother the land, depressing the crust of the earth into deep, wide basins.

During millions of years, the glaciers advanced and retreated again and again. In the harsh, frozen part of the cycle, the land was buried under an unbelievably large expanse of ice. Wet, warm pluvial times, the interglacial periods, melted the ice, creating deep lakes and violent torrents that sped off to the sea, scouring the mountains and plains that lay in their path.

Only great animals could survive in such a rugged climate. The giant wide-horned bison, the woolly mammoth and the huge beaver Castoridae, eight feet long with twelve-inch incisors, strode upon the land. They were mighty animals, perfectly adapted to the alternating cold and pluvial eras, and thrived. Just one enemy, the saber-toothed tiger, could pull them down. The vulture condor matched the scale of the other beasts, gliding down on twelve-foot wings to clean up the scraps after the kill.

Then a change occurred in the climate, the continental glacier retreated and the deluge came, but the next phase of the cycle did not arrive. Instead the land grew drier and drier.

The gigantic bison died, so too did the mammoth, saber tooth and the scavenger condor. However, in the genes of the beaver there existed the potential for change—and each generation of the Castoridae grew smaller, adapting to the lessening feed, becoming a perfectly miniaturized replica of his ancestor, but weighing forty pounds or less.

In this new time the beaver had a different foe. A brown-skinned man came into the mountains and began to stalk the animal's lakes and lodges. He was skilled and killed some of the soft-furred animals. With his limited tools the brown man was no threat to the existence of the Castoridae.

The hundreds of audacious white men that invaded the terrain of the beaver in the early 1800s were a different matter. They were hard men and brought with them strangely shaped steel capture instruments. Each mountain man, using four to six of these traps, could and did take all the beaver from long reaches of tumbling streams, leaving behind deserted lodges and decaying dams.

In 1825 there were approximately one hundred and twenty-five trappers in the south end of the Rocky Mountains. That year one man sold seven hundred pelts for five thousand dollars at the rendezvous on the Green River in Utah. The trapping year 1832–33 saw this soft gold selling for six dollars a pound. The price dropped precipitously to three dollars and fifty cents in 1834. The value continued to gradually decline over the next ten years, bringing one dollar a pound and making trapping uneconomical about 1845.

The white trapper came into the mountain country, carried out his binge of beaver killing and vanished, all in less than twenty-five years.

BOOK I
THE TRAPPER'S
WINTER WOMAN

CHAPTER 1

October, the Moon of
the Changing Season, 1843

The buckskin-clad man rode a strong black horse and led two heavily loaded pack mules across the lower slopes of the tall mountain. He carried a long-barreled .50 caliber Hawken rifle ready in his hands. He moved warily through the ponderosa pine forest, avoiding every clearing, for he was intruding into the land of the fierce Mountain Ute.

Luke Coldiron pulled his animals to a halt as the top limbs of the trees began to tremble to the first faint puffs of the day wind. He turned his head from side to side, his keen ears sifting the sounds on the slow breeze for danger. His alert eyes probed out from beneath the broad brim of his hat and pierced deeply into the pine woods that surrounded him.

He twisted in the saddle and cast a glance backward across the wide flank of the mountain, intently scrutinizing the route he had just climbed up over. There was no sign of an enemy and he relaxed a notch and breathed deeply of the resiny smell of the pine needles and concs. The spicy odor was a welcome change after the endless miles of dry grassland that lay behind him.

Through an opening in the woods, he scanned down over a day's ride of rolling foothills. Beyond that his gaze ranged out another fifty miles upon the great plains, a vast land, hazy with distance and pressed down by the sapphire-blue bowl of the sky. There his partner, George Tarpenning, had parted from him to hunt for the winter camping grounds of the Ute in the valley of the Arkansas River. Tarpenning was a daring man and a fearless fighter who intended to stalk the very teepees of the Ute braves and take a valuable prize from them.

Luke glanced up at the topmost rocky crest of the mountain, looming above him two miles high and already bearing a white frosting of snow from an early winter storm. He knew there were dozens more peaks just like it in a string north and south. They made the great mountain range the Mexicans called the Sangre de Cristo.

He turned back to his original course to the west and rode guardedly ahead. The horse and mules made no noise on the thick carpet of needles beneath the evergreens. Only a gray squirrel on a high limb noted the silent passing of the young rider.

He came to a steep bluff and stopped in the edge of the timber. After tying his animals securely to a tree, he crept up to the lip of the basin, crawling the last few feet through knee-high grass. He parted the slender reeds slightly and looked down into a valley some quarter mile wide and stretching both left and right for many miles.

The past spring, he and his partner had discovered the stream, filled with scores of beaver lodges, as they had been packing out their catch of fur, heading for Independence, Missouri, to make a sale. Greatly surprised at the virgin find, for few streams now existed that had not been trapped by the widely roaming mountain men, they had immediately laid plans to return and set their traps in the beaver-rich water.

Luke examined the flat land of the valley bottom spread at an elevation some two-hundred feet below him. Dozens of beaver ponds, glinting like a chain of silver coins under the rays of the morning sun, stretched along the meanders of the creek. Small dark spots on the surface of the tiny lakes marked the location of the numerous beaver lodges.

Many cottonwoods, some truly giants, and dense patches of willows lined the bed of the creek. Back from the stream, the valley bottom was dominated by meadows, the grass now dead and brown. Long curving fingers of dark evergreens cut the meadowland into a hundred pieces, ringing each with a wall of tall trunks.

To the right, the valley gradually grew very narrow as it climbed up between the forested shoulders of the mountain. A sprinkling of small groves of aspen, having already felt the frosty hand of the coming winter, shined like nuggets of new gold among the pine. The mountain maple growing at the base of some rock outcrops were brilliant patches of purplish red.

The lower, more gentle slopes of the mountain lay to the left. In that direction the valley gradually widened as it ran off to the far south. Beaver ponds were visible as far as Luke could see.

A band of fifteen or so elk came out of the timber on the same side of the stream as the man and started across the floor of the basin. Two gray wolves also left the cover of the forest and trailed along a couple hundred yards behind the elk.

A cow in the rear stopped and looked in the direction of the large predators. The wolves slowed, fastened their malevolent, meat-hungry eyes on her and came on at a walk. As they drew close, she wheeled nervously, and with her head frequently turning back to watch behind, trotted to catch up with the rest of the herd.

The elk climbed the bluff of the far side of the valley and entered the deep forest again. The wolves still followed.

Luke studied the meadows and timber. Had the Ute warriors already taken their families and horses and migrated down from the cold highlands to the warmer elevations of the plains? Or, since the autumn had been mild, might some of them still be camped on this stream?

Even as he cogitated, he spotted a man on horseback emerge from a clump of timber, a long rifle shot to the north. He traced the rider's progress along the edge of the valley, wondering if another trapper had arrived before him and staked first claim to the beaver in the stream.

The rider came nearer, his route coming in close to the bluff and then along its base. Luke made out an Indian on a good gray pony. Now and then, bright flashes of sunlight reflected from the iron head of the long lance he carried. A strung bow hung across one shoulder and a battle shield was tied to the back of the horse behind him.

Luke caressed the walnut stock of his rifle. One Indian could mean many more were near. His hand moved to briefly brush the butt of the pistol in his belt.

From the top of the bluff, he watched the warrior ride steadily forward. A large black feather tied in the man's hair fluttered alongside his head as the wind caught it. The Indian brushed it away from his ear with a sweep of his hand.

Luke noted the direct, purposeful course of the horseman. He hoped that meant the Indian had a destination to reach far from this valley.

The rider was now straight below Luke. At some unseen signal from his master, the pony came to an abrupt halt. The Indian's view swept the meadows, then up to the top of the bluff. The quick eyes in the dark-copper face evaluated the border of the timber and the grassy knoll where Luke lay hidden. Slow, deep breaths of air were pulled in as if he were testing for scent.

Luke saw the tightness in the man, his striving to sense things hostile. Luke did not move, staring tensely down through the grass. He felt the wind blowing up the slope of the mountain. The Indian could not catch his odor, if that was what he was trying to do.

One minute passed, two, half a dozen. Mustang and brave stood perfectly motionless, studying the top of the hill. The man twisted to range his sight behind and out across the valley.

The Ute turned back to throw one last, short look up at the ridge above him. Then he spoke to the mustang and the animal stepped forward in a swift walking pace.

Luke had seen countless numbers of horses and knew the pony below was an outstanding animal. Better than the one he owned, he judged. For a moment he considered killing the Indian for his mount. But he rejected the thought. He had come to trap beaver, not to fight.

The Ute drew rapidly away. The mounted figure grew very small with distance, then vanished altogether.

Nothing further caused Luke alarm. He retrieved his animals and guided them down the steep hill onto the floor of the valley. Heading upstream, he began to search for the rendezvous point he and Tarpenning had agreed upon.

In less than a mile, he reached his destination, a sandstone ledge with a large cave under it. Dismounting, he walked into the shadows beneath the arching rib of strong brown rock.

It was as he remembered, a high-ceilinged hollow the size of a large room. With a measuring eye, he surveyed the dimensions of the sheltered zone. He calculated one day's work from sunrise to sunset would be required to cut logs and wall in the open front and level out the dirt for a floor.

Coldiron remounted and continued north. Not knowing but what there might be other Indians in the valley, he took the pack mules with him to keep them safe.

The creek climbed steadily, the steep borders of the valley gradually crowding in. As Luke progressed, he studied the ground closely for signs of man or horse and he made note of the number of beaver lodges.

Finally, high on the side of the mountain, the terrain became too rough and rocky for the beasts to keep their footing. He led them up out of the narrow ravine the stream now splashed through and headed down along the west side of the basin.

He found the trail of the Indian. It came from the west and crossed the basin straight as a beeline. The man was merely passing through.

Later, opposite the sandstone outcrop, he halted to examine the cave from the far side of the valley. The noonday sun shined directly upon the wall of his new home. Luke was pleased. It would be a warm, snug bivouac even when the arctic winds and snow struck. The best he ever had for a winter's trapping.

He kicked his horse onward. Ten miles farther south and two thousand feet lower, the creek had grown substantially larger, having picked up the flow of several streams. Reasonably certain he was alone, he rode down into the bottom and hurried toward the sandstone cave.

Two deer, a fat dry doe and an old buck with a massive spread of antlers, spooked up from a clump of willows. They stood near each other, watching him, their nostrils quivering and sucking at the gentle breeze for scent.

Luke jerked his rifle up and shot the doe. In the complete stillness of the wild land, the crash of the gun rang loudly, rushing away to die in a series of echoes against the far ramparts of the mountain. The startled buck sprang away from the doe, thrashing in death throes on the ground, and hurtled from the place of slaughter in great frightened bounds.

Luke reloaded swiftly, pouring a measure of powder down the barrel, pressing the wad and lead ball into place, ramming it down with one firm tamp of the hickory rod. He flipped off the spent percussion cap and slipped a fresh one over the nipple. Hurry, always be prepared for another shot.

He field dressed the deer, glad he had passed up the tough flesh of the buck. Near the heart, he found the round lead ball, misshapen from hitting a rib. He dropped it into a pocket for later remelting and pouring.

The mule with the lightest load was led up and the deer carcass tied across the packs. The beast groaned at the added burden. The man laughed, mounted his horse and dragged the complaining mule after him.

Darkness caught him before the cave was reached and he felt his way the last mile through the gloom. A cold wind moaned down from the mountain as he unpacked the mules and unsaddled the horse. There would be ice on the creek in the morning.

All the animals were hobbled with leather straps around their front legs and released to graze on the abundant grass. The packs were carried inside and piled near the rear of the cave. Flint and steel were struck to drop a spark onto a piece of punk screwed into a nest of fine grass. He gently blew on it. A tendril of smoke rose, a flame came to life. Soon the liver of the deer sizzled in a frypan over a hot cooking fire.

While waiting for the meat to cook, Luke dug a handful of dried apples from a stock of them in one of the packs. Then with his moccasined feet extended to the fire and his back leaning against the pile of supplies, he chewed on the tasty slices of sweet fruit.

He thought of Tarpenning, some two long days' ride away to the east on the upper reaches of the Arkansas River. Was he having success in accomplishing his share of the preparation for the coming winter? The man had not failed once in the four years they had trapped together.

The meat finished cooking. Luke lifted the pan from the fire and ate the tender flesh with high relish.

He rested, luxuriating in the feel of a full stomach and the sound of the crackling flames. The fire died to a bed of embers. Now and then the coals glowed red through their covering of ashes as the wind gusted into the cave and fanned them.

Luke stirred himself, found his buffalo sleeping robe and spread it near the fire. He laid his weapons near his hand and pulled the warm fur over him. Sleep came immediately.

In the grayness of the early dawn, the crescent of the sinking moon, white as a grizzly bear's tooth, hung low on the western horizon. The twilight was disturbed by the soft thump of elk-hide moccasins striking the ground, the swish of grass upon buckskin leggings and the sigh of the wind.

The three young Ute warriors ran effortlessly, their strides long and hearts beating slow and strong. A flat plain surrounded them and stretched on all sides mile upon mile. The north wind cooled them and tossed the long prairie grass into thousands of waves, crests pursuing troughs as though they were part of the surface of a great sea.

Echohawk led the way. Tall Elk followed second in line. Though he was the oldest and strongest, he was not ashamed to let his young comrade guide. Echohawk would be chief one day and everyone in the clan knew he was the very best in finding the trail to unknown places, or to lead the way when the face of the sun could not be seen through the storm.

Thunder That Rolls trailed last. He was the youngest. Only sixteen winters had passed over his head.

It was the beginning of the third day since they had left their tribe's winter camp on the bank of the Arkansas River. Already they had run more than a hundred and twenty miles. Each evening they had traveled late into the dusk, until all light had leaked away to the sky, leaving only darkness. Then rolled into sleeping robes of finely tanned buffalo hides, they slept. The first hint of day found them up and running again.

Ten days before, the Ute tribe had come down from the mountains where the nights were freezing rimes of ice on the edges of the creeks. The three braves had halted long enough to help the other men kill the buffalo and elk and store away a supply of meat for the long winter soon to come. Then carrying short, powerful hunting bows, a quiver of arrows and steel-bladed knives, they left for the flat eastern plains. They searched for their enemies, the Arapaho.

It was bad to live in a time of few battles, thought Echohawk as he set the pace. Neither he nor his two comrades had yet faced enemies in combat. However, this raid on the Arapaho to steal ponies would provide them the opportunity to prove their bravery against a worthy foe.

The land was unknown to Echohawk. Yet that bothered him not at all. The older men of the tribe had given the direction and described the wintering places of the Arapaho. They called it the Buffalo Hills because the great beast took shelter in the valley there, protected from the frigid snowy storms that swept down from the north.

An hour later in the light from the yellow orb of the rising sun, a series of low broken hills took form. Wanting to come into the hills upwind, Echohawk veered off to the southeast for two miles or so. Then he angled back to the north. Almost immediately after turning, he caught a whiff of smoke on the wind. He broke stride and stopped. His companions stopped beside him.

"We are close," said Echohawk, facing his friends. "Do you smell the fires of the Arapaho?"

They both nodded solemnly, realizing soon the courage of all would be tested.

Tall Elk spoke, sliding his hand flat and slowly toward the source of the odor. "We will go in silently as the hunting owl."

"Let us do it while the morning is still young and all the Arapaho are in their camp," said Echohawk.

Using the low swales between the hills so as to not become skylined, the Utes carefully approached the camp still hidden somewhere among the short hills. They knew if they should be so unfortunate or so careless as to be discovered, their enemies on their swift ponies could easily ride them down. To be caught would mean death.

In a gully, the Utes happened upon a small clump of bushes and hid their bulky sleeping robes there. They continued onward, moving slowly and slinking close to the ground. The odor of smoke on the wind was very strong now. The camp of their foes must be very near. They dropped down to crawl up the slope of the next small hill.

Reaching the top, they cautiously parted the thick grass and peered over. An Arapaho village containing a few score of teepees lay in the bottom of the valley. A small stream wound through the middle of the camp. Smoke from morning, warming fires rose up in wavery columns.

"We have found them," said Echohawk.

"You have led us straight and true as the wild duck flies," responded Thunder That Rolls and grinned.

"Look out there," said Tall Elk, pointing to another village of lodges clustered beside the creek a mile east. "The Arapaho are many."

"We do not fear them," said Echohawk. He swept his hand to indicate much of the terrain spread before them. "See the mustangs on the hillside. The Arapaho warriors must be rich to have so many. That band there," he nodded his head at a herd on the valley floor directly below them, "contains enough mustangs that if we owned them, we could all buy wives."

Thunder That Rolls grinned in agreement. "They are excellent ponies. See that one of many colors. Ah! I would give much to own him."

"They are very close to the camp," cautioned Tall Elk. "It will be very difficult to steal them from a place where many Arapaho eyes can see us."

Echohawk scanned the valley. "The mustangs were brought in close to the teepees so they could be protected during the night. But there the grass is mostly eaten away. The mustangs must now go beyond the ridge to find new grass. We will wait."

Echohawk and his two compatriots rested silently in the dense grass on the crest of the hill. Below them the village continued to come to life. Children began to come outside as the sun warmed. Their sharp young voices in play floated up to the enemies on the hilltop. The smoke from the teepees increased in number, curling up blue-gray. As it drifted past the Utes, the aroma of cooking meat teased them.

Here and there in the village, a pony was tied near a lodge. They stood and stared anxiously after the free mustangs as they ambled away, picking at the sparse grass. Gradually the horse herds dispersed and moved out of sight of the camp.

An Arapaho warrior came out into the open. He stretched leisurely and looked in the direction the ponies had gone. Taking a long lance from where it leaned near the entrance, he swung astride his mount and trotted it up to a peak of the hill, one ridge distant from where the three Utes lay hidden.

"A guard," said Tall Elk. "That will make it more dangerous. If there is only one, we still should be able to take several mustangs. But we will have to kill him so no alarm can be given until we are far away."

"He is in a very open place," said Echohawk. "Even halfway awake, he will still see us before we can get close."

"We will wait some more," responded Tall Elk.

The sun rose up the sky for the distance of one finger. A hunting hawk, catching the updrafts where the wind was shunted skyward by the flanks of the hills, sailed noiselessly toward the Utes. Spotting the forms of the humans in the grass, he changed course, swerving abruptly aside.

Echohawk hastily looked to see if the guard had noticed the bird's sudden change of direction. The Arapaho was staring down at the village. The Ute followed the man's line of sight and saw a skirted figure climbing the hill toward the lookout.

"Soon his attention will be on other things," whispered Echohawk and nodded at the woman. His voice hardened. "When they begin to talk, we will kill him."

She approached the man and handed him something. They spoke together for a moment and he began to eat.

"Now we take the horses," said Echohawk.

CHAPTER 2

The Utes crept back from the ridge of the high ground. Without once showing themselves, they crossed the swale to the adjoining hill and wormed their way to within a few yards of the Arapaho. The man was very young, yet with a sturdy frame. The female was small of stature, slender-limbed and barely a woman.

The guard had seen nothing, so engrossed was he in the girl. His mustang had neither heard nor scented the wary enemies. However, reacting from the learned experience of countless generations of wild ancestors, the pony stopped feeding and raised his head to search about himself for any menace. He saw the strange forms, partially hidden in the grass, things that had not been there a moment before. With alarm he stiffened and pricked his ears directly toward the Utes.

The lookout was holding the hand of the girl and speaking softly to her. The pony's flag of alarm went unnoticed.

Echohawk made a signal for Tall Elk to help him kill the man and for
Thunder That Rolls to quiet the woman. He nocked an arrow in preparation to shoot.

In one fluid motion Echohawk rose from cover, pulled the stout bow
to full draw and released the shaft. The flint-tipped missile leaped across
the short distance and drove completely through the sentry from back to
front.

With long knives drawn and poised, the Utes sprang to their feet and
charged upon their intended victims. The pony bolted away down the
hill as the three hurtled past. The Arapaho brave, spouting blood from
his wound, struggled erect. Vainly he tried to swing his lance to impale
the nearest attacker. But the Utes were in too close. Echohawk brushed
the weapon aside and Tall Elk grappled with the man, crushing him to
the ground.

Tall Elk pinned the guard's arms and Echohawk plunged his knife
into the center of the already bloody chest. Tall Elk continued to hold
the stricken Arapaho until he ceased struggling and went limp, then laid
him down gently.

"He was very strong to withstand the arrow and still fight us," said
Echohawk, breathing hard from the excitement and danger of the contest.

"Yes," agreed Tall Elk, "but he was careless and let a woman blind
him." He raised his knife and brought it butt first to strike the center of
the Arapaho's forehead with a light thump. "First coup," declared Tall
Elk, his voice strong so the other warriors could hear him and the spirits
of his ancestors could also hear and know he was worthy of them.

Echohawk nodded, accepting his comrade's claim. "More glory would
have been had for only one of us to do the deed."

The voice of Thunder That Rolls called from behind them. "Come
look at her." His voice had a strange, awed tone.

They swung their view to Thunder That Rolls, sitting astraddle the
woman. He held her mouth shut with a hard hand and was gazing
intently down into her face.

They moved quickly up beside Thunder That Rolls. Echohawk made
the sign language for the woman not to cry out. Thunder That Rolls,
tensed to again muffle any sound, slowly removed his hand.

As the full face of the female became visible, Echohawk felt his breath
quicken and his heart begin to pound against the cage of his chest. He
froze there, overwhelmed by the unbelievable loveliness of the Arapaho
girl. "O Great Spirit, do not tease a young brave with such beauty," he
whispered.

Tall Elk reached out a hand and ran his fingertips along the smooth, delicate curve of her chin. He traced the outline of the perfect lips. She watched them intently, her black eyes trying to hide her fear.

"Is she a full woman?" asked Echohawk in a husky voice.

With a swift movement, Tall Elk reached out and ripped the front of the girl's buckskin dress open to expose her from throat to waist. "Yes, she is a woman," he said and his muscular hand began to caress one of the firm round mounds of her breast.

Echohawk felt the heat rise in his veins and he grew angry at Tall Elk for fondling her. "I must own her," exclaimed Echohawk in a rapid voice, afraid one of the others would speak first. He looked searchingly into the faces of his comrades.

Neither responded, continuing to hunker there on the ground and stare at the eye-filling handsomeness of the young woman. Tall Elk moved his sight to the dead Arapaho and then down at the Indian village. "Because she is so fair that a man's body grows hot, a brave warrior lies dead and we remain on the hilltop in full view of our enemies —like good friends, we should all take our pleasure with her. Then tie her so she can make no sound, and leave quickly with many ponies."

"No," cried Echohawk. "I will take her back to our people and make her my wife."

"Some women are too beautiful," cautioned Tall Elk. "They bring much bad fortune among their men. She is one of those."

"I do not believe that," said Echohawk and looked at Thunder That Rolls. "I must have her. What say you? Will you give up your claim on her?"

Thunder That Rolls studied his friend's stricken face, seeing the great yearning there. He made the sign for gift giving. "You have what is mine," he said in a husky voice.

Tall Elk rose to his full height. "You make a very big mistake, Echohawk. A man needs a woman that is pretty enough that he wants to return to his teepee, but not so beautiful other men will be envious. I will say no more. Let us hurry away from this place." He trotted off down the slope on the opposite side of the hill from the village and toward a large herd of horses.

The other two men followed, Echohawk pulling the girl along by the arm. They quickly selected six of the best mustangs, two for each of them. A pony apiece was haltered by throwing a loop of rawhide around the lower jaw halfway back in the mouth and then passing the long ends up across the neck.

Echohawk lifted the girl astride his second animal. With swift threatening motions of his hands, he told her not to try to escape or he would kill her.

Mounted and leading their second ponies, the Utes hastily retrieved their sleeping robes. At a ground-eating gallop, the cavalcade drew hurriedly away from the jeopardy of the Arapaho encampment.

With the first golden rays of the morning sun streaming into the valley, Luke began to swing his ax in a grove of cottonwoods near the creek. The powerful strokes rang loudly over the basin and frightened a flock of ducks on the nearest pond, causing them to swirl up, beating the air with strong wings and quacking loudly. He ceased chopping and watched the noisy calling birds until he could no longer hear them and their angular flight pattern had faded to only a black smear on the blue sky.

Enemy ears could also hear his work he knew. He began to labor again, always keeping his weapons within easy reach.

By noon Luke had cut and dragged, with one of the mules, enough logs to the cave to wall up the front. He began to shape the lengths of timber with skillful blows. The sharp blade of the ax sprang chips as large as his hand from deep, precise notches near the ends of the logs.

Inside the drip line, where the water that fell from the roof of the cave struck the ground, he started to lay the timbers. He muscled up the sweet-smelling cottonwoods and laid one notched end into another. Here and there he was forced to slice off a hump of wood or flatten a side so the round boles of the lengths could rest snugly against the next one below.

Where the logs touched the rock walls, he beveled the ends to match the contour of the stone and pressed the wood in to fit tightly. Mud, mixed with grass to furnish strength to the mixture, was plastered in all cracks to create a windproof outer wall.

In all previous winters he and his partner had spent the season in a hut constructed of deer hides, heavily smoked to make them waterproof and stretched over long willow poles. Now as he worked he began to look forward to the completion of this new type of shelter in the cave and to spending the first night in it.

The sandy soil inside the enclosure was scraped level and stamped down firmly to make a floor. Two rectangles of logs were notched together and filled with a foot-thick mat of fresh meadow grass. Luke tossed his buffalo sleeping robe on the bed nearest the entrance.

The weather was still relatively warm and he made no effort to close the narrow opening that was the door. In the pack was a thick piece of hide that would do as a door when the need came.

The sun was a red ball resting in the tops of the pine trees on the far side of the valley when Luke completed his labor. He backed away a few yards and examined his handiwork under the rock ledge, a half cabin–half cave. He was pleased.

He sliced a thick steak from the carcass of the deer and placed it over a low fire to simmer slowly. Then taking up his rifle, he walked along the bluff until he could see the trail his partner should use when he arrived in the valley. The route down the slope from the woods lay empty. Tarpenning would come when he came. Luke returned to his new home.

He left early the next morning mounted on one of the horses and carrying his sack of a dozen steel traps and a pouch of beaver scent. He rode the horse to the very highest beaver dam. Then hanging two traps around his neck by their chains, he dismounted and waded into the ice-fringed water behind the beaver dam.

The high valley would be trapped first before the winter froze a thick slab of ice over the water of the creek. As he caught all the beaver out of a pond, the trapping would gradually move downstream to warmer elevations. During January, The Moon of the Strong Cold, and perhaps for a longer period, it would not be possible to trap the water animals at all because of the ice. That did not bother him, for during that time he would take mink, martin and fox on the land.

In February, The Moon When the Snow Begins to Melt, the taking of the beaver could begin again. The trapping would start in the lowest reaches of the creek and work upstream as the ice broke up.

Luke made his first set under the water directly in front of the beaver slide, the path used by the animals of the pond to drag their winter food supply of cottonwood and willow branches near to the lodge and there to sink it below the deepest ice. The chain of the trap was securely fastened to a small sapling on the bank.

A second trap was set at the edge of the dam, at the point where the animals passed from deep to shoal water. A stick with a drop of luring scent, the sweetish musk secretion from the scrotum of a male beaver, was stuck into the creek bottom. The scented end of the stick extended from the water and hung over the trap. Any beaver in the pond would come to investigate the male odor.

With a length of string, Luke tied a small float stick to the trap to help in locating it in the event a beaver dragged it into deep water.

He set the remaining traps in likely places as he waded downstream from one beaver dam to the next. Not once did Luke leave the water to tread the dry land, for that spot would most likely be avoided by the suspicious beaver for days.

He returned to his horse and donned dry, warm moccasins. Stepping upon his mount, he headed for camp. On the way, an easy shot at an elk was passed up. The hunt to lay in a store of meat would not start until the first snow fell in the basin. Luke believed that would be soon, for the wind was damp and cold and the clouds were building on top of the mountain.

At a quarter mile distance from the cave, he turned aside and guardedly circled around it. There was no sign of man or horse. Yet his rifle was held at the ready as he rode slowly and cautiously in.

The camp was undisturbed and he began to cook the first food of the day. He stepped outside to glance along the trail to the east. It lay deserted.

Large fleecy snowflakes began to fall out of the clouds scurrying in from the northwest. He went back inside his shelter and found the piece of hide that would be used for the door.

The Ute camp, more than a hundred lodges strong, rested in a broad bend on the east side of the Arkansas River. The teepees were dark gray, stained by the smoke of many fires. Scores of children and dogs romped and played among the pyramids of skin.

There was a constant flow of women to and from the dense stand of trees that bordered the river. On each return trip, they toiled up the slope, packing heavy loads of wood in leather straps on their backs. Their steps were nervous, hurried as if some primeval instinct warned them there would soon be much need of the fuel to hold back the frigid cold.

George Tarpenning had hidden his horse in a narrow wash a mile from the village. Before daybreak arrived he was already in hiding in the trees near the edge of the river. He had lain and watched the sun, squashed and blood red, float up from the eastern horizon. He shrugged off the thought that many men believed a red sunrise was a bad omen.

As each woman entered the woods and began noisily to break the dead and down timber into lengths she could carry, Tarpenning slipped near and from concealment measured the comeliness of her dusky face and figure. So far none of the females had satisfied his demanding eye.

Shortly after noon, black clouds began to build in the northwest. Within an hour the temperature started to drop rapidly and the wind commenced to whip the limbs of the trees. Tarpenning smelled the snow on the air.

The Indian women also sensed the imminent arrival of the storm and called out to the children. Soon every child big enough to walk was coming into the woods for fuel. The children played at the work and the women scolded them in shrill voices for being so slow. It seemed to do little good.

Snow began to fall, large damp flakes slanting down on the stiff wind. From the east, a party of ten hunters ghosted in through the snow. Their ponies were heavily laden with huge chunks of some beast—buffalo, Tarpenning judged.

The millions of snowflakes obscured Tarpenning's view beyond a couple hundred yards. He retreated back through the woods toward his horse. Under the cover of the storm, he would bring his mount up very close. Then when he took the woman, he could withdraw on his swift pony.

He found the arroyo, a narrow gash in the earth, and dropped down into the bottom. The gulch was less than a dozen feet wide with vertical rock walls more than head high. Trailing his rifle, Tarpenning broke into an easy trot, climbing up and away from the river.

Snow was accumulating quickly, nearly an inch of white already blanketing the ground. The wind had strengthened, becoming colder, and the flakes, which had been large at the beginning of the storm, were now small and icy. Vision was reduced to less than the range of a moderate rifle shot.

He came upon his horse unawares. The snow-plastered animal snorted and tried to spook away at his unexpected appearance.

Tarpenning caught the leather lead that held the pony tied to a bush and, pulling the animal in close to him, gentled it down by stroking the long head and talking softly.

So he would not be seen from the plain above, he walked and led the horse down the grade of the stream course. The mouth of the draw emptied out upon the river a quarter mile upstream from the Indian village. That would be an easy distance to take a captive even if she had to be carried.

He cast a glance backward, as was his habit, to check his back trail. In the thickly falling snow just at the limits of his sight, some large animal moved in the arroyo. Tarpenning stopped hastily and, throwing a hand up to shade his eyes from the cut of the icy pellets, strove to get a better view.

An Indian on a pony became discernible through the blowing whiteness. Then another rider, and yet a third. All in a line and coming straight toward Tarpenning. Each had a spare mount. The Indians were almost to the location where they would see fresh tracks in the snow.

Tarpenning hurried down the arroyo dragging his horse. The brute could not climb out of the steep ravine and he would not relinquish the valuable mount. Yet to follow the course of the draw would mean to be driven into the enemy camp.

The warriors must be using the low passage to escape the brunt of the storm roaring across the flat plain little more than an arm's length above their heads. This near their home the Utes would not be overly alert. However, Tarpenning knew their sharp eyesight would soon spot his sign.

The wash curved sharply to the right. Tarpenning passed around the bend and, seeing a break in the rock sides that a man could climb, halted. He dropped the reins of his horse and ordered the brute to stay.

Digging into the cracks in the rocks with moccasined toes, he scrambled up to the top. Then he hurried back along the edge of the wash for a few steps and knelt, peering down into the wind-driven snow. The storm was at his back and in the face of his foes. That and a surprise attack might help to even the odds in the battle soon to come.

The three horsemen had gained upon Tarpenning and he saw them cleary. Large buffalo robes encased them from head to toe. Snow lay thickly upon the backs of the ponies and the shrouded forms of the men.

The lead rider discovered the tracks of a horse, a shod horse, in the new snow. He forced his mount back on its haunches and yelled a shrill cry of alarm to his friends.

Tarpenning jerked his rifle up and fired. The warrior farthest away screamed and tumbled backward from his mount.

Echohawk snapped his head to the rear to see Thunder That Rolls fall. Then swiftly Echohawk looked back to the fore to spot the smoke from the rifle fast being whipped away by the wind on the high ground ahead. He called loudly to Tall Elk and sped his mustang ahead along the wash toward the ambusher. Tall Elk sprang his horse into quick trailing position after Echohawk.

The Utes were attempting to race past before he could reload, Tarpenning knew. He dropped the empty rifle and yanked out the primed pistol. With one practiced movement he brought up the short weapon and shot through the center of the nearer buffalo-robed horseman, tumbling him from the mustang's back.

The last horseman, bent far forward and flogging his mustang, was almost even with Tarpenning. He must not escape to warn the braves in the village. Tarpenning launched himself down upon the figure speeding past.

His powerful arm caught the man, ripping him from the back of the horse. They fell heavily. The white man instantly sprang to his feet and pulled his knife.

The Indian was nearly as fast, surging erect, his robe falling away. He screamed his challenge, hand reaching for his own cutting steel.

Tarpenning lunged forward and stabbed his blade deeply into the brown body. Tall Elk shuddered under the deep wound and his hands were suddenly clumsy, fumbling at the handle of his weapon. The white man wrenched his knife free and stabbed again. The Indian fell backward to the snowy earth.

For a long moment Tarpenning stood, his lungs sucking great droughts of air and his eyes scanning the battleground, searching for any sign of life in his foes. None of the fallen men stirred.

He whirled about and scurried back up the rock face of the arroyo side to the plain. He found his pistol and rifle and jumped back down into the wash. Sheltering the weapons from the snow and wind with his body, he hurriedly poured powder, rammed the balls down and fitted the firing caps.

The buffalo hide that covered the Indian shot with the pistol began to stir. Tarpenning crept noiselessly upon the shrouded figure struggling to rise. With a sharp jerk, he tore the fur cloak aside. His knife drove forward even before the robe was clear.

At the last second Tarpenning recognized the target of his knife as a female. He caught the thrust of the iron point a scant fraction of an inch from her soft flesh. Slowly he withdrew his weapon, appalled at how near he had come to killing her.

He dropped his sight to the man lying motionless in the snow. The girl had been wrapped inside the robe with him. She had been very lucky the pistol bullet had missed her to drive through the warrior.

Tarpenning looked back at the girl. He reached out and caught her face, tilting it up to confront him directly. Critically he evaluated her.

She stared back at him with eyes not in full focus, still full of pain from the force of her fall from the horse. Cold snowflakes swirled down to settle startlingly white upon the dusky skin.

She forced her sight to concentrate on this new threat. To see the hairy face of a white man. Her people had talked of such strange men. Never until now had she seen one.

Tarpenning laughed deep in his chest. God! What a beauty! He backed away a step to look her over from head to toe. A little on the small side but perfectly formed. He moved in close again and took her by the shoulders. He laughed at the unexpectedness of the great find, glad he had not shot her.

The Arapaho girl shuddered at the meaning of his laugh. The alien blue eyes and long red beard of the white man so near repulsed her. She tried to draw away but he held her with a firm grasp.

"Now don't do that, my pretty girl," Tarpenning said, and his white teeth flashed at her through the red beard.

He swept a sharp-sighted look into the falling snow all around. The intensity of the storm had increased even more. The wind whistled like a keening banshee just above his head. No man, regardless how shrewd a tracker, could trail him through this blizzard.

He brushed the layer of white from the saddle of his horse. With ease the girl was lifted up and set astride. He saw the fear in her eyes and the exhausted droop of her shoulders. In her throat an excited pulse was beating visibly like a tiny trapped animal. Using the Ute tongue he spoke to her. "We will stop and camp after a few miles. Then you can rest." She seemed not to understand what he said.

Tarpenning moved to the nearest Indian, grabbed up his robe to shake off the snow and wrapped it about the girl to cover her completely, only her face showing. With lengths of rawhide, he girdled the fur in snugly to her waist and tied it warmly around each leg.

Quickly he strode to Tall Elk's crumpled body and pulled the robe free to drape about his own shoulders. He made a selection from among the half-dozen ponies hemmed in the draw and climbed upon it. He glanced one last time at the three dead men. Take their woman and take their horse. He had already taken their lives.

The Indian girl heard the red-bearded man laugh at something. Then his hands were reaching out and a leather thong was fastened around the neck of the pony she rode.

Tarpenning led off up the arroyo. Once he stopped, just long enough to lean down and drag Thunder That Roll's buffalo hide up to hang across the withers of the horse in front of him. Every bit of shelter would be needed to survive the storm.

The moment they climbed up out of the protection of the draw, Tarpenning turned directly into the teeth of the north wind. The blizzard assaulted them with terrifying fury. Wind clawed at their garments and ice crystals stung their unprotected faces. They had to cover their mouths with the robes to catch a breath of the air.

Tarpenning steered a course for the shallow crossing of the Arkansas River. He found the ford, but the placid water he had crossed the day before was now a crazy, churning maelstrom of white-capped waves that sped before the wind and completely masked the direction of the current. The blizzard of snow had swallowed the far shore, hiding it from man and animal.

The wise mustang Tarpenning rode fought against going into the water. It could see no land on the opposite side, so to it no land existed. Finally, unable to force the pony ahead, Tarpenning traded mounts with the girl. His obedient animal, though fearful and needing constant coaxing, waded in to lead the others through the fury of wind, water and snow.

They climbed the opposite bank. Knowing this section of the river extended north to south, Tarpenning used it as a base direction and faced unerringly to the southwest. A long distance out there through the bone-chilling cold lay the beaver valley, his friend Luke and a shelter with a crackling fire.

He felt the force of the wind against his right side. He would keep it there as he traveled, for the storm was new and should not change course for many hours. By then he should have reached the mountain and could use it as a guide to give them the final heading for the remaining miles.

He kicked his horse ahead into the snow that streamed across in horizontal layers in front of him.

The Arapaho girl thought, just for a moment above the screech of the storm, she heard the man laugh again. She shuddered—not at the cold.

CHAPTER 3

From the doorway of the cave shelter, Luke peered out into the blizzard that had mauled and lashed the beaver valley for two days. Large drifts of snow, many waist deep and still being added to, were piled in the wind eddies behind the trees and patches of brush. The land lay deserted, all life hidden, waiting for the snow to slacken and the wind to abate.

He had not run his traps since the frigid cold had settled in and this lost opportunity to catch beaver, and the lost dollars that represented, bothered him. However, there was one beneficial aspect to the winter storm—he believed himself relatively safe from Indian attack.

Night was approaching swiftly from the east and in a very few minutes would fill the valley with darkness. Before that happened, he had several chores to do. He left the cave and walked several times through the white mounds to the woodpile and carried a large quantity of fuel inside the shelter.

Picking up his rifle and hunching his head down into the collar of his heavy wolf-skin coat, he strode back out into the blustery weather. He breathed the frigid air, feeling the tiny bits of icy water enter his nostrils to melt and be drawn, cold and damp, onward deeply down into his lungs. Around his legs, thick currents of crystalline snow flowed, hissing and whimpering like a thing alive.

Luke shoved aside the fact that trapping could not be done in such weather and, at some primordial level, savored the turbulent world of wind and whiteness that buffeted and stung him.

He found the horse and mules yarded up in a thick patch of brush. The meadow grass was buried under more than a foot of snow and out of reach of the animals. They were surviving by browsing the twigs and shoots of the tasty willows and cottonwoods.

His pony nickered to show his enjoyment at the presence of his master. The staid mules merely turned to identify the newcomer and then went back to feeding. All three beasts wore shaggy winter coats, their growth hastened by the arctic wind.

Luke aimed his steps in the direction of the bluff and the trail that led in from the east. Tarpenning was out there someplace in the midst of the cold and snow. Though he was a hardy man, the blizzard was a mean one, enough to test the best of all mountain men. If the storm was not enough, he was not impervious to a sharp arrow or lance point.

The wind pouring down from the north was keeping the west-fronting bluff swept nearly free of snow. Luke remained at the bottom of the grade, staring up. An extra violent surge of wind struck him and he spread his legs to withstand the pressure. Wind tears formed in the corner of his eyes. The gray dusk faded into night.

The darkness was held back by the snow that generated a faint silver light all its own. Luke used the luminescence to look for the form of a man or horse on the ridge line above. Nothing was to be seen. The only sounds were the strength of the wind in the trees and on the face of the bluff and the grains of ice sweeping over the crusted white ground.

He returned to the shelter under the rock ledge. At the sight of the empty room, a tinge of worry for his friend came creeping in. A sense that he should be doing something to guide the absent, maybe lost, man home lay heavily upon him.

Luke knew he was very much indebted to Tarpenning. The older man had befriended a skinny inexperienced kid from Ohio, had taken him into the mountains and had taught him to live off the land, trap beaver and use rifle and horse. They had partnered for four years, romping through two rendezvous on the Wind River, one at Taos on the Rio Grande and the last year at Independence. Six battles with Indians had been fought, three the very first year with the Crows in the north mountains.

He tied the door flap shut behind him and stoked up the fire. Seating himself, he began again to work on a pair of snowshoes partially fashioned earlier in the day. The framework consisted of two broadly forking limbs of pine. They were being carefully shaped and soon would be ready for seasoning over the fire to strengthen and lighten them. Lastly he would web them with tough beaver gut.

He worked methodically, the flesh-colored chips falling free under the razor edge of his knife. The fire was refueled as its light and heat diminished. From time to time, he would raise his head to listen for some sound other than the storm.

A sharp, powerful blow, as if something had fallen against the logs, jarred the wall. Several pieces of dry mud cracked loose and fell to the floor. Coldiron scooped up his rifle and sprang away from the light of the fire and into the shadows near the door.

Above the roar of the wind outside, a hoarse voice shouted. "Luke! Are you in there?"

Luke moved toward the door, calling out loudly. "George, I'm here. You've made it, fellow." He jerked the ties loose and hurried into the stormy night.

His eyesight wrestled with the darkness.

In the gloom near the log wall of the cave, two exhausted ponies stood spraddle-legged. A pair of riders slumped, snow-covered and weary, on the backs of the brutes. One of the figures stiffly swung his leg over, stepped down and immediately fell weakly to his knees.

Tarpenning shoved his robe clear. "Help me, partner. Seems my feet and legs have turned feeble on me."

Luke lifted the man up and, supporting most of his weight, helped him into the shelter. "Rest here near the fire," he said and lowered his friend down.

He piled several pieces of wood on the fire and the flames leaped and crackled. Tarpenning scooted himself closer to the heat and began to fumble at the bindings on his moccasins.

"Need help?" asked Luke.

Tarpenning looked up with sunken, bloodshot eyes. Through the white frost and ice matted in his beard, he tried to smile. Only a strained grimace came. In a voice slurred by cold, stiff jaws, he spoke. "Damn, I'm glad you had a fire burning. I homed in on the smell of your smoke." He pointed to the door. "She'll need more help than I will. Go carry her in."

Luke nodded and hastily went again into the night. He stepped up close to the figure half sitting, half lying on the back of the horse.

"Come with me," said Luke in the tongue of the Ute people and reached out to take hold of her. At his slight tug, she toppled to the side. He caught her and was astonished at the lightness of her weight. Less than a hundred pounds, he judged. Gently he carried her inside and laid her down in the warmth of the fire.

"Never complained once in over two days of the toughest winter traveling I've ever been through," said Tarpenning. He pulled his last moccasin off and extended his bare feet to the heat of the flames. "Check her toes right away to see that they haven't frozen."

Luke stretched her on her back and undid the straps of her foot coverings. The small slender toes were like ice and appeared bloodless. He clasped first one foot and then the other between his hands to drive away the cold.

The heat of the fire and the man's hands roused the girl from her fatigued stupor. She opened her eyes and saw the evil white man was still with her. But he had changed. Though the eyes were still blue, the red beard had become black and it was thick and bristly like the chin hair of the bull buffalo. She quivered.

Luke felt the girl tremble and looked into her face. Her eyes were wide with fear and fatigue. He could see she was hanging to consciousness by a thread. Yet he sensed a fierce defiance smoldering in her. She tried to draw her feet away from his touch.

He shook his head no. "I must thaw your feet or you might lose some toes, so lay still," said Luke, still speaking the Ute language. He continued to hold his warm hands firmly about the weakly struggling feet.

She gave no indication of understanding him.

Tarpenning had observed the girl's efforts to pull free and Luke's lack of success in communicating with her. "She's Arapaho," he said. "I figured it out after a while. Had to kill three Ute bucks that she was with. They must have been coming back from a raid on some Arapaho camp. Appears she was their captive."

"I see," said Luke. Neither he nor Tarpenning had learned the language of the Plains Indian. The fright of the girl greatly bothered him. "So they kidnapped her and then you did the same. Not easy on her."

"She'll get over it," responded George. "The Ute and Arapaho are always stealing each other's women. I wouldn't be surprised but what she has seen some captured women in her village. Her mother could well be one."

"Maybe she will get over it," said Luke. He released her feet. "I think she'll be all right. Nothing is frozen too bad. Looks mighty young."

"Old enough," said Tarpenning.

The girl tried to sit up and partially made it. She endeavored to speak, but no sound came. Her eyelids closed heavily, her strength vanished and she wilted to the ground.

Tenderly, Luke gathered up the limp form and placed it in his own sleeping robe. From the ring of stones around the fire he extracted one moderately warm one and positioned it inside the covering near her feet.

"She's completely worn out. And me, too," said Tarpenning. He shook the melting ice from his beard and it sputtered when part of it landed in the fire.

"I'll unpack the horses and fetch your gear," said Luke.

The jaded mustangs had not stirred. He removed their loads, led them into the brush thicket and left them near his animals. The new ponies would be very unlikely to leave the company of those used to the area.

Luke found Tarpenning asleep on the dirt floor near the fire. He coaxed him half awake, mostly carried him to the second bed and rolled him in the large furry skin.

Tarpenning mumbled something and Luke leaned over him. "What did you say?"

"Keep the fire burning hot. Don't let her get sick." His voice trailed off.

"I'll do that." Even as Luke spoke, Tarpenning's low snore sounded.

Luke moved to place more wood on the flames. Then he seated himself on the opposite side of the fire and sat for a long time looking at the two sleeping forms. All was now in readiness for the winter.

Finally he began to labor on the snowshoes again, working in the ruddy flickering glow of the fire. The wood shavings curled before the edge of the knife blade and fell to the floor.

Outside in the night the raw wind droned past the cave.

Luke slept lightly, unconsciously listening for some sound or call from George or the girl. He awoke early and threw back the flap of the robe he had taken from Tarpenning's pack. The fire was only a bed of embers and he promptly fueled it with a generous supply of pine knots.

Both man and woman slept heavily. The whisper of their breathing was a pleasant sound, their presence enjoyable. Luke knelt to look at the face of the girl. At his first sight of her during the night, he had been deeply impressed by the fragile beauty of her features.

Her jet-black hair had strayed across her face. With utmost care so as not to wake her, he lifted aside the strands to see her better.

In deep slumber, she lay relaxed. The fear that had strained her delicate countenance was temporarily erased by sleep.

Tarpenning! You woman-stealing son of a gun! You have outdone yourself this time.

Suddenly the girl tensed, her hands clenched and beneath the closed eyelids the round orbs of vision swept rapidly back and forth. Luke watched her live the disturbing dream. He felt pity for her. How unfairly she had been treated—correction, was being treated. A bothersome thought came to him. Her predicament was partially his fault.

He stood up and drew back. Too late to change things now. The deed was done.

Something else caught his attention. There was a difference in the sound of the storm. He cocked his head to listen. The difference was, there was no sound.

He threw open the door. The sun shined dazzlingly bright on a quiet, snow-cloaked land. A slow wind blew in from the southwest. The temperature was warm, nearly up to the freezing point. Creek noises sounded clearly across the distance.

It was a perfect day to run his traps, to remove the catch of beaver and to reset for the next unwary beast. He went back inside and put beans to soak in a pan of water. Then, mounted on his horse and with the sun warm and gentle on his shoulders, he rode up the course of the stream.

Luke worked steadily all day. By mid afternoon all the traps had been visited and he had skinned seven beaver. Most were kits, the young of the season, but almost as large as the adults. A good catch. He saved the flesh of all seven broad, flat beaver tails.

The fair weather gave many signs that it had come to stay awhile. The temperature had continued to climb. On the south-facing slopes the snow was melting rapidly. The rims of ice along the banks of the stream were breaking loose to float down with the current.

The beaver were stirring and in many places had broken trails open to willow clumps and cottonwood trees. That would make for another large number of animals to be taken in the next day or two.

Merciless predators, other than the man, were also hunting. Tracks of four wolves were in the snow along the creek. One of Luke's beavers had been dragged from the water and devoured. Only a few tufts of hair marked the site of the feast. Coyote tracks were plentiful, mainly concentrated in the brush thickets where the rabbits abounded.

Luke returned leisurely down the valley, pleasuring in the contrasting colors of white-blanketed meadows, green pine woods and the yellowish-brown sandstone ledges of rock in the side of the steep bluffs.

The horse moved noiselessly in the soft melting snow. In a dense string of timber, man and mount came unseen upon a young bull elk. The beast never heard the shot with which Luke killed it.

He field dressed the large animal. After cutting out the tenderloin—the delicious strips of meat on both sides of the backbone—he mounded the cold snow over the carcass. In the shade of the tall trees, the flesh would remain fresh for many days. With his human scent everyplace, no animal would bother his kill before he could return and claim it.

He put the elk flesh with the beaver tails and rode directly to the cave. Taking care to make no noise, Luke entered the rock and log shelter. The man and woman still slept.

Silently Luke drew the beaver pelts, hair side in, over stretching hoops, lengths of stout willow bent back upon themselves almost in a circle and some two feet in diameter. During the next day and before the hides became stiff, the flesh that had adhered to the skins would be scraped away. Then the pelts would be taken off of the frames, turned fur side out and replaced over the stretchers for thorough drying.

He rekindled the fire. The most tender beaver tail was cut into bite-sized pieces and dropped in with the beans. In a short while the mixture was bubbling merrily over the fire and the aromas wafting to the farthest corners of the cave.

Luke faced to look at the girl. During the warming day, she had partially worked her way out of the sleeping robe. She lay on her back and her breast rose and fell with the rhythm of her breathing.

"Beautiful, isn't she?" spoke Tarpenning.

Luke jerked with the unexpected sound and swung around toward his partner. Tarpenning was propped up on an elbow and watching him.

"Yes, very beautiful," responded Luke smiling. He walked over to squat down near Tarpenning. "We have a pretty woman, a snug camp for the winter and the trapping is good." He pointed at the new pelts and then continued to move his hand to indicate the cave. "What more could a man want?"

Tarpenning did not return the smile. A somber expression held his face stiff. His eyes slipped away to look at the sleeping girl and then back to Luke. He kicked off the covers and got up abruptly. Barefooted he circled to the far side of the fire.

Luke rose to his feet and waited, trying to interpret Tarpenning's actions. Something serious was troubling the man.

Tarpenning lifted his head to face Luke squarely. "I can't share her with you," he exclaimed in a rapid stab of words. "God, man, I just can't do it. She's not like all the other women we've had."

Involuntarily Luke backed up a step at the intensity of the man's voice. And the pleading tone of the words sent a chill up his spine. George had never begged for anything in his life. It was not in him. What had the brown-skinned girl done to him?

Tarpenning spoke again in the same imploring voice. "Luke, try to understand. Anything else I have is yours, my rifle, my horse, just ask. But don't ask for her!"

"George, she's just a captive Indian girl, someone you stole. She would kill you if she got the chance. Whether one man or two loves her won't make any difference."

"Yes, she would knife me now, but I can change that. Luke, I've never had a feeling like this. Don't try to force me on this." His voice rose, a tinge of warning forming in it like a steel edge.

They both noticed movement and pivoted to look as the Indian woman sat up. Their loud voices, rumbling and echoing in the cave, had awakened her. She was frightened, her eyes wide and shiny with fear. She swept her view from one hairy face to the other. O Great Spirit, how she wished them both dead.

Silence held among them, to be broken by the sound of the pot boiling over into the fire. The spilling liquid landed upon a burning log and it split with a loud pop. A flame of escaping gas hissed. The girl lurched half erect.

"George, she's scared to death of us."

"Some of them have been before. Remember when we had to whip that Cheyenne squaw to stop her from following us when we tried to leave? Well, I'll get this one to act the same way. I'll be gentle and come spring she'll do anything for me." His eyes became clouded. "You do understand, don't you. She must be all mine."

Luke stooped and straightened the pot. As he stirred the stew, he retraced the last four years with Tarpenning. They had shared every danger, every dollar and often when women were scarce, those too. Yet deep within, he knew that there could come a day when a man took a woman to himself alone. It seemed George Tarpenning had reached that time.

Luke climbed to his feet and spread his hands. "That's the first time you ever asked me for anything. Hell of a partner I would be if I didn't give it to you." But Luke knew their partnership was now different and would never be the same again. Already they acted like half strangers, an odd feeling after all these years.

"I think I'll go for a long scout down the creek." Taking his rifle from where it leaned against the wall, he turned and walked out the door.

CHAPTER 4

Luke sat unmoving, had remained in that exact position for better than two hours. His rifle rested ready across his legs and he scanned the beaver pond for a target. The range was short, less than fifty yards, and he had charged his weapon with only a half measure of powder.

Not a ripple disturbed the small lake behind the dam of expertly interwoven brush, reinforced with a ballast of rocks. The beaver lodge, made from the stems of saplings surrounding a carefully designed hollow, reflected clear and distinct in the mirror-like surface of the water.

Within its home, the beaver awakened. An almost imperceptible undulation trembled the shiny top of the pond. The beaver had entered the water.

Swimming sleekly and effortlessly near the bottom, the beaver made his passage. He came up to the air at the edge of the dam and looked about in all directions. He saw no enemies.

As a cautious builder should, he began to inspect his dam for zones of weakness. If the structure should rupture, the lake surrounding his lodge would vanish downstream. Then his swift, fish-like water movements would become a slow, clumsy land waddle and one of his many foes could easily catch and devour him.

The beaver crawled along, inspecting the position and effectiveness of the wood and the rocks. At times he pulled himself to the top of the dam to examine it from that perspective. He ended his investigation at the end near the human.

The man raised his rifle. A plume of smoke erupted from the barrel and the speeding round ball tore through the beaver's lungs, to stop beneath the skin on the far side.

Luke trotted forward, lifted the forty-pound animal onto the bank and began to skin it.

It was the middle of November, The Moon of the Falling Leaves. Luke had spent not one night in the cave shelter since Tarpenning had arrived and laid sole claim to the Arapaho girl. He had returned just before dark that first day, packed the necessary gear to establish a camp elsewhere and left.

The weather had remained mostly fair. Ice froze at night but melted under the daytime sun. Nearly all the snow had disappeared from the valley. However, the upper mountain slopes were still sparkling white and each day the sun zenithed a fraction of a degree farther south.

It had rained once, all day, and Luke had taken refuge in a small slit of a cave beneath a rock outcrop. All the other nights he slept where the darkness found him, merely spreading his robe on the ground or sometimes laying a bed of pine boughs for a softer sleep.

His traps were checked every day and, if sprung, immediately reset. Every third day or so he hauled his catch of pelts to the cave and turned them over to Tarpenning to flesh. Luke always left after a brief conversation with his partner. Not once had he seen the Indian girl.

Luke knew he had the more difficult chore. That did not bother him. Tarpenning had offered to exchange tasks but Luke had refused, telling him he was satisfied with the arrangement.

With no one to wile away the time with, Luke found there were spare hours in the day after running the traps. To make profitable use of those periods he often took station near a beaver pond and slew any unwary beaver that exposed himself.

His diligence with trap and gun had eliminated the beaver from several miles of stream. Already more than a score of ponds lay empty, forlorn and sterile, the dams gradually falling into decay.

The three horsemen, heavily armed with rifles and pistols, followed the sign of their strayed animals through the pine forest on the side of the mountain.

"I'm going to kill that damn mule," hissed Lacy to the two riders beside him. "He won't stay put and he always takes some of the horses with him."

Sidlow, the leader of the group and the man nearest Lacy, spoke in disgust. "He's your mule, but if you don't shoot him, I'm going to."

"At least ten miles we've chased that dumb animal and still haven't come up to him yet," said the third man, Stauber. "He must have taken off the minute we turned him loose last night."

Sidlow growled angrily in his chest and kicked his mount faster along the trail of disturbed pine needles.

As the men tracked the lost beasts easterly, they left the basin where they hunted, crossed the water divide and entered a basin strange to all of them. The land became less broken and flattened out to slope moderately to the south. Glancing ahead, Sidlow could see the new drainage was wide, most likely containing a fair-sized stream. Perhaps it contained some beaver that could be trapped.

"There they are!" exclaimed Sidlow, pointing to a large brown mule and two horses grazing in a small grassy opening in the woods.

" 'Bout damn time," said Lacy. He pulled his rifle from its scabbard beneath his leg. "You fellows catch the horses and hold them so they won't stampede. I'll make coyote meat out of that mule."

Sidlow and Stauber quickly put lead ropes on the horses. The mule's owner raised his weapon and sighted down the long barrel.

From the valley not far away came the sound of a shot, flat and dull. Sidlow called out hurriedly, "Wait, someone is near. Don't shoot."

Lacy caught his trigger finger. He aimed hard eyes at the mule. "Saved again, but just for a little while. You'll not make it back to camp." He threw the loop of a rope around the mule's neck.

"Let's tie up all these critters and just sneak ahead through the trees and have a look," said Sidlow.

All the animals were stoutly tethered to trees and the men stole forward to halt where the slope angled down to the valley bottom.

"There, see him?" said Sidlow. "By the pond and bending over something on the ground."

"Yes, I see him," answered Stauber. "Looks like he's skinning something. Probably a beaver."

Even as they spoke, the man finished and stood erect with a pelt in his hand.

"Damn fast man with a skinning knife," said Sidlow. A twisted smile flitted across his face. "A right ambitious gent for he must be using traps as well as a gun. What say you fellows, come late February and before he pulls out with his fur, we come and take his whole winter catch?"

Stauber looked at Lacy. "I reckon we can't find fault with that plan, can we, Lacy?"

Lacy chuckled his agreement and said nothing.

"We should know how many friends he might have," said Sidlow. "Stauber, you work your way upstream and see if anyone is up that way. Lacy, you stay here and keep an eye on this hombre. I'll go south. In four hours or so, let's all meet back at the horses. Now don't get spotted for we don't want him to find out we're here."

Stauber nodded and disappeared into the brush and trees. Sidlow slanted off to the right, dropping down into the valley.

In less than an hour, Sidlow found the freshly cut logs beneath the ledge of sandstone. A man sat fleshing skins in the sun near the entrance. Sidlow concealed himself in a copse of trees, watched the trapper and waited to see if another person was present inside.

The day wore on and the worker completed his task with the skins. Taking his rifle, he walked to the creek to wash his hands. He returned and entered the cabin.

Time passed and the man did not return to the outside. Sidlow left his cover and proceeded along the valley. When he was certain the man at the camp could not see him, he began to course back and forth on both sides of the stream looking for tracks. He found no sign of another hunter in that direction.

Long east-pointing shadows were growing. The four hours Sidlow had specified were spent. He broke into an easy long-stepping run, quickly crossed the valley and climbed the bluff.

His men were waiting, squatting near the horses and talking when he came in silent as a night homing bird. He looked at Stauber. "How many men did you see?"

"None. Lot of sign. Some a day old and up to several days old. Saw no person though."

"Lacy, did you see anybody else?" asked Sidlow.

"Nope," said the man, shaking his head.

"Well, I saw one more. I'm not sure he was the last one, but it's a good guess he was because there was no trapping going on downstream from the cabin. The three of us can take their fur easy. Now let's get out of here and let them trap beaver for us." Sidlow laughed, contemplating the heavy pocket of gold he would have in the spring when he sold the fur catch of the two strange trappers and added that coin to his share of his own crew's winter take.

They mounted and kicked the horses into a rapid pace along the return course toward supper and bed. They stopped briefly once, to kill the mule that always ran off.

It was late November and mid morning. The weather was nippy but fair. Luke approached along the creek toward Tarpenning's camp. A heavy load of freshly skinned pelts rolled flesh side in were tied in a bundle on his back.

Rounding a clump of bushes, he came upon the Arapaho girl. She was on her knees, her back ·to him as she worked with a digging stick in a patch of cattails in the edge of the stream. A half bushel of the edible root was piled beside her on the bank.

Luke stopped and stood motionless watching her at her chore. She took hold of a stalk of a cattail, jabbed the end of the stick down into the water near it, pried the root loose and withdrew it from the mud by the plant stem. She broke the root off, tossed it onto the heap with the others and turned to repeat the action.

He remained motionless, keenly enjoying the feminine movements of the girl, the toss of her head to clear the hair obstructing her vision, the supple swing of her arm and hand to take hold of another stalk, and the round buttocks plainly outlined where her buckskin skirt pulled tight. Though he could not see her face, his memory had etched upon it the lovely features. But she was Tarpenning's woman. He had promised that.

The digging stick halted its probing in the water. The small body tensed. Then, very slowly as if afraid to look, she turned her head to cast an uneasy look up the bank of the creek. At the sight of Coldiron she leaped erect and swung the sharp stick of wood to point at him.

Luke felt sorrow for the girl, that she had at first glimpse of him become fearful and thought only of defending herself.

"Hello," he greeted her in English, smiled and passed around her to continue to the cave.

As he dropped his burden of skins next to the door, he glanced in her direction. She was examining him, but as his eye touched her she turned away and began to labor again at digging the cattails.

Tarpenning emerged from the pine on the ridge top above the shelter and descended to the valley floor. Luke watched him advance and, knowing the sharp, vigilant nature of his partner, believed it more than likely he had observed the episode with the girl at the creek. However, Tarpenning gave no outward indication he had seen anything.

"Twelve more hides," said Luke, chucking a thumb at the mound on the ground. "I'm now about five miles above the cave. If the good weather holds, I should have taken all the beaver down level with the camp in another month or a little less."

"It's a good season so far," responded Tarpenning. "The fur is excellent quality and should fetch a fair price."

"Yeh, if the market stays strong next year."

"Yes, it was getting soft there toward the last of the sale. Down to $2.50 a pound. Still that's better than working for wages at $1.50 a day. Next summer we'd better start looking for another way to make a buck. Silk has just about taken over the hat-making business."

Luke looked at the mule and horses grazing on the brown grass of the small meadow that fronted the camp. "I always thought I would like raising horses for the army. Sooner or later the government is going to send soldiers out here to kill off the Indians. Those troopers will need fast mounts to do that job."

"You might have something there," agreed Tarpenning.

An awkward silence settled between the two partners. Tarpenning picked up a stick and began to idly trace designs on the sandy ground.

Luke broke the uneasy quietness. "I'll pack a few supplies and be off up the creek. Still a lot of beaver to catch."

Tarpenning threw the stick with a long overhead swing toward the meadow. He did not look at Luke as he spoke. "Take time for something to eat. She's cooked a stew of elk, wild onions and three or four other kinds of roots. Damn good food and you look gaunt." He ranged his sight to check the location of the girl and then led the way inside the shelter.

Luke filled his pack from the store he and Tarpenning had hauled so many miles from Independence. Then seating himself near the fire, he unabashedly ate almost the entire pot of stew. It was delicious, the best meal he had had for many days. Tarpenning was fortunate to have found a woman who cooked so well. She would now have to concoct another batch for him.

The girl entered as Luke finished eating. She found a resting place in the rear of the cave and sat soundless and unmoving.

Finally, his hunger satisfied, a hunger much greater than he had imagined possessing, Luke climbed to his feet. "See you in three or four days," he said.

"I'll be expecting you," said Tarpenning. He followed the younger man outside and watched him stride up the valley swiftly, as if he was in a hurry to put distance between them.

A dark sky rained pellets of sleet upon Coldiron. The icy nuggets, the size of small peas, bounced from his shoulders and the brim of his hat with a noisy popping rattle. December, The Moon When the Snow Drifts into the Teepees, had arrived.

In all the length of the creek there was one cataract, a quarter mile of jagged rock where the water, white with froth, cascaded noisily down. Luke had set a goal to kill all the beaver above that change in the stream's gradient before the end of November. That objective had been accomplished except for one giant male, a sly, dark-colored animal turning gray about the muzzle.

Immediately above the cataract, the beaver had built a large dam to block the flow of the water to create a lake, one that inundated more than two acres of land. In the center of the body of water stood the animal's lodge.

Every last one of Luke's steel traps was set, placed at the most likely spot to catch the old beaver. Still after two full days the wise one was still alive and healthy.

He had not surfaced once during the daylight. If he came to the land at night, he avoided the traps. At times Luke could hear the beaver gnawing the bark from tree limbs within his lodge.

The hours passed, cold and damp. Luke controlled his impatient desire to take up his traps and move them below the rapids. He waited, primed to take advantage of any mistake his opponent should make.

On the other side of the lake from Luke, the water silently parted and the beaver's head appeared. He was going to his feeding yard, but he avoided all his recently used paths, taking instead an old route mostly grown full of water grass and reeds.

"You tricky old bastard," whispered Luke to himself. The beaver had crawled along the bottom from his home nearly to the bank without once disturbing the surface of the water. Even now, on the top, the animal made only the slightest of ripples.

The beaver reached the shallow water and touched the floor of the lake. With a crunching snap, something clamped an iron vise on his right paw. His tail smacked the water like the crack of a rifle shot. He lunged backward to be jerked up short. His tail exploded sound again and the water splashed up in a curtain of mist.

"Got you!" yelled Luke. "Outsmarted you, didn't I?"

The snared creature fought like a thing berserk. The water churned up muddy. He spun himself, only to suddenly stop and hurl his weight back against the steel grip of the trap. The powerful tail added many pounds of force to his efforts to tear loose. His entire body rose above the water in his violent exertion. The sapling to which the trap was chained swished and bucked as if in a fierce wind. Still he could not break the shackle that held him.

Many seconds passed and the animal continued its ferocious fight to be free. Luke held his rifle at his shoulder, waiting for a shot to end the battle. But the tortured, hurting beaver was a whirlwind of movement in its attempt to escape.

The water stilled, the waves radiating away, becoming quiet and losing their strength on the banks. Luke searched the surface for a target. Nothing showed. The beaver must come up for air in a moment.

However, nothing came to the top. Instead there were sounds of movement from within the lodge.

You did it, old fellow, thought Luke. You broke loose, but I bet you have one hellish sore foot. I'll come back and get you later. He rose to his feet and circled the pond, gathering his traps.

He slung the steel-jawed instruments of capture over his shoulder and started down the bank beside the cataract. He stopped just before he lost sight of the pond and looked back across the water at the home of the beaver. I won't be back, he called without voice. At least not this year. So breed and multiply, so when I do come again there'll be plenty of skins for me to take. I'll leave you some females in the next pond down the creek.

CHAPTER 5

On a morning in late December, Coldiron woke trembling with cold and with frost, white and thick on the hair of the buffalo robe where his breath had condensed. He poked his head outside. During the night a foot of new snow had fallen and the temperature had plummeted far below zero. Not a whisper of air stirred. Not one bird or animal was visible. The valley lay frozen, motionless in the dead of winter.

Luke climbed out, dug his camping gear out of the snow, packed it and headed for the stream to retrieve his traps before they became locked solid in the ice. His hands were stiff claws by the time he had dragged all his steel from the rapidly freezing water and started toward the cabin.

He was glad when he saw strong smoke pouring from the hole he had left for that purpose between the top log and the roof of the cave. He smiled in anticipation of the warm fire.

Tarpenning, as if he had been watching for his partner, lifted the hide door and came outside. "Come in and warm yourself," he greeted Luke. "I've been expecting you since early morning."

"Thanks," responded Luke. "I guess I'm here to sleep a few nights. This time I believe the cold will hang on for a while."

"I think so, too. Stay as long as you like."

They entered. Luke dropped the traps just inside the door and his sleeping robe on the closest bed, one that appeared to be unused.

The cave looked very much lived in. Several pounds of meat hung curing up near the smoke hole. Tarpenning had obviously been pouring lead balls for the rifles, for a pile of them lay near his mold and a small pot of molten gray metal sat in the fire. Bales of dried fur were stacked in the rear of the cave. Knowing his partner's penchant of putting ten pelts in each bale, Luke calculated quickly and arrived at a figure of two hundred beaver that had already been trapped. Thirty green skins were hanging and drying on the front wall. He was pleased with the catch so far.

Three beaver pelts had been stuffed with grass and lay near the fire as seats. Luke selected one and slumped down to extend his feet and hands to the flames. Slowly he began to thaw out.

Though the girl sat barely ten feet distant on the far side of the fire, Luke made no acknowledgement of her existence. From the corner of his eye, he noted she was sewing some type of buckskin garment.

Tarpenning flopped down beside her and looked at Luke. "How far from the cabin have you trapped to?" he asked.

" 'Bout a mile downstream," answered Luke.

"Is there enough game other than beaver to make it worthwhile to continue trapping?"

"I think so. Tomorrow I'll take meat bait and make some sets."

"I have a deer hanging in that first neck of woods up on top of the bluff. That should make good bait."

"I'll go cut some chunks off it tomorrow."

Tarpenning nodded and pointed. "There's grub. We've been keeping it warm for you, knowing you would be coming."

"Thanks, I appreciate that," said Luke.

At Tarpenning's gesture toward the food, the girl got up hastily and brought Luke a tin plate and spoon. With eyes downcast, she handed them to him and retook her place beside Tarpenning.

While Luke ate, Tarpenning tried to make conversation, but it did not come off well and finally he fell silent. Luke knew why. The presence of the woman was a palpable, disturbing thing. The smooth-working relationship of the partnership was missing. He wished for the old days.

After satisfying his hunger, Luke found the half-finished snowshoes he had stopped work on that day long past. He labored on them and now and then held desultory conversation with Tarpenning.

The well-seasoned wood, light yet strong, took final form under the blade of his knife. A webbing of tough beaver gut was stretched across the frames, anchored in place by notches cut into the outside edge of the wood. Straps to bind the snowshoes to his feet were added and he laid the contrivances aside. They would be much needed during the next two months.

Tarpenning yawned, "Guess I'll turn in."

"Me, too," said Luke.

The fire had burned down to a low glow as the night grew late. In the distant light, Luke watched as Tarpenning joined the girl already bundled into a robe on one of the beds. He lay down on his own mattress of grass and pulled the skin covering up.

Luke was aroused from a deep sleep by the sounds of Tarpenning and the girl's lovemaking. He could not but listen to their excited, hurried breathing little more than a body length away.

He felt himself stirring and, with an oath, sprang from his bed, jerked on moccasins and coat and plunged through the door into the night. He ran through the sub-zero cold, with the rays of a full moon bathing the night in a weak silver light and the snow crackling and crunching beneath his heavy footsteps.

For a long distance he raced through the trees and over the snow-covered meadows, cooling his hot, lusting blood with strenuous action. Finally with his throat and lungs burning from the intake of the frigid air, he halted.

He stood in the stark, silent valley and let the last of his fiery passion drain away. Around him the dim shapes of the nearer objects, framed by the snow, could be seen. With distance, the snow and trees faded into an amorphous gray whiteness. Against the sky to the north, the tall mountain blocked out a hand's width of twinkling stars.

His frost-nipped ears began to ache, for he had left without his cap,

and he cupped the aching organs in his hands. He turned and started the
return journey to the shelter.

Much later he entered the cave. All was quiet. He found his bed and,
closely wrapping his nearly frozen body in the heavy cover, shivered
himself to sleep.

The arctic wind hurtled downward from the cold crown of the mountain. It drove into the hearts of the mules and horses, robbing their
bodies of flesh and fat. The brutes stood pressed together in a tight
clump as if trying to draw heat from each other. Even with their dense
coats of heavy long hair, the animals' bony ribs showed painfully.

Coldiron left the smoky warmth of the cave shelter and went outside.
More snow had fallen during the night and was now more than crotch
deep, smothering the valley and hiding the grass and low-growing shrubs.
He donned his snowshoes and with ax over his shoulder, mushed to the
grove of cottonwoods near his starving beasts.

He began to swing his ax to girdle a broad-trunked cottonwood just
above snow line. Finishing, he pried the thick bark away from the
wooden inner bole of the tree for a few inches. Later he would return
and fell the tree so the animals could get at all of it.

Hearing the sound of the ax upon the tree and dredging up memories
of previous snowy winters and how he had been fed, Luke's pony pulled
away from its mates and waded through the white drifts toward the man.
As Luke moved to a second cottonwood to repeat his procedure to provide feed, the horse came up to the first tree and sniffed at the projecting
strips of bark.

The starving animal had tried unsuccessfully several times to break the
bark on the round trunk of a tree. Now that task had been accomplished
for him. With the odor of the sweet cottonwood strong and tantalizing
in his nose, the horse clamped his big teeth on a strip of bark, swung his
muscular neck mightily and ripped a length fully five feet up the tree
before the woody covering broke off.

The pony chewed, gradually drawing the quarter-inch-thick strip of
the skin of the tree in between his broad, ridged molars. Luke glanced at
his mount and grinned at the half-closed eyes, the contented munching.

The mules arrived next with the remainder of the horses close behind.
They ringed the cottonwood, tearing and hauling away at the bark of the
ancient tree, taking its life to preserve their own.

Only the swish of Sidlow's snowshoes betrayed his passage through the
silent woods. He came up to the edge of the bluff and looked down into

the valley where the strange trappers had been discovered. He found a well-screened vantage point and stopped to scan the white-mantled land spread below him. He located the log wall of the shelter and the figure of a man, a tiny black spot moving against the snow near a patch of trees.

A narrow finger of pine stretched from a point just below Sidlow to far out onto the valley bottom. He slid down the steep slope and skulked through the trees. As he neared the creek, the sound of ax strokes came to him and he peered out to see Luke chopping in the grove of cotton-woods. Recognizing at once what the man's intention was, Sidlow counted the animals as they came in to feed, for their number might tell him how many hunters were in the camp.

A tall man left the cave, went to a large pile of wood and began to fill his arms. In some surprise, Sidlow saw yet a third person appear in the doorway. He locked his sight on the last figure, tracking the small skirted figure as it moved up beside the man and took a load of the fuel.

"A woman, by God," whispered Sidlow to himself.

For several minutes the three people worked at their chores. Sidlow observed first one person and then another, but most of his time was spent eying the woman, contemplating what her presence meant to him and his cohorts.

He had come across the snowy mountainside to check on those trap-pers who were unknowingly gathering furs for him. He did not want them to leave without his knowledge. Now the existence of the woman put a new ingredient, a strong spice, into the game.

How could he win two objectives, taking the woman from the men and at the same time keeping them trapping furs? However he accom-plished the first goal, the men had to remain alive.

With the animals chomping noisily on the tough but nutritious cot-tonwood bark, Coldiron returned to the shelter. Tarpenning and the woman finished carrying wood for the fire and also came inside.

In the thicket of pine on the far side of the creek, Sidlow stole slyly away. Soon he was out of the valley and hurrying westward through the deep forest. He chuckled low and savage. It was a luck-filled day for him and his partners.

The winter day was fast fading when Sidlow came down into the valley and reached his bivouac. He unstrapped his snowshoes and jabbed them to stand erect in the snow near the entrance. Stooping low, he entered the round shelter, a circle of tall willow poles leaning inward to meet at an apex and covered with tanned deer hides.

Half a ham of a deer was roasting over a fire, the juice dripping and spluttering in the flames. His two comrades slept on pallets of fur. They drowsily raised their heads when the wave of cold air came in with Sidlow.

"Are they still trappin'?" asked Lacy.

"Yep, and better than that," responded Sidlow. He lifted the piece of venison from the fire and sliced off a thick slab. The deer haunch was still raw deep inside so he replaced it on its support to continue cooking. He blew on his chunk of meat to cool it, took a large bite and began to chew.

"What do you mean, better than that?" impatiently questioned Lacy.

"They've got a woman," said Sidlow with a full mouth. "From what I could see, an Injun woman."

Lacy sat bolt upright. Stauber looked at Sidlow and laughed gleefully. "Now what more could a man want when it's midwinter, the snow is ass deep and he's just laying around getting fat?" He laughed even louder.

"I thought you fellows might like the news," said Sidlow grinning widely. "But do I need to remind you she's with two other men and we don't know how mean and tough they could be."

Lacy shook his head in a deprecating manner. "I've never met any man I was afeared of," he said.

"Why worry about them?" asked Stauber. "We can simply shoot them from ambush. They won't know what hit them. They'll just suddenly be dead."

Sidlow shook his head in the negative. "Now don't get too fast. They can't trap beaver if they've dead. Why don't we take a bunch of skins over there and buy her?"

Lacy and Stauber looked at Sidlow with disbelief that he should propose such a plan.

Before they could speak, Sidlow continued. "Now think it through. What do we plan to do about all the fur they have in the spring? Take it away from them, right? Well, whatever we give we'll get back. And we'll have the woman in the meantime."

"That's a good thought," acknowledged Lacy.

"I'm for it, too," said Stauber. "How many pelts should we take?"

"Let's be generous," Sidlow smiled crookedly. "Forty skins should buy her with little doubt. We'll pack up and go over there in the morning."

"The calendar stick says tomorrow is Christmas," said Stauber, pointing to a foot-long length of wood with a series of notches cut in it that was hanging on a sinew from the ridge pole of the shelter. "I've been keeping good count of the days. What say we take fifty skins for her because it'll be the day for gift giving." He chortled and tugged happily at his beard.

The other two men laughed heartily.

Luke sat eating breakfast. Soon as it grew light, he would leave to run his trap line. Because of the extreme cold, the catch of upland fur had been small. Still he had nothing better to do and George and the girl needed their privacy.

Tarpenning came up beside him and found a seat. Luke stopped eating, expecting his partner to begin talking. But the man fiddled with the ties of his moccasins and said nothing.

"Something bothering you?" asked Coldiron.

Tarpenning's eyes wandered about the shelter as he started to speak in a low but firm voice. "Luke, I've been trapping beaver and riding and walking over the mountains for some fifteen years. I've made every trapper's rendezvous they've had except last year when you and I went to Independence."

Luke remained quiet, looking at George.

Tarpenning resumed speaking. "I've had many women, Indian, Mexican and white. Drank gallons of whiskey and killed my share of men. It's time I settled down and raised a family." He cast a finger at the young woman sitting nearby sewing a blouse for herself. "I don't remember telling you her name. It's Morning Mist."

Coldiron nodded his understanding. There was more to this conversation than the woman's name.

"She's with young and I have decided to keep her and the child when it is born. What do you say to that, partner?"

Coldiron controlled his surprise at George's disclosure of the woman's condition and his plans to deal with it. He hesitated, mulling over the ramifications. How could he answer his friend?

"I wish you the best of luck," said Luke, deciding to stay clear of voicing any evaluation of the proposal.

Tarpenning looked inquisitively at Coldiron, expecting him to go on. Then he realized the question put to his comrade was unfair. This was a very personal decision. He dropped his head and poked at the fire with a stick. "Well, I wanted you to know. We'll talk more about it after you have a chance to think on it."

He stood up without further discussion and stalked around the fire to find a seat near the girl.

Luke closely observed the expression on the woman's countenance. The beautiful dark features gave no hint as to what thoughts crossed her mind. She continued to methodically punch holes in the joining seam of two pieces of buckskin, push a narrow strip of binding hide through and pull it tight.

Luke believed she knew he was watching her; however, she gave no indication of it. Did she understand Tarpenning's intended plan for her? Would she resist it?

Coldiron put his food down without finishing it and left the cave.

Coldiron traveled up the western rim of the valley, stopping at each of his traps. He halted instantly when he saw the three sets of snowshoe tracks crossing in front of him and going down into the bottom. He hesitated only a moment to glance left to see where the trail came out of the woods and then right to sight along it. The presence of anyone at this time of year meant danger and he had to warn George. Dropping the pelts of two gray foxes he had caught, he raced along the stretch of disturbed snow, moving as swiftly as the clumsy snowshoes allowed.

He passed a spot where the three men had stopped to spy on the cabin. Now he knew without doubt they were enemies and he increased his pace to the maximum, plunging recklessly ahead. He crossed the ice-locked creek and climbed the bank. He charged past the horses. Startled, they threw up their heads and trotted aside, floundering in the deep snow.

When within fifty feet of the shelter entrance, Luke halted, removed the snowshoes and slipped forward silently. He lifted aside the door flap and peered in, his rifle cocked.

Tarpenning and the Indian woman sat on the far side of the fire, facing the entrance. Three large men, their backs to Luke, rested on bales of beaver skins, skins it appeared they had brought with them. The men were eating.

Their rifles leaned against the wall near the door.

"Luke, come in," called Tarpenning, spotting Coldiron in the doorway. "I want you to meet some gents who are trapping on the first creek to the west."

Coldiron thought he detected relief in George's voice, but it was well concealed. He crossed to casually place his rifle on the packs in the rear of the cave. Then he came to stand beside Tarpenning.

"Sidlow, Lacy and Stauber," said George, swinging his hand to point out the men as he called their names. "This is my partner, Coldiron. Luke, I've invited them to have something to eat."

The strangers grinned with full mouths and bobbed their heads in greeting. Their eyes did not match their smiles, as they measured Coldiron with cold stares.

"Howdy," said Coldiron, returning the hard looks. He judged them brutal men who would not hesitate to kill for something they wanted. He noted each of them was armed with pistol and knife. George had only a knife on him. That was bad. Luke unbuttoned his coat to expose his own weapons ready to his hand.

As they ate, the strangers let their eyes slip to the other side of the fire to rove over the girl, examining her in long, intimate detail.

The woman smelled the raunchy odors of the trappers. Their eyes were like fingers probing her. She cast a stealthy glance at them and saw their ears moving and wobbling in time with their chewing jaws, like so many animals. They were disgusting and she was afraid.

The men finished eating and wiped their beards clean on the sleeves of their buckskin shirts.

Sidlow openly allowed his sight to rest on the woman. "Right pretty Injun girl you got there."

Tarpenning shrugged his shoulders but said nothing.

Sidlow smiled shallowly. "Me and the boys here haven't seen a woman for months now and we could stand some lovin'."

"Probably could find some Ute woman not more than a hundred miles east of here," said Tarpenning.

"Never could get there and back this winter with all this snow," said Sidlow.

"Man's got to plan ahead," said Tarpenning.

"That's the best way all right. But right now I got a better idea. We'd like to buy the woman here for the rest of the winter. Forty good beaver pelts for her. What do you say to that?"

"She's not for sale," answered Tarpenning in a flinty voice.

Luke recognized the dangerous tone and glanced at his partner. Tarpenning's eyes were hot, full of warning, if the men could only read them.

"Now don't be hasty," said Sidlow in a mollifying voice. "Forty pelts is far more than an Injun is worth. But just to show we want to be fair, we'll give ten more pelts, fifty in all for her."

"No!" Tarpenning's eyes were furious, his voice strained and intense as he snapped the word out.

Luke felt the hair move on the back of his neck. He knew the wild, fierce nature of George. And the fact they were outnumbered three to two would mean nothing. But it would be worse than madness to fight

with knives and pistols in the small, confined space of the cave. All of
them could be killed.

The strange trappers stood up as if on a signal. Sidlow spoke through
stiff lips. "Then just let us borrow her for a week or so and then you can
have her back."

"No!" repeated Tarpenning and he put his hand on the butt of his
knife.

CHAPTER 6

Luke's muscles tensed. Damn it, George, he thought. Don't provoke
them, don't start a fight inside. You're correct, we've got to kill them.
But pretend to give them the girl and then we will shoot them outside.

"Coldiron, what do you say to our offer?" questioned Sidlow, leaning
forward slightly and aiming a cold stare.

The sudden query caught Luke off guard. He hesitated, not knowing
how to answer.

Some instinct within Sidlow read with undoubting sureness Luke's
true relationship with the girl. "Damn my ass. You haven't had her
either. Lived and slept right here within easy arm's length and didn't get
her." He laughed coarsely. "Now we will share her with you."

Tarpenning swept eyes that burned with unreasoning fury over
Coldiron and then Sidlow. He shouted, "Kill the bastards, Luke," and
leaped across the fire, whipping out his knife as he landed, stabbing it at
Sidlow.

With a flick of his hand, Sidlow yanked his knife and warded off his
attacker's first thrust. He sliced at Tarpenning but was off balance and
his stride was short. Tarpenning rushed upon his opponent, intending to
make a short fight so he could help Luke.

Sidlow stepped stoutly forward. They clinched, each catching the
other's knife arm. Breaths whistled between their teeth and muscles
strained as each man strove for an advantage.

Though Luke had been expecting George to attack, the swiftness of
the move had allowed him no time to immediately support the assault.

Lacy and Stauber were also caught unawares. They turned hastily to the struggling men and grabbed their hand guns.

Coldiron's hand blurred as it dipped down and came up with his pistol. As he drew, he saw that Lacy was the quicker opponent, his gun already free of the holster and lining up on George. Luke's pistol bucked in his hand as he fired a ball into Lacy's body.

Even before the stricken man could fall, Coldiron shifted his attention and hurled himself across the short distance and upon Stauber. Luke swung his heavy pistol savagely, felt it connect with Stauber's head and heard the crunch as the skull cracked. Even as he died, Stauber completed the triggering of his weapon.

Tarpenning was aware of the probable attack upon him by either Lacy or Stauber and hurled himself backward, dragging Sidlow down with him. As they struck the ground, George wrenched his hand loose and drove his knife deeply up under Sidlow's ribs. Tarpenning sprang erect just in time to take Stauber's bullet through the chest. He collapsed heavily to the ground.

Lacy, in great pain, forced himself to a sitting position. He looked around and through a haze saw one man moving, Coldiron rising from on top of Stauber. With strenuous effort, Lacy lifted his pistol and drew bead on Coldiron.

Luke looked to check how the battle between Tarpenning and Sidlow was going. He sensed movement out of the corner of his eye, locked onto it and, from not ten feet away, found the deadly black eye of Lacy's gun pointing directly at him.

Coldiron hurled himself to the right. Something tugged at his arm as he fell. There was no pain, just the force of the blow.

He jumped to his feet and charged upon Lacy. Jerking his knife as he moved, he drove the long blade down into the hollow of his enemy's neck and felt the man shudder under the impact of the piercing point of steel.

Luke hastened to Tarpenning and lifted him to lie on his back. "How bad is it, George?" he asked as he tore away the front of the bloody shirt to see the wound.

"Don't, Luke," said Tarpenning, his voice low and broken. "It's too late for me."

"Not yet, partner," objected Luke. But he was looking at the dark red hole in George's chest and knew he lied.

"Don't waste what time I've got," whispered Tarpenning. He coughed and bright red blood came into his mouth from the horrible injury. "Promise me you'll take care of her and the young one when it comes. Find a home for them."

"Sure, George, I promise. Anything you ask."

Tarpenning tried to speak again but failed, his words gurgling as his throat swelled with the ascending, choking blood.

Coldiron stifled a sob and turned away. His partner was dead and it did not have to happen. If Tarpenning had used reason, he and Luke could have tricked the three and killed all without danger to themselves.

Coldiron went to check the strange trappers. All were dead. He cursed the sons of bitches once and then again.

He stood motionless, subduing his sorrow, and watched the coils of gunpowder smoke rise lazily to the ceiling and work their way slowly out through the vent hole.

His arm began to ache and he looked down to see blood dripping from the ends of his fingers. He rolled up his sleeve to examine the wound where Lacy's bullet had struck him. A deep groove had been torn through the outside of his arm just above the elbow. It gaped open, bleeding profusely.

He cut a strip of buckskin from his shirttail and looped it around the arm, just above the injury. Awkwardly he attempted with one hand to tie the thong as a tourniquet.

The Indian girl stepped forward and took the ends of the sinew from his hand. At her touch, Luke's anger flared hot and he whirled upon her, grabbed her by the shoulders and shook her roughly.

"Damn you! You are the cause of George's death. You blinded him until he could not think." He shoved her roughly away.

She staggered backward, tripped and fell against the wall of the cave. Her head struck the stone and she crumpled with a moan to the ground.

He ignored her. With his teeth and one good hand he finished the tourniquet, inserted a short twig into it and twisted it tightly until the bleeding stopped. Then the free ends of the string were tied over the stick so it would not unwind.

Unceremoniously Coldiron dragged the bodies of the three dead men outside, found a deep drift of snow and dumped them into it. He located another white mound, even deeper, and after excavating an icy crypt placed his friend into its cold center. With a firm hand he tamped down the icy snow to seal him in. Come spring, when the ground thawed, a proper burial would be made. The other three would be hauled off and left for the buzzards to pick their bones clean.

The girl sat where she had fallen, when Luke once again looked at her. Blood was matted in her hair. A surge of disgust at himself for being cruel swept over him. She was a victim of the men, not the reason for their death. Her beauty was not her fault. The men who fought to possess that beauty were at fault. They had killed themselves, was his judgment.

Coldiron squatted down before the woman, wondering what he should say to her. He held his good hand out toward her as a gesture of peace. She flinched and drew back. Fear was ugly in her eyes. Luke agonized over that reaction, but knew he deserved it.

He said in English, "Please forgive me. I have promised my partner I would take care of you. That I surely intend to do. Can we be friends?"

Comprehension flooded her face and the fright diminished. Then the faintest of smiles trembled at the corners of her lips and she reached out with her fingertips to brush the palm of his hand. "Friends," she said.

Luke laughed gently at her understanding of the word and acceptance of his offering. Tarpenning must have been secretly teaching her English in preparation for the day when he would take her among his own people.

She climbed to her feet and pointed at the wound on his arm. Quickly she went to the roots dug earlier in the winter and sorted among the varieties until a special specie was found. In a moment it was mashed to pulp and she indicated it was to be smeared on the injury.

Coldiron loosened the tourniquet slowly. The scab of coagulated blood held and no new bleeding occurred. Deftly she pressed the poultice over the raw lips of the damaged flesh and bandaged it in fresh buckskin.

The trail in the snow was easy to follow and Luke made rapid progress. It was five days since the battle in the cabin and he was backtracking the three trappers to their camp.

Where the land angled downward into a valley, he slowed his pace, snowshoeing cautiously and silently between the tall pines. Just maybe there was yet another member of the gang.

He found the teepee of the men, screened by a fringe of trees on a south-facing slope. There was no smoke or any other sign of life. Seven horses stood near the shelter as if waiting for the men to return and feed them.

Within the hide structure was a large cache of furs, food supplies and two rifles of good quality, one with two barrels. No traps were discovered. Luke figured they must be set someplace for game.

Coldiron decided to take possession of all the belongings of the dead men. Half would be moved today, with a second trip made soon, before the scent of man lessened to the degree that some animal would invade and destroy the remaining goods.

He girdled several cottonwoods for the hungry horses. Then with practiced speed he packed the most valuable portion of his booty, the furs and guns, on two horses and struck the trail home. It was after dark before he and the weary pack beasts struggled through the last mile of deep snow and reached the warm cave.

January, The Moon of the Strong Cold, arrived. With it an ice fog settled into the valley. For many days it endured, restricting the range of sight to a few hundred feet.

Luke left the cabin only when it was absolutely necessary, and then for only brief periods. He taught the girl English, and for each word and phrase she learned she told him the Arapaho equivalent. Often the pantomime actions or drawings used to explain the meanings struck them as funny and they laughed together.

The girl was very clever and quick to learn, and Coldiron was pressed to keep pace. Until now he had never given serious thought to the intelligence of women. He found great pleasure in seeing the sparkling black eyes comprehending what he was saying, many times grasping the idea before it was fully stated.

The ice fog was finally swept away to the south as a new storm swirled in with wind and snow. The two humans continued to be locked within a few yards of the cave. Luke and the mules and horses stripped the bark from many cottonwoods. The large boles of the trees were frozen through from bark to core. Now and then, as Luke chopped upon an icy trunk, the wood would pop open, splitting itself with an explosion that made his ears ring and the animals bolt off through the deep snow.

In February the winds swung around to come in from the southwest and water noises began to sound beneath the ice on the creek.

"Soon I can start to trap again," Luke told the woman. "The beaver will be coming on the land for food."

"You have many traps and will catch all the beaver in the stream," she said and brought her hands together with a clap to show how the steel jaws, propelled by the strong springs, would close in great force upon the leg of an incautious animal.

Coldiron smiled at her lively spirit and nodded agreement. He actually had far more traps than he could properly handle for he had found most of those belonging to the dead hunters. The extra traps could be sold for a nice sum at the rendezvous or in Santa Fe.

He stopped at that thought. No, he would not be taking the girl to the rendezvous in Taos. Already she was showing signs of the developing child. In a few months she would need the assistance of a midwife to help at the birth.

Taos would be bypassed and they would travel straight to Santa Fe. Also prices for his furs would be better in Santa Fe than at the rendezvous because many trains of freight wagons traded between Independence and the Mexican town and competition was keen.

In the middle of February, the ice on the riffles of the creek in front of the cabin began to melt. However, the quiet current-free water of the ponds remained locked under more than a foot of ice. Luke packed up his equipment and moved some fifteen miles downstream and two thousand feet lower in elevation. There the water behind the tiny beaver-built dams was ice free and he set his traps.

Success was high. The first day he caught six beaver. After the long freeze-up, the animals were out hungrily foraging for fresh bark and the tender limbs of trees and brush along the banks. The second day was even more productive than the first, with eight pelts taken.

Days passed with Luke laboring from sunup to dusk, wading the cold water to place his traps, fleshing the skins and stretching them to dry. In the bleak, damp days of February, the furs would only partially dry in the open. So periodically he returned to the shelter with his pelts and left them there for the woman to finish caring for in the warmth of the fire.

The weather warmed rapidly with the coming of The Moon of the Big Wind, March. One day followed another with the sun apexing farther and farther north and higher in the sky. All beaver were killed from pond after pond as Coldiron trapped his way up the course of the stream.

One sunny day in the last part of the month, Luke lifted a trap and a drowned beaver from the creek and laid them on the bank. The quality of the fur had deteriorated rapidly during the past week and he knelt to closely examine this latest catch. Along both sides of the body the fur was thin, caused by some shedding from the warming days and from the animal rubbing itself coming and going about its routine. The pelt was not worth skinning.

With a powerful grip of his hands, he compressed the metal springs of the trap to release the jaws enough for the beaver to fall out. He left the body for the next hungry bobcat or wolf and slung the trap over his shoulder.

All trapping was finished for the year. He removed all his steel from the water and returned to the cabin. Soon as all the pelts were thoroughly cured, he would take the woman and leave the valley.

The pack animals, two mules and four horses heavily laden with bulky bales of furs, stood waiting in front of the cave shelter. Coldiron finished loading a fifth horse with the camping gear and the many extra traps and firearms that had come into his possession. He tied a spare pony to the end of the pack string, to be used in case one injured itself, and then saddled two riding horses, using Tarpenning's saddle for Morning Mist. All the other animals would be left free to fend for themselves.

Morning Mist came outside and put a small bundle of her personal belongings into the pack containing the sleeping robes. She retied the straps and turned to look out over the meadows beginning to turn green with new spring growth. "The Moon of the New Grass Appearing, the time you call April, is here."

"Yes and the Ute will be coming back into the mountains soon. They may pick this valley to camp in this summer. We should leave at once."

He was edgy and anxious to be gone. The responsibility of the pregnant woman weighed heavily upon him. Already she was commencing to become awkward on her feet from the off-centered weight of the developing child, and there were many tough miles to travel. There would be no relief for him until he had her safely among other women.

"Let's mount up and ride out of here," said Luke.

"I am ready," responded Morning Mist and moved up beside her pony to mount.

Luke stepped quickly to her side, caught her under the arms and lifted her gently astride. He swung upon his own mustang and glanced at the long caravan. A small fortune existed in the hundreds of pounds of fur, that is if he could transport it the one hundred and fifty rough, dangerous miles to Santa Fe and sell at a fair price.

Taking up the rope of the lead animal, Luke headed down the east side of the valley.

"Luke, wait," called Morning Mist and urged her pony past all the other animals and up close to Coldiron. "I don't want to be last in line for then I cannot talk with you. It is alright if I ride beside you?"

He grinned at her. Her company was pleasant and she would be safer near him. "Fine by me," he said.

Not wanting to tire her, Luke set a slow pace. Often he examined her face to judge how she was standing up under the journey.

Their course paralleled the snow-covered crest of the tall mountains that formed the Continental Divide, lying some ten miles away on the right. After several hours the high backbone of the land veered to the west and the terrain fell away gradually before the travelers. The stream turned eastward in the direction of the winter camp of the Utes. Luke wanted to go south and at the same time lessen any possibility of encountering the Indians on their migration to the mountains. He guided his caravan straight ahead, leaving the smooth bottomland and entering a series of low forested mountains.

The young woman spoke often to Coldiron and pointed out things to him that caught her interest, like the newborn fawn the horses almost stepped on while it lay frozen immobile, or the log that a bear had ripped open searching for grubs. Luke had already spotted these things before she indicated them, but he always acknowledged her statements as if they were something new to him.

It was strange to journey with someone who constantly chattered. Tarpenning and he had ridden in silence, rarely speaking, moving noiselessly so as not to attract the attention of hostile Indians.

More than once, he almost told her to be quiet. But there was little likelihood they would encounter other humans for another day or so, and besides, he greatly enjoyed her pleasant, melodious voice. Reviewing the weeks they had lived so closely together, he realized that not once had she ever complained, argued or hesitated to do her share of the chores.

Tarpenning had fallen under her spell for good cause. She was a very fit mate for a mountain man.

Shortly before dark they came upon a small spring in a cove on the side of a mountain. It was well hidden and surrounded by an acre or so of meadow. Luke dismounted to scout and found no sign of man, only the tracks of deer and the round pad marks of a bobcat in the soft soil near the water.

"This looks like a good place for us to spend the night," he said to Morning Mist and stepped up and lifted her to the ground.

"You know I can mount and get down from my mustang by myself," she said. "The women of my people ride and work to the very time of giving birth."

"I'm sure you could do it, too," said Luke. "But please always let me help you. You start a fire and I'll care for the animals."

After hobbling the mules and horses, he climbed to a rocky knob above the spring and surveyed the surrounding land. To the east, short wooded mountains fell away for forty miles or better to where they faded into the great plains. Somewhere near the edge of the plain, freight wagons would be bumping and rattling along the Santa Fe Trail.

A series of mountains stretched to the south, until at the extreme limit of his vision a great flat-topped mountain, its crown blown away by some gigantic volcanic explosion millions of years in the past, reared majestically up into the clouds. He knew the mountain, for Santa Fe lay at its east base. To the east of the tall caldera reared the highest peak of all, Sierra Mosca. Beyond this rocky prominence the mountain chain, growing ever smaller, extended deeply into Mexico. Half a day's ride to the west the crest of the Continental Divide still glistened white in the failing light.

With each passing minute, daylight leaked away to the sky and a gray darkness hurried in from the east, filling the troughs of the valleys. The gloom grew deeper, overflowing the depressions, engulfing the low hills and hiding them from Coldiron's view. Before the light disappeared completely, he went down to the camp to eat a delicious meal with the woman.

Late into the night they sat and talked of many things. Luke described the towns he had seen, the far north mountains he and Tarpenning had trapped, and he even spoke briefly of his home in the East. Morning Mist listened, enchanted. Every one of the places sounded so very interesting, but she knew it was the man who sat and talked with her that made it all so wonderful.

CHAPTER 7

It was the second day when Luke and Morning Mist rode into a forested valley with steep rocky sides that contained a small stream. As they approached the water to allow their mounts to drink, Luke reined his horse to a fast halt. In the dirt before him were the tracks of many unshod mustangs, perhaps seventy animals. Creasing the surface of the ground and cutting through the hoofprints were the drag marks of several travois.

"Ute," Luke said to Morning Mist and pointed down at the sign of the Indians' passage. "They went by here recently, this morning I would guess. From the number of teepee poles they dragged, I judge twenty lodges strong."

He looked in the direction the Indians had gone. Nothing indicated danger. There were only the peaceful sigh of the wind swaying the boughs of the pine trees and running water making noise in the creek.

Had he and the girl been one day earlier, the Ute would have been crossing their trail instead of the other way around. His own animals were now unshod, same as the Indian ponies; however, in this season of early spring, his north to south course would have told the Indians that the odds were high a trapper with a load of furs had passed. More than likely a band of warriors would be in fast pursuit, looking for scalps and loot.

Coldiron allowed his animals to drink while he kept watch both ways along the valley for stragglers from the Indian band.

"We need water," said Morning Mist in a hushed voice.

Luke nodded. "Get some quickly and get back on your horse."

She guided her mustang up beside a fallen log and climbed down on it. With hurried steps she went to the creek above Luke and submerged the necks of the canteens. She lugged the dripping containers back, hung them over the pommel of her saddle and remounted the pony.

"I'm ready," she said.

Luke led off immediately. At the first place where the walls of the valley were less steep, he picked a well-used game trail and followed it as it climbed up and down over a ridge.

In the afternoon, thunderheads began to build over the crest of the mountains on their far right. They grew rapidly, towering white columns boiling up with threatening gray centers. Misty streamers of rain started to fall. Only the fringe of the cool moisture touched Coldiron and the woman, not enough to bother them to pull out a covering to protect themselves.

The third day their southerly course entered Nuevo Méjico, territory claimed by Mexico. Luke only guessed when they crossed the border, for it was unmarked and no one knew for sure its location in the deep mountains.

Also the first humans were seen that day. The mules and horses were blowing from a hard climb, and Luke had walked out to a projecting point of land to reconnoiter ahead when two trappers, leading three packhorses piled high with bundles of fur, came out of a fringe of trees. Luke slunk down into a leafy patch of brush and watched them pass not a hundred yards below him.

Normally, had he been traveling with Tarpenning, they would have called out and hastened to join up with the strangers for the trek out to the rendezvous. But these were perilous days and the Mexican Govern-

ment enforced no law north of Santa Fe. The strength of muscle and
sharpness of the shooting eye guarded one's valuables. And Tarpenning
was not here to help in any fight that might occur.

With the girl's safety his responsibility and the furs to protect, he
planned to avoid all contact with Indian or white man.

"Can the mustangs make it through?" asked Morning Mist as she
peered past Luke at the boulder-choked gorge.

"Doesn't look like it," he replied. "You wait here while I take a look-
see." He stepped down to clamber forward over the large brown boulders.

Their route had been in the bed of a stream all afternoon. Bit by bit it
had descended into a narrow rocky chasm. Not wanting to backtrack,
and with the bottom remaining flat and easily navigated by the animals,
they pressed on.

Coldiron returned. "About a hundred yards farther on around that
bend, the gully widens out into a level basin. I can place some rocks to
bridge between the boulders for the horses to walk on and we can be
clear through in a couple of hours. Find yourself a shady spot while I get
it done."

The animals were skittish, not liking the feel of the stones, some
unstable and wobbly, that Luke had laid as a footpath for them. But they
permitted themselves to be coaxed upon them and onward, betwixt the
large round boulders and out into the valley.

The canyon floor was mostly flat, approaching five miles in width and
stretching south many times that distance, extending so far that it was
impossible for Luke to see its end. A few small hills, capped with pine,
were scattered randomly about. On every side high sandstone ledges,
tens of feet thick, rimmed the valley in with smooth vertical walls. A
creek at grade and meandering in long looping curves crossed the full
length of the valley.

"Oh! How beautiful this place is," exclaimed Morning Mist.

"Yes, a good-looking land and all set off by itself."

"Look, wild mustangs," Morning Mist pointed.

Coldiron turned his view to where she indicated and then continued
to skim as much of the basin as he could see for more horses. "There are
at least twenty bands within sight. Over there near the edge of the
woods is a band of elk. They don't seem excited. We may be the only
humans they have seen for a long time, or forever."

"There are beaver ponds in the creek."

"Not enough to be worth the effort to set traps and the pelts would not have any value this time of year."

Morning Mist smiled and waved her hand at the pack animals heavily burdened with furs. "You already have enough riches to buy many women."

Luke did not respond to her teasing.

"Let's find a place to camp and stay here a few days," suggested Morning Mist.

She saw a doubtful expression come to his face and hastened to continue. "It is nearly two moons before the child is to be born. We have plenty of time to stop and then go on to the place you call Santa Fe."

"It is a pleasant-looking place," agreed Luke. "We should be safe here." Though they had traveled slowly, a third of the distance to their destination had been covered. Morning Mist had stood up to the ride quite strongly. Still, a couple days' rest would do her good.

He guided the way to the left and along the base of the rimrock. On the warm west-facing slope they came to a meadow of flowers. The yellow blossoms, two or three acres of them, bobbed their tiny round heads in the gentle wind like thousands of butterflies trembling on the verge of flight. The mountain honeybees droned a low sleepy hum all around. As the hooves of the horses waded the golden turf, a sweet, tantalizing aroma rose up to delight the sense of smell of the man and woman.

"The first flowers we have seen," said Morning Mist and breathed deeply of the odor. "And there is a spring just over there. Let us camp here."

The burdens of the pack string were dropped to the ground. As Luke began to hobble the animals, he glanced at the nearest band of wild mustangs standing on a nearby hilltop. Seeing the watchful attention of the harem stallion, Luke took particular care of the hobbles on the tame mares, pulling the straps extra snug around the ankles. Better to prevent the opportunity for his ponies to run off and join the wild bunch than to try to round them up later.

Soon as Luke had finished with the horses, he dug into one of the pouches and rose up smiling, holding a hook and line in his hand. "I bet you there are trout in that creek. Be back in a little while."

A long slender willow was cut for a pole and a plump white grub from under a rock went on the hook as bait. At the first cast a trout, hungry after the long winter, took the juicy offering with a rush and splash of water. The second and third fish were caught nearly as quickly.

The trout were roasted to a golden brown and Morning Mist and

Coldiron were soon eating, savoring the delicious change of food. She chewed the last tiny morsel of her portion and grinned at Luke. "Good, very good. Why does the first fish of the spring taste so wonderful?"

"After all the red meat we have eaten this winter, our bodies crave something different. And surely I agree with you, it is a mighty fine taste. I'll catch another batch tomorrow." He leaned back to contentedly lie on the ground.

The yellow sun slanting in from the west was warm and pleasant on Morning Mist. She reclined beside Luke. She thought of their destination. "How much longer for us to ride to Santa Fe?"

"We can make it in four to five days without making it too hard on you."

"Will it be hot there?"

"Yes, much warmer than here in the high mountains."

"I like friendly people, Luke. Are the people friendly there?"

Not to Indians, reflected Coldiron, and sometimes not to gringos. "Most of them are friendly," he said.

"How many people live there?"

"When I was there two years ago, about two thousand, maybe twenty-two hundred. I have heard the town is growing fast. Quite a lot of trading goes on between the Americans and the Mexicans. The Santa Fe Trail coming down from Independence, Missouri, ties in to the El Camino Real of the Mexicans. The El Camino wagon road goes hundreds of miles deep into Mexico, to Chihuahua and on to Mexico City. The American traders take south with them manufactured goods such as print cloth, boots and iron wares. The Mexicans swap gold, fur and mules for these items. Something interesting is always happening in Santa Fe. I think you will like it there."

I do not believe I will, thought Morning Mist. Yet she said nothing. This man had been a very good friend and she did not want to cause him concern.

"I do not understand some of those words you spoke. Iron wares. Does that have something to do with your name Coldiron?"

Luke laughed good-naturedly, began another lesson in English and got his lesson in the Arapaho tongue in return.

Luke rode the wash, staying hidden, trying to slip as close as possible to the herd of wild mustangs on a low ridge half a mile ahead. They were not yet aware of his presence and the wind was from them to him.

Coldiron had loafed one whole day after arriving in the valley. Then his cautious nature had roused him and he had saddled his mount to scout the land. He must know if Morning Mist and he were alone. He had been at it two days, but the long roundabout route examining the area below the rimrocks was nearly complete.

He was amazed at the great number of wild horses and even more surprised at the large quantity of dead ones. Within a short distance after leaving camp, he had come upon the first skeleton of a horse. The skin of the carcass, though dry and cracked, still covered most of the bones and he knew the beast had died during the past winter. Scores more bodies were soon discovered and the degree of decomposition ran the gamut. Some bodies were years old and consisting merely of a few bleached bones; others still had the smell of rotting flesh, dead not more than a month.

Now he was getting close to the band and he stood up in the stirrups and cautiously peeked over the lip of the ravine. The mustangs still grazed the wild grass on the side of the hill. On the highest point a tall roan stallion stood solitary watch.

The large black eyes in the intelligent head of the stud saw everything that moved in his domain. From his elevation he could view the flat bottom to where the stream entered the basin from the north and in the opposite direction where it left in the south. On the far side of the valley, to the east, the steep rimrock rose abruptly to block his sight.

Once in a summer drought, when the grass had grown only an inch when it should have reached a foot, he and his dam had climbed up a steep trail, through a gap in that rocky face so narrow their shoulders touched on both sides and out onto a great level plateau covered with trees. There had been no grass there either. Disturbed and feeling unsafe in that unknown place, they had turned and clambered back down into the country where both of them had been born. Better to stay where the dangers were known than to wander in an untrod land.

The colt had been strong and had survived that long dry summer and the winter of starvation that followed. Over the next four years, when the grass was tall, he grew into a large animal. He acquired his harem of mares a month just past.

Big wounds on his neck and withers were almost healed. Large white splotches, like some terrible disease, showed where the scabs had sloughed away. The injuries had been made by the vicious mouth of the giant black during the fight when the red one had stolen the black's harem. Those sixteen females, their rumps glistening in the afternoon sun, grazed the green grass on the slope below his lookout. From time to time they would look up and prick their ears toward the stallion, listening for any signal from their king.

The swale gradually shallowed until Luke could no longer remain out of sight. He leaned forward over the horse, holding himself tight against the neck, trying to blend himself with the brute. Then reining his mount directly toward the band of mustangs, Luke kicked him up into the open.

The watchful stallion spotted the strange horse the instant his head showed above the top of the wash. The stud snorted nervously and stamped the stony ground. He almost charged down to challenge and drive away the intruder, but the unnatural hump on the back of the newcomer worried him and he held back.

Luke drew closer, less than two hundred yards separating him from the mustangs. Unable to endure the nearness of the strangely shaped animal, the harem stallion spooked down the hill, bugling a loud commanding whinny out across the grassy slope. The mares instantly came to attention. Sweeping across the rear of the band, he nipped and crowded them in the direction he had selected for escape. Sensing quickly the intention of the master, the lead mare broke from the milling herd and raced away, the others immediately following.

The stallion sped straight through the group and took up station three lengths in front. He increased his pace, drawing the rest behind him like metal filings after a magnet.

The band of horses flowed past Coldiron in a flat-out dead streaking run, their long unpruned tails streaming out behind. The stud was a fine-looking beast in moderate flesh. The mares were in varying states of physical condition. The stronger ones were in middling shape like the stud. The very old and very young were thin, and several were worse than that, being bony and scraggily coated.

Trailing the mares and trying desperately to keep up was one sickly colt, all that remained of this year's crop of young. Luke shook his head sadly at the stunted little fellow. There were too many horses for the amount of grass that grew on the land. The strong survived while the others died, horribly.

One thing about the mustangs pleased Luke. A wide variation of color was present, with the predominant shades being black, bay and roan. The roans had a fair amount of gray mixed in. As a total, there were enough color and pattern that a good breeder of horses could develop an outstanding herd.

Luke ranged his eyes over the thick rock ledge rimming the basin. Five trails he had counted by which the wild ones had found entrance to this place. They were steep trails, passable now, but with snow on the ground, the period when food was most scarce, the hard hooves of no horse could climb that sharply angled grade. The stream's exit from the valley was the same as the bouldery entrance, closed to the passage of a hard-footed mustang. Almost completely locked in, they had bred and multiplied until now; except in the best of years, they were always half-starved.

Luke evaluated the rough, narrow access ways into the valley. With two weeks of work a man could wall up these trails. That would make the herds of mustangs his.

The sun rose, its shaft of golden light striking across the rimrock, ready to melt the purple shadows from the valley. In a cavern beneath the ledge of rock, the big male mountain lion slept. His stomach was full, for in the darkness of the early dawn he had killed a colt and gorged himself. From time to time his long tawny tail lifted and twitched. The great white claws half unsheathed themselves as he relived the final charge, the crunch of bone between his teeth and the taste of tender flesh.

Luke led a slow pace along the horse and game trail that slanted up the pine-covered slope toward the rimrock. Morning Mist followed close behind him, riding astride her soft-stepping steed. Plodding last was the pack train, each beast tied with a short length of rawhide to the one just ahead.

"Luke," called Morning Mist, "we could have stayed here for a few more days. It is still more than a moon before my time to give birth." She was happy in the companionship of her male friend and wanted to lengthen it.

Coldiron twisted in the saddle to look at his small companion. They had spent eleven days, quiet spring-filled days, in the valley. She had grown ever more beautiful as her pregnancy had advanced. She seemed extremely healthy.

He smiled at her. He knew they would not have left had he not insisted upon it. "Maybe we are moving on more for my peace of mind than yours," he said. "But, I imagine you will also feel more at ease once you are with other women."

I do not think I will like Santa Fe, thought Morning Mist.

The pathway grew narrow, barely wide enough for one animal, and crowded in close to the base of the cliff. The slope of the hill fell away steeply on the right.

Morning Mist called out again to Luke, her high-toned woman's voice sweeping out through the woods and piercing into the semidarkness of the cave where the lion drowsed.

The sound penetrated the sleep of the lion. He awoke instantly and sprang to his feet, muscles bunched. His savage eyes darted out through the opening in the rock and into the lighted world just outside.

A line of mustangs with two riders were passing not thirty feet distant. The smaller human in the rear was making alien mouth noises. The lion, cornered within the cave, swished his tail in frustration and growled threateningly. He crept to the very brink of the light.

Then no longer able to endure the nearness of the horsemen, the lion roared its fury and hurtled from hiding in one long bound. He struck the earth near the horses, coiled himself and leaped again, passing in back of Luke's mount and in front of Morning Mist's, his body brushing the pony's face. He vanished among the dark trees.

In mortal fear of his ancient enemy, Morning Mist's pony flung himself to the right. His feet lost the trail and slipped on the sharp-angled side of the hill, and he fell, rolling, crashing down through the trees.

Morning Mist was pitched from the saddle by the sudden swerve of the panicked mount. She struck the ground, tumbled once, twice, striking hard and stopping against the trunk of a large pine.

Luke saw Morning Mist fall, but he could do nothing, for his own frightened mount was bolting ahead. He caught the leather reins up short and pulled them into his lap. The mustang fought the steel bit so mercilessly cutting its mouth under the powerful arm of the man.

Coldiron hauled the horse to a sliding halt and instantly whirled him around to speed back to the location where Morning Mist had fallen. He dropped to the ground and jumped down the incline to kneel beside her.

Morning Mist struggled up to a half-sitting position and propped herself against the base of the tree. "Oh, Luke, I am badly hurt," she said, her face strained with the shock of her fall.

"Easy does it. Let me see." Luke gently began to examine her, steadying her slight body against him on the steep hillside. His heart ached when he saw the upper right arm bent at an impossible angle. From the way she winced at each breath he judged she also had broken ribs. How much other internal damage there was could not even be guessed at. She was bloody from many scrapes and bruises.

"I must carry you to a level spot. I'll try to pain you as little as possible."

"All right," she answered with a tortured whisper. "Do you think my baby is hurt?"

"I don't know. The hardest blow seems to have been on your arm and above your stomach. Maybe the baby is okay." But it will be a miracle if it lives with you injured so badly, he thought.

He lifted her up in his arms. The agony of the movement added its toll to the growing shock of her body and she fainted. Luke dug in his toes, climbed to the trail and continued in under the rock ledge.

In the soft dirt where the lion had slept Coldiron tenderly eased the battered girl to the ground. He set and splinted the broken arm while she was still unconscious. He decided not to try to treat the fractured ribs. She was cold and clammy to his touch. He was greatly disturbed, for her condition was precarious, her survival in great doubt. Hastily he went to fetch a canteen and a sleeping robe.

The pack animals had heard the maddening growl of the cougar and Luke found that the front ones had surged backward to become entangled with those behind. Two were down, thrashing, kicking the ones still standing. Half the packs were dislodged and dragging the ground. So snarled were the animals with each other they had been unable to stampede.

"Whoa now! Stand still you ornery bastards," commanded Coldiron as he strove to fashion order out of the mix-up. As soon as they were straightened out, he hurried to return to Morning Mist.

As he placed her on the buffalo robe, her eyes came open. "I am so very cold," she said and a shiver shook her.

Luke tucked the thick warm hide in snugly. "I will build a fire."

"Wait. Don't leave me," she whispered in an urgent voice. "I am having pains like I have seen women have when birthing a baby. But it is too early."

Luke touched her cheek, wishing there was something he could do to lessen her hurt and the growing fear.

"The injuries and the strain may be hurrying the child along."

"You will stay with me?"

"You have my promise on that. I'll do everything I can to help you."

CHAPTER 8

A tiny girl child was born in the first full darkness of the night. Luke gave the baby the best care he knew how, cleansing her, tying the umbilical cord and swaddling the little wrinkled body in tanned deer hide.

In that hour just before dawn, when a human's vitality is at its lowest ebb, Morning Mist died.

Beneath the ledge Luke dug a grave down to solid rock. He wrapped Morning Mist in a robe and tied it firmly about her in several places. With trembling hands he lowered her into the hole and covered her with the excavated soil. Using all his strength, he dragged a large rock, a slab of the overhang that had spilled down from above, over the grave. Upon that, many more rocks were piled until a great mound had been constructed.

He knelt beside the burial cairn, his hat in his hands and tears in his eyes. The realization lay heavy upon him that had Morning Mist lived he would have kept her with him and never let her go.

He thought of Tarpenning. I am sorry, old partner. I could not honor my promise to keep her safe. He turned away and hastened from the grave.

There were important things to be done and many miles to travel if he was to keep the child alive.

A soft beaver fur was shaped into a carrying pouch. The tiny infant, weighing less than his pistol, was tenderly slipped inside the hide bag and hung over the horn of the saddle.

Coldiron jerked the pack string into line and left immediately, up through a gap in the natural barrier of rimrock and then across rolling wooded hills.

In mid morning Luke gave the baby a drink, dipping his finger into the neck of the canteen and then quickly withdrawing it to allow the water to drip into the small mouth. Several times he repeated the procedure until confident the infant had consumed sufficient liquid.

He noted the baby was being jarred by the step of the horse on the downhill stretches of trail. He cinched his shirt in tightly with his belt, lifted the baby from the carrying pouch and placed the minute speck of life inside, next to his chest.

No stop was made for lunch or rest. At one short halt the baby was watered again and Luke changed mounts. As the day wore long the pack beasts grew tired and tried to slacken the pace, but he forged ahead, towing them on a tight rope and not slowing at all.

The baby had not cried once. Nor had it moved for some time. Coldiron reached inside and held his fingers on the frail chest until he felt it expand with a breath. How many hours could a newborn hold on to life without food? Was there some other care or assistance he should give it? He spoke to his mount and that willing horse stepped out more smartly, putting even more strain on the lead line and the necks of the animals wanting to slow up.

As the darkness threatened to obliterate the trail, a bright white moon sailed up over the hills to the east and Luke continued on into the night. Finally clouds obscured the moon and he stopped. He dropped the packs from the backs of the animals and laid the baby on a soft bale of fur.

It was a dry camp with no water except from the canteen for the baby and himself. Fifty long miles had been traversed, a tough, hard day. The horses and mules should not be treated so harshly, but not one minute of daylight could be wasted by stopping early simply for them to have water.

The animals were hobbled with extra care, for he did not want to have to search for a stray come the morning. When released they did not graze, only wandered off a few steps and stood with drooping heads.

Luke picked up the child. The premature body hung limp in his hands and for a frightening moment he thought she was dead. Hastily putting his ear close to the mouth and nose, he held his breath to listen.

A soft puff of air touched his face as the diminutive chest exhaled. The underdeveloped human, a minute speck of life, still clung to the world of the living.

A coolness came in with the night. Luke swaddled the baby with a second thickness of tanned deer hide. She stirred and a hand came free of the covering and the thumb found the mouth. Coldiron smiled. The gloom that lay all about, that had forced him to stop, was now more endurable.

As he sat holding the girl infant, a listening silence fell upon the wooded hills. The hush held, broken once by something that passed close in the darkness, like the flight of a bat.

The first paling of the stars found him moving. When the sun was a quarter of the way up its arc, he came down through the patchy woods and into the valley and upon the wagon road. Only one such road, worn and rutted with the passing of many wagons, existed in this remote land —the Santa Fe Trail.

Luke looked north toward Independence, Missouri. The trail lay deserted as far as he could see. He guided his thirsty beasts south in the direction of Santa Fe.

Near noon he arrived at the turnoff to the Indian pueblo of Taos. The village was close, lying five miles to the east. But the fur buyers would be long gone by this late in the season and Luke pressed on along the main road south.

In mid afternoon, a small plume of dust became visible on the road ahead and he hurried onward to meet it. At half a mile three wagons could be made out, each drawn by three teams of mules. A man on horseback rode point, two hundred yards out in front.

As Luke scrutinized the wagon train it descended into a narrow stream channel and out of sight. The voices of the drivers calling and the iron rims of the wheels rattling and grating on the rocky creek bottom floated to him.

Shortly Luke's road fell away into the valley and he looked down upon the small freight caravan. The teams stood knee deep in a fair size stream, drinking. Faded canvas was lashed over large loads bulking up high above the wooden sideboards of the wagon beds. At the tailgates of the vehicles the drivers were untying spare mules to take to water.

Coldiron leaned on the pommel of his saddle and evaluated the scene as the drivers and their animals watered at the creek. He was disappointed for he had hoped to find settlers, which could mean a woman was with the party. A woman to wet-nurse the child, that was his desperate need.

The point rider had crossed the creek and now sat his horse part way up the far slope. He saw the trapper when he and his string of pack animals appeared on the brink of the hill. Quickly he called a warning down to the other teamsters.

Luke's thirsty mules and mustangs smelled the water and crowded forward, trying to get past him. He yanked them back into formation and led the way down the rocky side of the wash, the dust kicked up by the animals swirling up on the wind.

The point rider, a middle-aged man cradling a rifle in his arms, watched the trapper approach.

"Howdy," Coldiron greeted him.

"Howdy, yourself," answered the man. He examined the eyes of the young man for his intentions; he saw no danger there, only a tense and hurried look. He glanced beyond Coldiron and counted the bales of fur, noting the animals of the pack string were gaunt and had been pushed hard. The trapper was traveling at a mighty fast clip.

"Right smart bunch of furs you got there," said the point rider. "But you missed the rendezvous by nigh a month."

"I did that all right. Had some trouble that delayed me."

Luke continued past the man and down to the creek. His mules and horses took long noisy swigs of the water as he dismounted and ranged his view over the wagons and the teamsters in their heavy work clothes. On the sides of the wagon boxes in faded yellow paint were the words "Clark Freight Co."

Two of the drivers moved toward Luke and he fastened his sight on them. He kept his hands away from his weapons to show he was friendly, for he had ridden into their temporary territory. In the edge of his vision, the third teamster climbed back up into the high wagon seat and turned to watch the men on the ground.

The two men, big with dark heavy beards, greatly resembled the point rider and Luke judged them closely related. They appeared strong and alert, tough enough to look after their own. They drew up a short distance from Coldiron and, half warily and half friendly, looked him over.

The baby stirred against Luke's chest. His hand swiftly swept up to touch the bulge in the front of his shirt.

The teamsters' caution tightened at the movement, the younger one swinging up his rifle and earing back the hammer. What did the trapper hide inside his clothes?

"You got any women with you?" asked Coldiron.

"Now, why would you want to know that?" growled the younger freighter.

From the man's expression and his answer, Luke calculated there was indeed a woman with their party. He moved his view to the third driver. When that person had climbed into the wagon, he had thought that beneath the man's pants the hips were very broad. Now Coldiron intently scrutinized the tanned beardless face beneath the battered hat squashed down to touch the ears. A face with extraordinarily smooth skin. The imprint of two large breasts could be made out pressing against the cloth of the shirt.

The older man was angry at Coldiron's intimate examination of his companion. "Trapper, what's your problem that you want to know about a woman?" His voice was cold and threatening.

Luke noticed a minute shift in the man's stance as he readied himself for quick action. Slowly Coldiron inserted his hand inside his shirt.

The second driver jerked his rifle to his shoulder. The younger man shouted a warning. "Mister, hold it right there."

"Easy now," said Luke. "I don't want any trouble."

"Well, you sure are tempting hell. At this range, this old gun can blow a hole through you I could put my fist through."

"I've got a baby here in my shirt that badly needs a woman's care."

"Sure you do," scoffed the younger man. "Now just bring you hand out real slow like."

Coldiron lifted the infant into sight.

"Goddamn almighty! You do have a baby. What are you doing with that?"

"It needs something to eat and maybe some other help."

The younger man called over his shoulder, "Bess, this man's got a youngun, a might small youngun."

"All right if I show her?" asked Luke.

"Sure, go ahead." All belligerence had left the man.

The woman's wide brown eyes appraised the young trapper hurrying toward her. The two men of her family, the younger her husband and the other his brother, followed closely behind the stranger. She knew they came to protect her as well as out of curiosity. Her men folk could turn quickly violent if they thought harm threatened her. She was pleased to be a woman and, with the men's nearness, she felt safe in this wild land.

With a hopeful expression that stirred Bess's heart, the trapper held out the child. Her strong working hands gently took the infant.

Luke spoke hastily. "She's two days old and hasn't had a bite to eat yet."

"Appears like she came early," observed Bess. "Have you given her water?"

"Yes, several times. Is there anything you can do for her?"

"You are in luck. I got my own kid, a son sleeping back there in the bed of the wagon. He's six months old, so I'm still fresh with milk."

Paying no attention to Luke's eyes upon her, Bess opened her shirt and exposed a milk-filled teat. The baby's mouth was pressed to the tan nipple without delay. But the tiny mouth remained closed.

Bess rubbed the nipple back and forth along the crease between the lips. Still the child did not respond, lying listlessly. As she teased and toyed with the child, the woman's breast began to lose milk, white drops trickling down to land on the small mouth. Quickly she placed a finger on each side of the baby's face and pressed in on the cheeks.

The lips parted to accept the life-giving drops.

Bess smiled at Luke. "Her tongue is curling. She's getting ready to nurse." She lifted the baby slightly. "She is sucking! Not strong like my boy, but good enough." A pleased expression, very charming to Luke, came to her face.

The husband was growing angry at the trapper for watching his wife nurse the child. He started to move forward to pull Luke aside just as the trapper turned to face him. The teamster's hand fell back to his side when he observed Luke's eyes shiny with relief at having found food for the infant.

"I'm very lucky to find you and your woman," said Coldiron. "I owe both of you very much."

"Bess is a good mother. The young one will get a belly full real quick."

"God! I'm glad for that!" said Luke fervently.

They walked away from the woman and squatted down comfortably in the shade cast by one of the wagons.

The older man spoke. "I'm Jed Clark." He put out his hand to shake with Coldiron. "This is my brother, John. Bess is his wife. Albert is up there on the hill."

"My name is Luke Coldiron." He shook hands with both men.

"Since the trapper's rendezvous is long over with, I would guess you're going to Santa Fe," said Jed.

"Yes, to sell these furs. How's the price this spring?"

"Down a little from last year. Prime pelts are bringing $2.00 to $2.10 a pound. Looks like you got several hundred pounds."

Luke nodded his head. "The price is not like a few years back when a prime pelt fetched $4.00 to $5.00 a pound."

"Just about like hauling freight. Profit's gone. I think Sam Magoffin and Bent-St. Vrain with their big outfits are cutting prices to drive us little fellows out of business."

"Well, they sure as hell are getting that done alright," said John.

"How are the Mexicans and the American getting along?" asked Coldiron. "I heard some hard talk in Independence last fall about fighting the Mexes."

"Some folks are talking of war," said Jed. "But I don't believe it will happen. What's here to fight over?"

"Seems like wherever the Mexes are, there is gold and silver," said Luke.

"They do have good luck looking for those valuables," agreed John.

"How many other freight companies besides you and the two big lines?" asked Luke.

"Must be more than a dozen. We run into one on the trail now and then," answered Jed.

"John, Jed, let's set up camp here and spend the rest of today and tonight," called Bess in a firm voice as if she had given the subject considerable thought and had made up her mind. "That way I can feed this baby a few more times before we leave."

Coldiron saw the reluctance in the two men. Time was money. "You're right about the baby needing you," said Jed. He pivoted to look up at the walls of the narrow valley. "But it is not safe in this hole in the ground without a good lookout."

He walked out away from the wagon and yelled loudly. "Albert, Bess says we should stay here today. This man's got a child that needs care. You find a high point and keep guard. John and I will take turns with you after a while."

Up on the hillside Albert waved his hand in acknowledgement of the plan and reined his horse to climb to a better vantage point.

"Are you interested in buying my furs?" asked Luke. "You should be able to turn a fair profit by reselling them in Independence."

Jed answered. "I'd like to, but can't do it. We're plumb out of cash money and we're not hauling anything you would want."

Coldiron did not pry further. The usual merchandise going north was gold and silver, furs and mules. He saw no mules other than those needed to pull the wagons.

"You haul freight just between Santa Fe and Independence?"

"Yes, back and forth between those towns."

"Any Indian trouble?"

"No trouble I've heard of except the Comanche stole about fifty head of horses from a ranch south of Santa Fe last fall. In the spring like this, the tribes are short of supplies and are traveling around looking for new hunting land. A party of Ute bucks, squaws and children came onto us on our way south a few days back. We were hauling boots, calicos and some manufactured wares. So we gave them a few metal goods, pans and such and they went about their business. But a big fight is coming one of these days as more and more whites come into the country. Even now some of the smaller traders are joining up in wagon trains for better protection. That's what we plan to do next year."

"I still think we should go out to California and start a freight business," said John.

"We'll need to talk some more on that," said Jed.

"She's sleeping now," called Bess. "She nursed good and then dozed off."

The men returned to stand near her. Luke closely watched the face of the kindly woman as she held the baby. He was much impressed by the entire Clark family.

The evening passed pleasantly with the freighters. The woman nursed her own child and Luke's infant several times, her big breast always producing milk and the children sucking contentedly.

In the middle of the night, Coldiron climbed the hill to relieve Jed and take over the watch. In the hushed darkness, a warm spring night, he sat without moving and followed the stars as they wheeled across the sky. Daylight seemed to arrive early, the sun bursting up over the horizon in a spray of thin golden clouds. Voices sounded and soon Albert rode up. Luke spoke briefly with him and went into the valley to help break up camp.

An idea had been born in Coldiron's mind during the silent night. He knew that alone he could not be a proper guardian for Tarpenning and Morning Mist's child. Would the Clarks, who had spoken of having financial problems, be agreeable to raising the child for a fee? He would make them a proposition.

Luke prepared his own animals for travel and approached the men and Bess, who sat balancing tin plates on their knees and eating breakfast.

"Join us for some grub," invited Jed.

Coldiron did as he was bid and soon was savoring bacon, pancakes and coffee. As the last of the food disappeared and a certain anxiousness to be moving on began to stir the Clarks, Coldiron broached his idea.

"Folks, I have no way to care for the baby in a fit manner. Would you be interested in taking care of her and teaching her to read and write? I would pay you a fair yearly sum to help me with this."

With an astonished expression, John looked at his wife. Coldiron noted that Bess smiled slightly and did not seem surprised. She would not be one to be easily caught unawares.

"Bess, you already got one young one," said John. "Do you want to try two of them?"

The woman faced Luke. "Small as she is, she needs a lot of care and plenty of milk."

Coldiron examined the expression on Bess's gentle face. She was the more important one of the husband and wife team. Her age he guessed at near thirty. Apparently a late marriage. Her husband and she, from all indications, were on good terms.

"I would pay $200 a year," said Luke. That amount was a year's salary for a man on a wage, more than fair payment for the support of the child.

Bess held Luke's intense, measuring stare for several seconds. Then she turned to John. "She would make us a pair, a boy and a girl. With that much money, I could stay home and raise the kids. You, Jed and Albert could hire another driver to take my place." She swung her large brown eyes back to Coldiron. "We will do it. We will raise you a fine daughter."

"Yes, a fine daughter," echoed John and nodded at Luke and smiled.

Luke did not correct their wrong assumption about the child's parentage. It was not important at this time.

"Then it is agreed," he said, feeling a great relief yet with an unexpected tinge of sadness. It was very strange how one could become attached in two days to something so small and unprepossessing as that baby.

He went to the pack string and untied the rope of an animal with a heavy load of fur. He led it up and tied it to the tailgate of the wagon Bess drove.

"There's probably two hundred to two hundred and twenty-five pounds of fur on that mustang. The extra fur is yours for a first-year bonus."

"You are a generous man!" exclaimed Bess.

"There is something else I want you to have." He took Tarpenning's rifle, pistol and skinning knife from where they were stowed in a pack and handed them to the man. "These are some of the best weapons in these mountains."

"I can't accept them, for you have already given too much," the man said and stepped back.

"When a person truly wants to give you a gift, you cannot refuse," said Luke and offered the weapons again.

John nodded and took them into his hands. "They are truly the best I have ever seen."

Coldiron walked close to Bess and rested his sight on the baby, sleeping beside the boy on the blanket at the woman's feet. "I believe you are with very good people," he said to the uncomprehending child. He touched a soft cheek of the infant with his finger tips.

Hastily he spun away and strode to his horse. Stepping astride, he took up the lead rope of the pack string and came back past the Clarks.

"I'll see you in Independence in a few months," said Coldiron.

"We won't be hard to find," responded John. "Our place is right on the main street."

"Before you leave, what's her name?" said Bess.

"Tarpenning."

"You mean she's not your child?" asked John.

"No, she's the daughter of a very good friend. He's dead and I promised to see that she is raised right."

"What is her given name?" asked Bess.

"You pick a pretty one for her."

"You never said what happened to her mother."

Coldiron froze at that question. An innocent woman had been stolen and forcefully carried far away from her home and people. Never to return, but to be fought over, to die quickly. And he was as much at fault as any of the others.

"We killed her mother," he said through stiff lips and kicked his animals savagely away from the stunned Clark family.

CHAPTER 9

Coldiron rode slowly, letting his mustang set its own pace along the wagon road. The shadows of the ponderosa pine forest crowded in from both sides, a very welcome protection from the warm noonday sun. He was relaxed, more so than for many months. He knew the reason for his ease of mind was his arrangement with the Clarks. A more fitting guardian for the child could not have been found.

In front and off the left side of the road in the woods, came the muffled thumps of hooves, heavy enough to be either elk or horses. Luke dragged his mount to a halt and lifted up his rifle from where it was fastened with a loop of buckskin to the pommel of the saddle.

The sounds ceased and a silence stretched as if someone was listening. Then the noise commenced again. Almost immediately the limbs of a section of the dense pine forest broke open and two mounted Mexicans, heavily armed with rifle and pistol and leading three horses with Indian children upon their backs, rode out into the trail. The men—small, wiry hombres—spotted Luke in the shadows and whirled their steeds to face him.

The dark visages of the Mexicans evidenced no fear, only a cool wariness at the presence of the lone horseman. They shifted their rifles, carried familiarly in their arms, to a more ready position.

Coldiron saw them evaluate his packs of fur with covetous, hungry eyes. A cool warning tingle prickled the hair on the back of his neck.

Luke flicked one short glance at the children. Two girls, nine or ten years old, slumped tired and frightened on blanket saddles. A boy a couple of years older, hands tied behind his back and fresh bloody bruises on his face, stared back at Luke with sharp, inquisitive eyes.

Luke recognized what the men were, slave traders who stole Indian children and dragged them deeply into Mexico to be sold into backbreaking labor. He touched his horse with his heel and the animal moved forward, closing the gap with the Mexicans.

He smiled and nodded at the two slavers. Never show fear to strangers or enemies. Tarpenning had told him that once during their first hunt into the mountains and had laughed in his reckless way.

The children appeared to be Utes and he called a greeting to them in that tongue. The boy's mouth came open in surprise, and a smoldering gleam of hope came alive and flashed hot across his battered face.

Coldiron looked back at the Mexicans. He knew with certainty they were silently plotting to take his furs. To do that, they would kill him. The issue must be settled now before they rode off and lay along the trail and bushwhacked him. Another thought jelled in his mind, to take the children from the slavers and set them free, to do it for Morning Mist.

It would be useless to attempt to persuade the Mexicans to turn them loose. Worse than that, any palaver would put them on guard and more primed to fight. Two reasons to make the first move. Coldiron pivoted his rifle in the direction of the captors of the young Utes. As the weapon centered on the man on the left, Luke's thumb cocked the hammer and his finger pulled the trigger.

From less than thirty feet the large .50-caliber lead ball lifted the man from the saddle and slammed him backward to fall heavily on the ground. At the roar of the gun, Coldiron jabbed his heels into the flank of his mustang. The startled beast leaped forward toward the second Mexican. Luke's right hand turned loose of the rifle, snapped his pistol from its holster, pointed the gun and fired in one nearly invisible movement.

The Mexican died with his rifle only part way to his shoulder. His legs, clamped tightly around his horse, held him for a moment, then he tumbled sideways from the saddle.

The young male Ute sat frozen for a second. Then he skimmed a look over the dead men, to settle his eyes on Coldiron. "Did you kill them to keep us as your prisoners or to let us go back to our teepees?"

Luke did not respond, letting his violent emotions subside as he reloaded his weapons. The Mexicans had done nothing worse than the terrible wrong Tarpenning and he had done with the kidnapping of Morning Mist. Yet he had killed both of them without warning.

He let his gaze rest upon the two girls. With lowered heads, long black hair nearly hiding their pinched, frightened faces, they looked back at him from large dark eyes. Coldiron hated to see fear in a human; in a child it was even worse. He was glad he had killed the slave traders.

Luke said to the boy, "To send you back home."

"Then you have slain our enemies for us." The youth threw back his head and yelled out in a shrill young voice the victory cry of his people.

One of the girls began to cry and the boy shouted at her. "Be quiet. The white man has done us a great favor. We must be worthy of it." She sniffed twice more, then controlled her emotion and was silent.

Coldiron finished recharging his last gun and sat contemplating what to do next with the youngsters. They were a very long way from their home and he did not want to turn aside to lead them there.

"Can you find your way back to your village?" Luke asked the boy.

The Ute lad looked to the north through the heat-distorted distance to where the tall mountains met the great plains at a sharp angle. He faced back to the white man. "I am twelve winters old. I do not get lost in only three days riding from my village."

"Good. Then take their horses," Luke pointed at the dead men on the ground, "and go find your village." There were large identifying burn brands on the rumps of the animals and Luke reasoned the dead Mexicans were most probably from Santa Fe. For him to enter that town with their horses in his possession could well start a fight. And he only wanted to sell his furs and loaf a few days in peace.

"Take one of the rifles and a knife, too," Coldiron said.

The youth swung a leg over and dropped lightly to the ground. Stepping up close to Luke, he pivoted to turn his back and held out his tied hands. One saw of the trapper's skinning knife and the bindings fell away.

The Indian turned to stare up into Luke's face. "I am called Plenty Wolf. What are you called?"

"Coldiron."

"Cold Iron. That is a very fitting name. You killed those two and your eyes did not change at all. I will take the mustangs and thunder gun as you offer. I cannot use it, but my father is a mighty warrior and he can make it roar."

Plenty Wolf went to the nearest Mexican body and took a rifle, powder horn, bullet pouch and a scabbard and knife. "The sombrero, may I have the big sombrero?" he asked, pointing down at the broad-brimmed hat.

"Take both of them if you want," Coldiron told the boy. "And take the saddles and all their food and water. I don't want any of it."

The youth tied the sheathed knife to his waist and the long rifle to the saddle of one of the horses. Then with one of the big hats riding the top of his ears, he jerked himself astride with a long pull of his arms. His eyes shone with delight at the gifts and he looked at the white man. "Cold Iron, Plenty Wolf owes you three lives." He pointed at himself and at each of the girls. "My father would tell you he has the same debt."

"You owe me nothing," said Coldiron in a quiet voice. "I killed them for someone else."

"I do not understand what you say. Only that they are dead and we are free," said Plenty Wolf. "We go now back to our people." His hand rose in a signal of farewell and he led off to the north with the girls riding close behind.

Luke searched the dead men, taking a few silver coins and the remainder of the weapons. He swung upon his black horse and looked to the south along the chain of mountains the Mexicans called the Sangre de Cristo. Ahead half a day's ride, the tall pine-covered peak called Sierra Mosca reared high. At its base on the west, but as yet impossible to see, lay Santa Fe.

The wagon road passed under the end of a high, black, lava mesa and forded the Rio Grande. In the floodplain of the river, the wild grass was growing rapidly and already to the belly of his horse. A small herd of reddish brown cows raised their heads from the sweet grass and watched him journey by. All carried large brands on their flanks, and the ears were cropped and notched in various patterns to provide additional identification of ownership.

Coldiron noticed two mounted cowboys on a high knob. Both returned his arm wave of hello. They were the first humans Luke had found that were not traveling to some other piece of the country. Somehow that was a very satisfying discovery.

The density of cattle increased steadily as he drew closer to Santa Fe. Also bands of sheep and herds of good-quality riding horses became

common sights. So, too, did armed Mexican riders on guard over the
valuable animals.

Luke came out of the pinion pine and saw Santa Fe spread below him
a quarter mile away. A westering sun slanted in at a low angle to lie on
the town. The long main street, flanked with brown adobe buildings,
some quite large and two story, stretched along the bank of the Santa Fe
River. Dwarfed by the distance, a few tiny figures of men, horses and
oxen moved on the street. Coldiron felt his spirits lift and he realized a
sharp hunger for the company of other humans was about to be satisfied.
He hurried downward, leaving the woods behind.

Santa Fe was larger than he remembered it from two years before, and
still growing. Several new buildings were under construction in the
center of town. A sign in front of one partially completed structure
stated a cantina would soon be doing business there. Luke counted seven
already in operation.

A farmer driving a wagon drawn by a yoke of oxen stirred dust up in a
brown cloud. In the shade of one of the taller buildings on the west side
of the street, Mexican men in worn and stained cotton pants and shirts
sat on long wooden benches or slouched against the wall. Four caballeros,
Mexican cowboys, in tightly fitting leather pants, intricately decorated
jackets, leather boots and large-brimmed hats, stood off silently by themselves. Their brightly colored clothing was in sharp contrast with the
peons' dress.

In possession of a large shady section of the sidewalk in front of a two-
story cantina, twenty mountain men lazed about. With their long shaggy
hair and beards and fringed buckskin outfits they looked like half-tamed
wolves. No rifle or pistol was in sight, but a long-bladed skinning knife
was carried on the belt of each.

Separated more than a block from the men who worked for a living, a
group of *Los Pelados*, the town loafers, talked among themselves. From
time to time they surreptitiously checked the position of the mountain
men, for those Americanos badgered them unmercifully at every opportunity.

At the hitching rails of the stores, offices and drinking and eating
establishments, dozens of horses stood, heads down, half asleep, tails
switching flies. A man in a white shirt and tie came out of a building
with a big sign that stated Banco de Santa Fe and called something
across the street. In answer a young man started toward him, dust puff-
ing up around his boots with each step. He glanced down once at the
dirt and then ignored it.

A busy, prosperous city, thought Coldiron.

Several horsemen rode up fast behind Luke, split into two groups and raced past on both sides. He stopped until the dust settled and then continued his slow, watchful pace along the street.

A middle-aged Mexican woman and a younger one, very pretty, came out of a store and proceeded along the sidewalk in front of the trappers. One of the men stepped out to block the women's route.

"How about a kiss for a poor, lonely *americano?*" he said to the younger woman in a loud voice and spread his arms wide as if in preparation to give her a hug. A ripple of laughter ran through the mountain men at the fellow's daring.

A second man called out, "While you are about it, I could stand a little lovin' myself."

The women sidestepped to get around the man barring their way and continued along the wooden walk.

The young one smiled slightly to herself. All the trappers followed them with interested eyes. The caballeros watched the incident and talked among themselves in a resentful manner, but the mountain men paid them no heed.

A small man arose from the bench and pushed through the others to stand in the open. He studiously examined Coldiron. Then with a wild shout of greeting he sprang out into the street. "Luke Coldiron, by God! You damn young rascal. I never thought I'd ever see you again."

"Hello, Tom Kidder," Luke called back and, smiling broadly, slid from his horse and came to meet the man.

Kidder circled Luke, looking him over and stomping the dust up in a little fog. "Wow! Boy have you filled out. Must have grown half a foot since last time I saw you."

"Not quite that much, Tom, but a fair amount. But stand still or you're going to choke us in the dust." He was very pleased to see the small man. The first year Tarpenning and he had gone up into the mountains to trap they had found Kidder nearly dead from an arrow in his back. Just at nightfall one evening, an Indian war party had attacked Tom's camp on a high stream in the Wyoming Territory. Though grievously wounded, Tom had escaped into the darkness. Only because Tarpenning and Coldiron had chanced upon him, and thereafter cared for him for weeks, was Tom still alive.

"Come inside and let me buy you a drink," said Kidder. "How's your sidekick, Tarpenning? Out stealing a squaw or two?"

"Tarpenning is dead," responded Luke quietly.

"Damn, Luke, I'm sorry 'bout that. How did it happen? No wait, let's get something to wash this dirt down and jaw for a couple hours."

"I'd like that, but first I got to take care of my animals and store my fur until I can find a buyer."

"We'll have just one small one and then I'll help you." Tom turned toward a big burly man who had been watching them. "Ben Brown, meet Luke Coldiron. Saved my life once. I'm going to buy him a drink and save his. You keep an eye on his belongings for a few minutes."

"Sure, Tom, I'll do that. Glad to meet you, Coldiron. There should be enough of us trappers to keep your things safe." He grinned largely.

"Hello, Ben," said Luke. He nodded at three other men he knew from past rendezvous and followed Kidder into the cool shadows of the cantina.

A long, polished, wooden bar and enough tables and chairs to serve maybe fifty customers occupied the left end of a big room. The floor was of packed dirt. Three caballeros sat drinking tequila in the farthest corner. On the right a wooden platform deck for dancing was raised above the floor six inches or so. There were empty chairs for the musicians. Luke made himself a promise to return later and lift a fast foot to some music and see if the women of Santa Fe were as pretty as he remembered them from two years before.

The bartender watched Luke and Tom come up and lean on the shiny wood of the bar.

"Beer or tequila?" asked Kidder.

"Beer for me," Luke told the barkeep.

"Same here," said Kidder. He faced Coldiron. "Now, tell me about Tarpenning. I hope he died quick."

The time passed reminiscing with Kidder, a pleasant conversation once they got past the death of Tarpenning. Some trappers came inside and began to drink and talk. Odors of food cooking for supper drifted in from the kitchen in the rear. Coldiron turned to look out the door. Long shadows were settling into the street.

"It's getting late and I still got a lot to do," said Luke. "Where can I get a room?"

"Right here. The whole upstairs is full of rooms for rent. But damn, it's noisy until mighty late. Now me, I've found a quiet place with soft clean beds down at the other end of town. Just a small rooming house and run by a Mexican that speaks American. Let's go see if they got an empty room for you."

"Is there an honest man to buy my furs?"

"Yep. Sam Magoffin keeps a man named Tolliver here full-time during the trading and freighting season. He always pays a fair price. He knows if he is light on the weight or low on the price that some of the boys will simply meet him outside town and take back their furs to sell again to someone else. We still got plenty of daylight to do everything, but let's get to it." Tom began to move toward the door, then stopped. "You're going to be disappointed with the price. It's way down from last year."

"A $1.90 per pound, that's the most I can give you for the beaver, Coldiron," said Tolliver, a large man getting far along in years. Kidder and Luke were in the buying station of Magoffin's agent. Luke's loaded pack string stood in the street in front of the building.

"Hardly worth risking a man's neck for," said Coldiron.

Tolliver nodded his head in agreement. "I know, but my company won't get more than $2.80 to $3.00 after we haul the fur all the way to Independence. Also, I must pay the Mexican governor 25 cents a pelt for allowing us to buy here and ship north to the States. Now for the mink, martin, otter and fox, I'll pay an even $1.00 a pelt. If you want to look around and try to find a better price, that's alright. For $2.00 a day you can store your fur in my strong room." Tolliver pointed out a rear window at a small stone building with one heavy wooden door reinforced with iron straps.

Luke looked inquiringly at Tom, who shrugged his shoulders as if to say that's the way fur prices are today.

"No, Tolliver, I'll take your offer," said Luke. "Let's weigh the skins out. I have several traps, what will you give for them?"

"If they are in good condition, $5.00 each."

A quarter hour later the furs had been lifted off the backs of the grateful pack animals, gone onto the scales and then into the trader's strong room. Tolliver hung the traps on the wall with several others and seated himself at a small desk and began to write.

"Here's a bank draft for $2,025. First thing in the morning you can exchange it for gold at the bank."

"Good enough," said Luke accepting the paper. "Now for a bath and clean clothes."

"Then out on the town to find us a dark beauty apiece," laughed Kidder.

They went outside to the hitching rail and took up the reins and lead rope of Luke's animals. Kidder pointed ahead. "That fellow that runs the livery stable there on the right takes good care of horses."

"I'll trust your word for it," said Coldiron. "I've been dragging these damn stubborn critters over the mountains long enough and I'm ready to leave them with someone else."

An hour later Luke had a room rented and was soaking in a warm soapy bath. Several wooden tubs of water had been sitting in the sun all day in an area enclosed with a pine-slat screen behind the boarding house. Luke sat with his head back, eyes closed, enjoying the pleasant feel of the water on his body. Kidder sat just outside the bathing place in the shade of a cottonwood.

He spoke over the short wall to Luke. "Since you don't have a partner now, how 'bout us teaming up to go trapping next winter?"

"If I needed a partner, Tom, no one would make a better one. But I'm not going after beaver again."

"I know the price is plenty low and we would be working for little more than wages. But what else is there for the likes of us to work at?"

"Raising horses could make a man a living. A good riding animal can bring $200."

"Not five mustangs in a hundred will fetch that much money. And even then he has to be broke and worked with for a long time."

"Not wild mustangs, Tom. But horses bred by the best studs and trained for weeks. I saw the Mexican horses as I rode in. They were good animals. Those Mexes know how to breed them."

Kidder looked up at the top of Sierra Mosca, blushing with a tinge of orange in the last of the day's sunlight. "What you are planning could take a good chunk of a man's lifetime. I don't think I could ever settle down and stay in one place long enough to make that kind of business pay."

"I could and plan to begin in a few days. You are welcome to join me. There'll be more than enough work for both of us."

"I appreciate the offer. But I'll be back in the mountains next winter after the beaver and trying to keep my scalp from being lifted by an Indian."

"Soon the fur won't be worth carrying to market," said Luke.

"I know that," said Kidder.

Coldiron arose and began to towel off. "Tom, would you tell that washer woman to bring my clean buckskins?"

"They haven't had time to dry out and will still be damp."

Luke raised his head up and laughed happily at the sky. Damp buckskins, as if that had any meaning to a beaver trapper. Here he was fresh from a bath, talking with a friend, looking forward to a hell-raising night in Santa Fe and with enough money to start a horse ranch. He laughed even louder, balled up the towel and threw it over the wall at Kidder.

That worthy understood the absurdity of his statement about the wet clothing and, chuckling deep in his chest, went to find the laundress.

The brawny Mexican blacksmith struck skillfully, the clang of his hammer ringing half-musically, shaping and bending the red-hot metal he held in a pair of heavy tongs. Heat from the forge radiated out, pressing like a force on Luke where he leaned against one of the supporting posts of the building and watched the man work. The odor of the burning charcoal was so dense he could taste it.

The iron turned from bright red to dull red and the smith stabbed it back into the yellow and orange coals, to bury it deeply in the hottest place. He looked down for the last time to check Coldiron's drawing of the design he wanted. Obvious satisfaction lighted his face. He wiped his forehead with a calloused finger and flicked away the sweat droplets.

"Soon, señor, the branding iron will be finished. It will be beautiful, for I am an artist." His grin broadened at his boast. "Better than beautiful. It will be a brand that will be very difficult to change to look like any other. All thieves will be angry."

Again the iron rod with its six-inch head of intricate weave of curving and intersecting metal pattern was extracted from the forge. This time a small hammer was used, the man tapping delicately here and there to make an arc more true or an edge more straight. With a flourish the smith tossed the hot iron into a trough of water, to sizzle and hiss and send the steam boiling up.

"It is done," said the smith and fished the branding iron out.

Coldiron accepted the two-foot-long branding iron, his brand, and hefted it in his hand. "Feels good." He stepped from the blacksmith shop into the street. With his moccasined foot he smoothed out the dust and pressed the brand directly down upon the ground.

The imprint of a steel trap, jaws opened wide and the trigger set, stared up at him. One day I will have this brand on a thousand brood mares, he vowed.

CHAPTER 10

The old gray wolf lay dying on the bluff above the creek. He was merely a skin bag stretched over a bony frame. He had not eaten for more than a month and even that had been carrion fit only for the buzzards. Though he did not understand what death was, his senses were failing rapidly and he knew something very strange was happening to him.

During the winter, when a wolf as ancient as he and incapable of hunting should have died, the carcasses of horses dead from starvation had fed him. Then the new green grass came out of the earth, grew ever more lush, and the horses waxed fat and strong. They stopped dying. The wolf stopped eating.

Two hundred feet down slope from the wolf and close to the creek, Coldiron crouched hidden behind brush and rock. Arrayed before him, primed and ready for firing, were a double-barred rifle and two single-shot ones.

On the far side of the stream, a deeply rutted horse trail led down the bank. The gurgle of water as it ran through the stones of a riffle floated up to Luke.

It was late May, The Moon When the Ponies Shed, and in the early afternoon. The time of day when the wild mustangs would begin to come in to quench their thirst at the cool snowmelt water that coursed down from the high mountains.

Luke had returned to the valley he and Morning Mist had stopped and lingered in the month before. He had brought with him a pack string of animals loaded with the equipment required to build his horse ranch. Tom Kidder had not accompanied him, staying behind to spend the summer in Santa Fe and then go beavering in the fall.

The pleasures of Santa Fe had enticed Luke to stretch his intended sojourn there from a week to a month. That loafing period was past now and he felt the pressing need to get to work.

The valley lay quietly beneath a warm yellow sun. The wild grass, beginning to form a seed head, nodded gently in a soft wind. As he viewed the long, somewhat oval basin with its brown rimrock and the scattered low hills with the patches of pine on them, he sensed he had found a home.

It was an isolated, dangerous home, and for a moment he wondered if his plan for a *grande rancho* was a foolish dream doomed to failure. Years could be spent breeding up a herd of horses and one raid by hostile Indians or white outlaws could destroy it all.

Yet the valley was ideal for his intended purpose. It contained at least one hundred thousand acres of grassy meadows and enough dense thickets of pine and cottonwood to protect the horses from winter storms. The elevation, at nearly seven thousand feet, would build deep chest and stamina. Excellent horses could be raised here.

Luke turned to look to the west as a new sound came to him. A black stallion followed by seven mares and two colts all in single file came down the trail toward the creek. At a hundred yards, the big stud stopped and his nostrils twitched as he sucked warily at the slow warm wind. His ears flicked nervously, for he detected for one short breath the faint odor of wolf. The stallion keenly tested the air for several breaths. The scent did not come again.

The mares came up to stand close behind the stallion. They lifted their heads and also checked the breeze for enemies.

Time passed and the importance of that one whiff of wolf lessened. Finally the stallion moved ahead down the rocky bank to wade out into the creek.

Coldiron critically evaluated the band, measuring each animal's height, the depth of its chest, length of leg and size and intelligence of the head. The strength and fleetness of his herd must always be the primary consideration. Color would be bred for when all other characteristics had been met. He picked up the two-barreled rifle and cocked both hammers.

The wild ones finished drinking and began to file up out of the creek bed. Coldiron brought up the rifle and centered it on the stallion. The horse was obviously very strong, broad and heavy-muscled, but with big feet like a plow horse. He could never run fast. Luke shot him through the lungs; he fell with a high shriek, struggled to rise, partially made it, then fell down dead. The second lead ball burst the heart of a lame mare just behind him and she tumbled backward into the creek.

Luke scooped up the second weapon and killed a stunted roan mare. The fourth shot dropped a barren gray mare far past her prime. He wished for one additional round to slay a mare with a thin, shallow chest.

The remaining frightened animals scrambled away, hurling clods of dirt from under their driving feet.

Slowly Coldiron lowered his rifle. His culling of the hundreds of horses that roamed the valley had begun. It would be a summer-long job, a terrible gut-revolting job. But he knew it had to be done. A hundred pounds of lead had been brought with which to do it. When finished, two goals would have been accomplished—the establishment of the base herd he desired and the number of animals reduced to be in balance with the amount of grass the land produced.

On the high ground the old wolf was jerked to consciousness by the roar of the rifle fire. He pulled himself halfway to his feet and listened. The strange sharp sound did not come again. His nose caught and sorted through the scents on the air. He smelled horses—dead horses and blood, fresh and near. He felt the blind yearnings of the flesh to exist and strength flowed into his string-like muscles. He stood erect. He moved up the wind along the stream of scent.

The smell of the creature that walked on two legs was mixed with the hundred other odors the wolf could identify. He had never been harmed in the few encounters he had had with man and his inborn caution was overridden by his total concentration upon reaching the source of the tantalizing aroma of food.

Coldiron saw the aged lobo totter from the brush on the ridge and stumble down the slope toward the dead mustangs. The wolf tripped and fell and required more than a minute to fight his way back to his feet. Luke did not understand how an animal so starved still lived.

The wolf, homing in on the center of the horse scent, came directly to the stallion. He lay down with his nose pressed against the bloody hole of Luke's shot. His tongue licked his gray chops once with the pleasure of anticipation and then his worn, dull teeth started to tear at the bullet-mangled flesh.

Coldiron watched the famished old lobo gorge himself. He soon had an opening into the stomach cavity of the horse and plunged his head completely inside to get at the rich, nourishing liver and kidneys.

With his stomach distended with an impossible fullness, the wolf crawled off into the cool shade under the creek bank and sank down. He took a deep breath of air and lowered his head to rest on his paws.

Luke chuckled silently to himself. He was pleased that some good was made of his slaughter. He went to his horse concealed in a copse of nearby pine and rode off.

After the killing of the wild horses Luke returned to his camp, located on a bench cut into the flank of a hill near the center of the valley and east of the creek. The site, at an elevation two hundred feet above the basin floor and overlooking a broad expanse of the land within the rock-walled world, was exactly right for the ranch house.

The bench was amply wide for house, barn and corral. The soil was very sandy and would make no mud when it rained. In an area of an acre or so, a large quantity of slab sandstone lay exposed on the surface, as if just waiting to be laid up into the walls of the house. Above the bench the hill rose up, capped with enough pine to supply all necessary building material and firewood for a lifetime. A spring gushed out of a rocky face in the bottom edge of the timber and flowed down the hill and across the bench.

Coldiron paced off the dimension of the foundation, an ambitious one hundred feet in length. The building was aligned to face to the south so the sun would strike it full-faced and thus help heat it when the frigid arctic winds struck. This first year he would construct the foundation of the entire building and one complete room with fireplace to shelter him during the coming winter.

The task was begun at once, using tools obtained in Santa Fe. One of the mules was fitted with a wide leather collar and, using a length of stout rope, the animal dragged large flat chunks of sandstone into place. Hammer and chisel were used where necessary to make a tight joint. Due to the plentiful supply of stone, the foundation swiftly took form.

The second day Coldiron slew a total of seven horses at two different stands. The lobo did not make an appearance. A pack of coyotes came in to feed as he departed from the killing ground.

That evening he constructed another compartment to add to the gun pouch, a deep saddlebag-like contraption in which the rifles were transported. Now he carried four rifles. Five rapid shots could be fired in less than three or four seconds. He wished he had more two-barreled guns so he could shave another fraction of a second from each round.

The lobo awoke, considerably stronger and languid with rest in the mid morning of the fifth day following the breaking of his fast. He felt the flow of faster blood in his veins and the returning of vitality and elasticity to his muscles.

The second day the coyotes had beaten him to the fresh horse slaying. They had also arrived first on the third and fourth days, an ever enlarging pack, becoming fat and lazy, not bothering to hunt, simply following the killer human and eating without effort. The wolf had been forced to eat with the repugnant scent of the smaller, half-scavenger animal tainting the flesh. Today would be different, for the lobo meant to be first.

Coldiron tied his roan in a hidden place back from the creek and carried his arm load of rifles to a shooter's vantage point. Each day his horse ambush point was moved, for he did not return to the same spot twice. The locations of these past killings were marked by the tight circling funnels of vultures sailing in to feed on the great supply of carrion.

The wolf walked in to take up a stand on Luke's right and downwind from the creek. The human saw the gray old animal hide himself in tall grass and knew with certainty the lobo was deliberately and purposefully there. Eat what I kill and survive this summer, thought Luke, but you will surely die come the winter.

A large band of bachelor studs appeared on the distant bottom land and came winding their course in toward the water. Through a gap in the brush, Luke eyed their approach. The group was composed of old male mustangs, not strong enough to capture a harem, and those young males run off from their dams by the jealous harem stallions. For jointly security and companionship the unwanted males had joined into a loose herd, members arriving and departing on whim at frequent intervals.

Luke counted nineteen bachelors as the herd came in slowly and cautiously to drink at the creek. One young dun was outstanding. At only a few months over a year in age, his chest was deep and his legs were long and extremely quick and nimble. Though he was part of the band, he was little led by the older animals; instead he examined the land around him with intelligent black eyes and moved ahead only when satisfied of his own safety.

Coldiron made his determination of those cayuses that were to die and raised his first gun and began to shoot. His aim went true every time and five studs died within yards of each other.

The instant the round ball left the barrel of his last rifle, Luke sprang erect and raced to jump astride his mount. With a shout and a sharp slap of his hand on its neck, he sent the big horse after the stampeding mustangs.

The lobo arose from concealment and hurried in among the dead horses. The thick odor of blood hung like a fog over the corpses and he inhaled deeply of it. He started to lick the savory red flow that gushed from a deep wound in one of the bodies.

Something flashed past, striking his shoulder and nearly toppling him from his feet. A sharp searing pain followed instantly. He spun around. A gray form of a coyote hit him again, biting, ripping. The lobo snapped at the attacker but the agile foe leaped clear.

The wolf whirled to put his rear end up against the bulk of the horse and thus protect his hamstring. His wise old eyes surveyed his enemy, the pack of fifty or more coyotes that had rushed in to surround him. His bristle came up stiff, his lips pulled back in tight deep folds to show his teeth and he snarled ferociously.

The coyotes, sleek and well fed, trotted around him, angry at his presence but nervous and afraid at the strong wolf smell. Early in life they had been taught the harsh rule that the king wolf ate first. Now, however, the coyotes sensed the weakness and vulnerability of their ancient enemy.

One dark male coyote, a splendid brute in the prime of life, had successfully made that first daring assault. Now growling menacingly, his tail rigid, he lunged in with a gleam of teeth, stopping short of the reach of the wolf's broad savage head and springing back. Most of the other coyotes became enticed into the battle and began a siege on the lobo. A handful of coyotes, with watchful eyes on the fight, settled down and began to feed on the horses most distant from the wolf.

The attacking coyotes dashed in and out, trying to pull the wolf out of his sheltered position against the carcass of the horse. The lobo was far too old and clever in the world, had been in too many battles, to forget his caution. He remained ensconced and snapped powerfully left and right at his opponents. His reflexes were slow and his teeth clipped emptily together with a metallic snap.

The dark coyote saw an opening in the lobo's defense. He charged in with great swiftness. His feet were silent as velvet as he came across the body of the horse that guarded the wolf's rear and hurled himself straight for the big animal's jugular.

The wolf finished an unproductive biting action to the left and pivoted right, his mouth open wide to bite in that direction. The coyote saw the suddenly developing danger to himself and tried to alter his course. Too late. His pointed head went straight into the trap of the wolf's mouth.

Quicker than thought, the massive jaws closed, crunching down. The wolf, surprised at the sudden thrusting of a coyote's head into his mouth, increased the force, vising ever harder. The brain matter squeezed from the crushed skull into his mouth. More pressure was exerted, his teeth entered the head cavity. The lobo felt a surge of strength like the old times and he shook the coyote, jerking it back and forth, flopping the body as if it were an empty skin.

Satisfied the threatening assailant was dead, the wolf tossed the body aside. His great head rose and a triumphant growl came from his big chest. He washed a challenging look over every foe that surrounded him.

All fight fled from the coyotes and they drew back. Keeping a wary sight of his many foes, the aged wolf began to eat.

Coldiron's roan mount saw the wild mustangs boiling away ahead of him and understood his task was to overtake them. He flattened out into his running stride, neck outstretched, eyes searching the ground for obstacles that would trip and throw him. He felt his master adjust his weight to a position to help him reach the fastest pace.

Leaning forward over the neck of the roan, Coldiron thumped him once in the ribs to show this was a serious race. He extracted a long Mexican lariat from its tie on the side of the saddle and held it handy.

Man and horse darted through the brush patches and across the grassy meadows and gained on the bachelor band. At one mile they had drawn to within four hundred feet of the ones in the rear. That nearness of the human spooked the slower mustangs and they began to peel off from the main bunch.

Luke sighted the young stud with the long legs out front beside the fastest stallions, as he had expected. Run hard, little fellow, but still I will catch you.

More horses turned aside as the race lengthened to two miles. Coldiron touched the rein to the neck of his mount, guiding him slightly right, and the big animal identified the single horse that was to be caught. He accepted the task, enjoying the challenge.

The last members of the band sensed they were not the target of the contest and angled away to safety. The yearling stud, now alone, glanced back once and saw the horse and rider closing ground between them. He pointed his nose in the direction of the far end of the valley and gave his all to outrun this strange pursuer.

Every foot the roan gained on the young mustang was hard fought. Luke was pleased at the speed and stamina of the yearling. With the roan carrying a burden of two hundred pounds it was a close race. Finally the nose of the roan drew even with the long streaming tail of the horse ahead. Luke encouraged his mount again with his heel.

The loop of the lasso snaked out and dropped over the head of the mustang. Quickly Luke spun a dally on his saddle horn and began to rein in. The roan dragged the small dun down to a trot. The young horse began to fight the rope, rearing and jerking to break free.

Every time the yearling struck the end of the lariat, the noose tightened more. Gradually his air passage was constricted and soon he stood spraddle-legged, choked, ready to fall.

Luke jumped down, grabbed the mustang by the head and twisted him to the ground. With short lengths of rawhide he tied its feet together. Hastily the strangling rope was snatched loose. The hoarse rattle of a full lung of air rushing into the young dun's throat gratified Coldiron. It would be a sad loss to kill such a fine animal.

He struck a fire, built it high and inserted the new branding iron into the hot center. While the metal heated, he went to the horse that lay intently watching him. Gently he rubbed its nose, passed his hands over its eyes and stroked its ears and forehead. Several times he breathed into its nostrils. Get acquainted with me, little stud, for I believe you will help me build a great herd of horses.

The hot iron was pressed firmly onto the right hip of the dun and rocked back and forth slightly to insure that the edges of the brand would come out. Smoke curled up from burning hair and flesh and the mustang struggled mightily at his binding to tear loose and escape the pain. Luke lifted the iron and touched the horse again with its hot edge a few inches away.

He examined the seared flesh in the outline of a steel trap and the number one close beside it. His first stud horse had a good clear brand. It was a very satisfying accomplishment.

The dun was released and it streaked off. Luke kicked dirt over the fire and hurried back to retrieve his rifles. It was not safe to be without his long guns.

CHAPTER 11

Coldiron reloaded his weapons and struck out at once for the ranch house. Many hours of daylight still remained and every one must be fully used. He wanted the construction that was to be finished this year completed soon. Then he could put most of his time into the heavy slaughter of the horses and get it completed before they ate most of the summer growth of grass.

Ahead two miles and within sight was the bench that contained the site of his ranch house. The roan gave Luke a smooth rocking-chair lope over the grass-carpeted land toward it. His course angled across the toes of three low pine-cloaked hills that extended part way out into the valley from the east rim. Luke knew the large center ridge had a horse trail on its top that led up and through the rock ledge to the plateau above. He drew even with the western most sweep of the timber.

Six riders charged out of the woods, six painted warriors on painted horses, yelling shrilly. Coldiron snapped a split-second look, estimated the number of the lithe horsemen, knew their deadly intent. He kicked his steed into a full run straight up the valley.

He leaned forward and called loudly and defiantly into the roan's ear, exhorting it to give its utmost. Though the brute had already run a fast race after the yearling, he took the primeval cry, his nostrils flaring and stride lengthening to the limit of his strength.

Coldiron twisted to look behind at the Indians strung out in a short line and bent over their ponies, flogging them with short leather whips. A large warrior on a magnificent black mustang and carrying a rifle was out front. A small brave, armed with bow and arrow and hardly more than a boy, brought up the rear behind the main group of riders.

The Indians had been lying in wait. From the rimrock the distance was not so great but that they could have seen his smoke or heard his shooting and come down to investigate. With their mounts running at full speed when breaking from cover, they had approached within a thousand feet.

The space gradually narrowed between Luke and his pursuers on their fresh, fast cayuses. He sighted back and knew they would soon overhaul him, and there was no place to hide in the grassy bottom and the low patches of brush.

A few minutes later the chase had driven him along the valley bottom and he was directly below the bench and ranch house. With a quick tug of the reins he spun his mount to the right and up the steep front of the hill toward the bench. The valiant horse, his heart grinding, took to the grade.

Blowing hard, the roan breasted the top of the bench a good four hundred feet ahead of the Indians. Coldiron plunged him through the door of the half-built end of the house. He swung down, snatched the rifles from their carrying pouch and dashed back to the front stone wall. He positioned the weapons against the wall and picked up the two-barreled one.

The big brave in the lead was near now and raised his rifle and fired.

The lead ball struck the rock near Luke's shoulder and ricocheted away, snarling like a small deadly animal. Luke swiftly returned the shot, knocking the man from his horse. His second ball slammed the next closest brave from his saddle.

The Indians jerked their ponies to a halt and, rapidly pulling their short war bows, let loose a flight of arrows at Luke. The sharp metal points on the stiff wooden shafts rattled on the wall and swished past Coldiron's head. As he ducked down behind the shielding stone, one well-aimed missile slashed the lobe of his ear. Bright red blood began to leak onto his shoulder.

He grabbed up another rifle, stepped sideways two yards and thrust it over and fired. At the sharp crack a warrior with his hair full of brightly colored feathers tumbled from his mount. Luke switched guns and shot a man going to the left.

Luke reached for his last rifle. All the Indians had to be killed, for they had seen his house, and if one escaped he would return with many warriors to destroy him.

The larger of the two remaining Indians shouted a warning to his small companion. That person whirled his mustang hastily and jumped it in a series of stiff-legged lunges down the sharp-angled face of the bench. Coldiron's shot killed the brave who had called out.

The last warrior made it to the base of the bench, pulled his mustang left and hurtled out of sight. Coldiron believed the man's goal was to reach the pine woods on the next ridge over and then, using that thick cover, take the trail up through the rimrock without being spotted.

Carrying his rifle, Luke jumped astride and dove the roan out the doorway and sped him up over the low ridge of the hill. By going across the top his route was shorter than the Indian's circular path around the point of the hill. Just maybe Luke could catch him. With the horse bounding across the uneven terrain he reloaded his rifle, guessing at the charge of powder that went down the barrel.

Coldiron came down from the hill and onto the bench again just in time to see the Indian within two horse lengths of the forest. The expert rider had made great speed. Luke fired swiftly as the brown form on the racing horse plunged into the trees.

At the edge of the woods, Luke dropped the reins of the roan to ground-tie him. On foot, he stealthily slipped into the dense stand of pine. The driving hooves of the Indian pony had churned up the needles to leave an easily followed trail.

Coldiron dogged the sign across a shallow draw and up to the top of a rocky knob. There in a small opening in the trees he found the Indian's mustang. Along the pony's back lay the brightly painted warrior, his arms locked about the muscular neck. Blood oozed from a round hole in the center of his small back and dripped down to splash upon the horse's shoulder.

Luke came up slowly on the pony's left side. The animal shied away a couple of steps and swung its head to watch the human suspiciously.

"Easy, boy," called Luke in a calming voice and caught hold of the single leather strap that made the bridle. He separated the stiffly interlocked fingers of the warrior's hand and lowered the body to the ground, face up.

He rocked back on his heels in shock at what he saw. The fiercely painted countenance of Plenty Wolf stared up at him with dead black eyes.

"No! Damn it, no!" whispered Luke savagely to himself. But he recognized without the slightest hint of doubt the boyish features beneath the stain.

For many minutes Coldiron sat in sorrow near the limp body. Why of all Indians did Plenty Wolf have to be the one that discovered him in this valley? They could have been friends. Never would he have knowingly hurt the young Indian.

The land was unpredictable, where events happened that no one could ever foresee and least of all prevent.

Coldiron turned to gaze in the direction of the cliff beneath the rimrock where Morning Mist lay buried. The spot was at a long distance and only the general outline of the thick ledge of rock and pine woods could be distinguished. But in his mind's eye he saw the stone cairn of her grave very clearly. Luke looked down at the boy who would be a warrior.

"Up there, Plenty Wolf, is a very wonderful person named Morning Mist. Go find her. Make her your friend in the spirit land of the Other World. You will find she is gentle and pleasant and will never make you weary of her companionship."

Luke Coldiron began to dig his second grave in the valley.

BOOK II
THE MUSTANG MAN

The Americans captured Santa Fe in 1845. Not a shot was fired. When the invading gringos reached the town, the Mexican Governor Armijo and his army had vanished, slipping stealthily south to Chihuahua. The governor's palace and the army garrison buildings sat empty. The American General Carleton declared all Nuevo Méjico to be the possession of the United States and immediately took up residence in the plush home of the Mexican governor. His soldiers moved into the deserted barracks and the capture of the land was complete.

CHAPTER 12

August, the Moon of
the Big Heat, 1863

The sun, not yet to its zenith, was already a fireball striking down with harsh brilliance to roast the long rimrocked mountain valley. The air lay completely still, filling the basin like shimmering liquid heat, distorting objects and space. No life stirred, all hidden away in shaded refuges, awaiting the coolness of the evening.

There was one exception to the absence of life. On the east side of the valley near its mid length, where a horse trail went up to the rimrock, a tall dun stallion stood motionless beneath the sun, his head drooping and body damp with sweat.

In the small shadow cast by the horse, Luke Coldiron squatted. He had been waiting thus for more than an hour.

Finally the patient dun tossed his head and sighted down at the man. Luke regarded the inquisitive black eyes of the animal. He knew the horse wanted to be moving, but they would wait some more, for Two Suns and Lightning Blanket might need help.

He shoved back his hat and with a curved finger scooped sweat from his forehead and held it out. The dun smelled at the liquid then licked the tasty brine with pleasure.

Luke chuckled. The big brute of a horse was the best mount he had ever owned. It was the select one from all the thousands of horses that had been raised on his rancho. When only a small colt, ten years before, the dun had shown his great potential and Coldiron had brought the small fellow and his dam into the ranch headquarters. His training had gone swiftly, for he was amazingly intelligent.

Something caught the horse's ear and he turned to look to the north. Luke also heard the sound of iron striking upon iron, like the ringing of several distant church bells, slightly dull and off key. There was not a church in two long days' ride. He stood up and, shading his eyes, spotted a column of tan dust a mile distant up the valley.

The earth cloud advanced at a steady pace and soon the tiny figures of a few score of horses could be seen framed against its outline. The half-musical clamor of the metal notes were persistent, growing stronger.

Coldiron mounted and rode to the top of a small hill nearby. One of two riders hazing the horses onward saw Luke and waved his big sombrero.

The herd of mustangs and their drovers, trailed by the slowly rising dust cloud, drew close, and Coldiron galloped down toward them. The ringing of iron was loud and it had a cadence that was in rhythm with the step of the trotting animals.

Suddenly the beat of the sound increased as the band of mustangs changed direction and whirled at a faster pace up the trail Luke had been guarding. He had expected them to break away along the well-used route and try to escape into the timber growing at the foot of the rock ledges rimming the valley.

The dun sprang off like a frightened deer, cut in ahead of the leaders and crowded them back in the direction they had been traveling. As Luke dropped back and followed behind, the Steel Trap Brand burned into the right hip of every animal was very visible. He always enjoyed seeing his brand.

The gait of the horses slowed immediately once they were headed south again. And for good reason, for around a front leg at the ankle of each animal was tied at least one horseshoe. The flare of the hoof prevented the encircling shoe from falling off. As the beast moved, the loop of iron bounced on the swell of the foot. A walk or trot created little pain. As the speed increased, the sharp metal edge of the heavy shoe struck harder and harder upon the tender flesh where the ankle met the hoof and the animal must slow to lessen the hurt. Some tough stallions could withstand the misery of one shoe and still run, so two would be put on, one above the other. The clanking of those two shoes, the top one driving the bottom into the flesh with agony, created the ringing sound.

Luke knew of other ways to control large groups of half-broken horses so they could be driven long distances through rough country. Some mustangers pierced the nostrils of the wild ones on each side and, stringing a length of rawhide through the wounds, tied the air passages almost completely shut. Only enough breath would be allowed to be drawn for the animal to go at a slow speed. Sometimes with this method a horse in a frenzy to escape would suffocate himself. Often the nostrils would tear open and leave a bad wound and scar. There were other practices that worked, all painful.

Coldiron rode in beside the nearest man, a Ute Indian in his early twenties, dressed in white man's clothing except for the moccasins he wore. "Two Suns, you are late."

The Indian nodded agreement. "The gray stallion gave us trouble. He broke free with only one shoe on his leg and we had to run him down. We then put three on him, but now he has only two and that's keeping him slowed up. He kicked Lightning Blanket."

"Bad?"

"He'll limp for a couple of days."

"How many cayuses did you bring?"

"All sixty as we planned."

As they finished talking, Lightning Blanket angled into Luke's other side. The two Indians were brothers and looked it. Both were medium height and well muscled, with dark bronze faces. Two Suns was the older.

"You okay?" asked Coldiron.

A little shamefaced, Lightning Blanket answered, "That's one damn fast mustang. Had me kicked before I knew he was thinking of it. But I can ride alright."

"Good. Let's move them south to Santa Fe," said Luke. "Two Suns, you stay on this side with me."

The three men separated, Lightning Blanket taking up station on the right flank just forward of the dust. Luke and Two Suns took up a similar position on the left.

An hour later Coldiron swerved away from the drove of horses and entered a clump of pine near their course. He emerged in a short moment, leading two packhorses, carrying light loads consisting of the men's food and bedrolls.

Just after noon, the men and horses left the valley. Where the stream had punched through the ledges of sandstone rimming the basin, a rock gap fence was thrown aside to allow passage along the creek. Luke remained behind to rebuild the fence.

As Luke lifted the slabs of sandstone back into place, he threw a short view across the land. Almost twenty years of his life, tough years of hard labor, had been spent building the ranch. From this spot in the extreme end of the valley, the ranch house and corrals could not be seen and the land looked the same as when he had first cast an eye on it. A beautiful land. All his.

He swung astride the dun and hurried to catch his men.

At the end of two days Coldiron and his Indian wranglers brought the band of horses into the outskirts of Santa Fe. A hot wind was gusting in from the west, whistling around the corners of the adobe houses, whipping up the dust from the streets and rolling it in great clouds over the small hills surrounding the town.

"Needs a rain to hold the dirt on the ground," observed Luke.

Neither Indian responded. They were always morose and silent when in a town near strange white men.

"Two Suns, ride ahead and get the gate open to the big corral at the army post," directed Coldiron.

"Right, Luke," said Two Suns.

The Indian, circling wide so as not to turn the cavalcade, sped off toward a cluster of two- and three-story buildings on the northeast side of town. By the time Lightning Blanket and Luke pushed close, several mounted soldiers had spread out in a large V from the wide gate and the horses were easily funneled into the large round enclosure.

Sergeant Stover, one of those helping with guiding the herd, galloped in as the gate was closed. Above the sound of the wind he barked out an order to a young private. "Anderson, go tell Major Whittiker the Steel Trap horses are here."

"Yes, Sergeant," answered the soldier and dashed off toward the major's residence at the far end of the compound.

The sergeant yelled at a group of uniformed men watching from the far end of the corral. "Hey, you troopers, get in there and help the Indians take those anklets off the horses. Take some liniment to doctor any sores."

The cavalrymen swarmed up and over the poles of the corral and hurried out toward the mounted Indians.

Two Suns tossed a long loop around the neck of the nearest horse. Immediately Lightning Blanket roped a rear leg and they stretched the mustang, toppling it to the earth. Three soldiers scurried up. One fell upon the thrashing head and pinned it to the ground. The other two grabbed and held still the leg encumbered with the horeshoe, cut the thong and jerked off the girdling iron ring. Liniment was dabbed on a raw wound. The Indians shook their loops free. The horse lunged to its feet and raced off to join its mates at the farthest extremity of the corral. It ran awkwardly, unused to being free from the pain and weight of the horseshoe.

Two Suns aimed his mount at a second mustang and began to swing his lasso.

The sergeant climbed up to the top rail of the corral near Luke. "Good-looking mounts you got there, Mr. Coldiron."

"Thanks, Stover. The Steel Trap brand has always meant the best and I intend to keep it that way," responded Luke.

"No question in this part of the country about that," said the sergeant.

Major Whittiker strode up and looked into the corral. "Hello, Luke, I see you have made delivery before the due date. How many animals did you bring?"

"Howdy, Tom. Sixty head, just as our contract specified."

"And the other conditions?"

"They are all guaranteed sound and are broke to saddle and ride. They are not trained to ground rein, nor to stand at gunfire."

"We can teach them that," said the major. He closely examined the horse herd, noting the uniform size and excellent conformation of the muscular bodies. Without doubt each animal would make an excellent mount for a trooper.

Whittiker glanced sideways at the tall black-headed man, whose enemies called him "Horse Killer." In his late thirties, he was lanky with rope-like muscles. Sun squints crinkled the corners of his eyes. His hands were square and heavily calloused.

Local gossip said that as a young beaver trapper Luke had lost his love in a remote mountain valley. He had returned there, walled up the exits of the valley and proceeded to slaughter almost every wild mustang that grazed in it. The story went that more than fifteen hundred horses had been slain that first year. With the remaining select herd, the present Steel Trap Brand began. Additional horses—throwbacks, mutants or those undesirable for any reason—were destroyed each year to continually improve the herd. More than horses had been shot. Some people guessed Coldiron had killed more than twenty men, anyone who dared to steal even one of his horses.

Thinking Coldiron would make an excellent officer and a very terrible enemy, Whittiker turned back to view the horses.

The major spoke past Luke to the sergeant. "Stover, saddle and ride six of those horses. Select them at random. Report to me within an hour your findings of their condition and training."

"Yes, sir," replied the sergeant and jumped down to call out an order to his men. "Andrews, Templeton, and you, Jewett, on the double, saddle and bridles. We're going to test some of those Steel Trap nags." He looked back to grin at Luke.

Coldiron moved his hand in acknowledgement of the joke about his famous steeds being mere nags.

The major said, "Come up to the office with me, Luke, and let's get out of the dust and have a sip of something while we wait."

"Sounds like a fine suggestion," said Luke. Lightning Blanket and Two Suns had come up to lean against the logs of the corral near the white men. Now Luke spoke to them. "You two go on into town. Take the dun and have that left front shoe reset. Give Dunstock at the General Store that list of supplies and tell him to have it all packed and ready by two days from now, early in the morning. Two Suns, leave your horse here for me to ride."

"Sure thing," Two Suns said.

Both Indians unbuckled their six-guns, wrapped the belts about the holsters and put them in the saddlebags of the horse left for Luke. They stepped astride their mounts and loped off.

"Aren't you afraid they will get into trouble?" asked Whittiker. "The recent Navajo raids on some of the outlying ranches have got the citizens angry and they can't distinguish one Indian from another."

"That's one reason they don't wear guns in town, to keep down trouble. Still, most everybody in Santa Fe knows Two Suns and Lightning Blanket are friendly and work for me," said Luke.

"The town is growing fast and there's a lot of newcomers. Lot of hard cases. Population is over eight thousand people. Things are changing in other ways, too. With the big war back East and my command reduced by nearly two thirds, the Indians are getting more bold. Besides the Navajo attacks, the Comanche have been raiding up from the southeast. There have been reports some Ute have been seen with war paint on. As I recall, that's the tribe your Indian riders are from."

"I will go into town soon as you pay me for the horses," said Luke, knowing the truth of Whittiker's statement.

They walked to the major's office near the center of the army compound. Relaxed in their long friendship, the two sat quietly in soft leather chairs, left by the Mexican governor eighteen years before, and pulled at their drinks.

"Luke, when the war back East is over, the Army will be ordered to go full force to bring these Indians under control. I would surmise they will all be put on reservations. Very likely my troops will be strengthened in number and I will be told to take to the field. This country is rough, with great distances to travel, and I want my men to have the best mounts. Think over what price you must have for an additional hundred head of your horses, delivered next spring. Before you leave Santa Fe, let's talk and see if we can reach an agreement."

"All right, Tom. I'd hate to see you and Emily leave."

Whittiker went to his desk and from a bottom drawer extracted a box of cigars. Luke accepted one of the offered tobaccos, ran it past his nose to savor the pungent aroma and struck a match to it. There was something to be said for living in town where the trade wagons came regularly.

"Emily instructed me to bring you out to dinner the very first night you arrived," said Whittiker.

"That's nice of her," laughed Luke. "How many unmarried females will be there?" Whittiker's wife was a delightful person and was constantly trying to marry him off.

The major grinned back. "She has never had more than three for you to select from at any one time. I believe she spends all the time between your visits arranging for these evenings."

"Some of the women have been very beautiful."

"Yes, I know. And she is mystified why you have not taken one seriously."

"Too busy building a ranch," volunteered Luke.

"You already have one of the biggest ranchos in all New Mexico. And without doubt, the best horses, even including northern Mexico. I heard rumors you found a gold mine out there in your valley."

"Just rumors, that's all there is to it."

"Three miners left here a month ago to check out the story. Did you see anything of them?" asked the Major.

Coldiron's eyes, guileless, emotionless like deep frozen water, rested upon his friend. The major and his troopers were the only law in the territory outside Santa Fe and this was not an idle question. "Everyone

knows I don't allow trespassing on my land. So those three probably
went some other direction."

The major's face was clouded and serious. "Luke, that's open government land. I hope you are doing something to get proper title."

"I have that land grant from the Mexican Government."

"Yes, I know. You rushed to Santa Fe one day ahead of the American
Army and bought it from the Mexican governor for a thousand dollars in
gold. Then that stout-hearted hombre put his tail between his legs and
dashed to the safety of Mexico. You know the Mexican Government has
never ratified the sale of lands he made those last few days. Your title
with his signature is more than likely not valid."

"It's better than anyone else has."

"Maybe so. But you should try and legalize your ownership under
American law."

"I'm working on it. Something called a Homestead Law has been
recently passed by Congress. I've got a lawyer looking into what's needed
to get ownership. He says considerable time will be needed to get title to
thirty miles of creek and seven springs. But once I get the water tied up,
the whole valley will be mine permanently. In the meantime, I have nine
points of the law on my side."

"What do you mean?" asked the major.

"Meaning I have possession of the land and I'll hold it until someone
strong enough to take it away from me comes along. That may take a day
or two." He laughed coldly.

A knock sounded on the frame of the open door.

"Yes, Sergeant, come in," said Whittiker. "Did Mr. Coldiron live up
to the terms of the contract?"

"Yes, sir. They are very fine horses. Several of the troopers wanted to
try one so we actually rode fifteen of them."

"Thank you, Sergeant. Stand by for a moment." The major turned to
Coldiron. "How do you want your pay?"

"I need about $1,000 in cash. A draft will be alright for the balance."

Whittiker spoke to the trooper. "Sergeant, have the quartermaster
bring $1,000 in gold and a bank draft for $11,000 as Mr. Coldiron
requested."

"Yes, Sir," said the sergeant and about-faced and left.

CHAPTER 13

Macrina Archuleta and his band of five *pistoleros* rode swiftly north along the El Camino Real toward Santa Fe. Their course led down from a chain of low hills and would soon reach the Santa Fe River a mile above its junction with the Rio Grande.

A stiff wind shoved at the backs of the horsemen, flopping the broad brims of their sombreros and grabbing the brown dust kicked up by the horses' feet, washing the men in a dirty mist.

"Madre de Dios!" exclaimed Fabio Cuadrado. "Why doesn't the wind change direction and blow the dust away?"

Archuleta twisted to look back at his second in command. "Patience, Fabio, we are almost there. In two hours you will be in the shade of a cantina and drinking large quantities of cool beer."

Cuadrado's teeth showed for an instant in his dust-covered beard. "I am not complaining, *patrón*. You and I have ridden in much worse weather than this small, warm wind. To take revenge upon the Americans, I would follow you through the dust so thick I would have to cut it with my knife to see."

"I know you are loyal," said Archuleta. He ran his eye over the lean faces of his men. Muniz was the youngest and fast with his pistol; only Archuleta himself was quicker. Trujillo, thick-bearded, sturdy and dependable, was always there to back the leader's hand. Ochoa had much Apache blood flowing in his veins. He rode with the Mexicans simply because he hated them less than the Americans. Barrera was the relentless fighter, never giving quarter or accepting it.

Archuleta spoke loud enough for all of them to hear him. "The reward for each of you when we finish this campaign will be very great."

"I have no doubt of that, Colonel," said Cuadrado. He had worked for Archuleta for eighteen years and knew the man was very skilled at planning raids, in designing the brave thrust, creating the false trail to mislead their enemies. This great robbery would be the biggest of all.

Archuleta faced back to the front. His strategy was sound. However, it was the men that were the key to success. With these gunmen, the very best in all the state of Chihuahua, he would not fail. The twenty-two vaqueros who had gone on ahead, in ones and twos, they were also good at their profession.

The plan, containing many segments and conceived over more than two years, was complete. All parts were in motion. The venture would yield much gold. He chuckled in anticipation even though he was hot and dirty and his tongue fuzzy with thirst.

He felt good, like the old days when he had been Colonel Archuleta of the Army of Nuevo Méjico. That was in 1845 before the cowardly Manuel Armijo, Territorial Governor, had retreated to Mexico without firing one shot at the invading American Army. He had hastily left before he even knew the gringo numbers or armaments.

The governor, no longer with the stomach for battle, gave up his post and retired to a rich rancho. However, that official's cowardice had tainted Archuleta's career, stopping all advancement. His friends would ask, "Ah, yes, Colonel Archuleta, weren't you at Santa Fe immediately before the Americans came?" Their coolness toward him followed, becoming an accusation. That led swiftly to withdrawal of support.

Archuleta resigned his commission, for no one advanced in the Mexican Army, no matter how clever a tactician and commander of men, without the support of friends in high places. He returned to the family rancho, a small one near the American border, and began to plot his revenge. Archuleta could not make a reprisal against the governor; however, more than once he considered calling him out for a duel of honor. The Americans were also to blame for his great loss. The colonel could make them pay, and for many years he had ridden north to wrest away that payment in cattle, horses and gold.

The colonel spotted where the fresh tracks of a group of horses had turned from the road and gone down toward the Santa Fe River. He halted his crew and sat for a half minute until the dust had blown away. Then he angled his sight to the right, along the sign where the riders had gone out onto the floodplain of the river.

On the subirrigated bottomland, lush meadows grew and the path left by the passage of the horses could be easily seen. Archuleta saw the large cottonwoods that marked the location of a long looping meander of the river channel.

"Out there where the tall trees are is the place where I told the gringos to meet us. It appears they have come before us. They know I will have much gold with me. Keep your weapons ready, for they cannot be trusted."

Each rider pulled his pistol from its holster, blew the dust off and began to check the action. They were skilled men and knew one misfire could get them killed.

As the colonel inspected his own handgun, he reviewed his agreement with the gringos. He had good reason to have one part of his plan be carried out by *norteamericanos;* so the month just past, he had traveled to Tucson to meet with a cousin living in the lawless town. His relative knew men who would do anything as long as the pay was good. Archuleta had met with one of those men, the gunman Kazian, and they had struck a bargain.

Now following the tracks, the Mexicans crossed through the grass and brush of the floodplain and came out onto a bare sandbar adjacent to the river.

The Americans had heard the approaching riders and stood waiting with hands near their six-guns. Archuleta noted the horses were still drinking, indicating they had just reached the water. Five men and five horses, the odds were there was no one hiding in the brush to fire upon them.

"Buenos días, Señor Kazian," said the colonel and climbed down from his mount. He faced the strong-looking man who had stepped out in front of the other Americans.

"Hello, Archuleta. I'm here with four damn good men, as I agreed." Kazian measured the colonel, tall for a Mexican, gaunt, with hollow cheeks. He let his eyes drift over the five *pistoleros* who had swung down to flank their leader. They were hungry-looking hombres, hard, staring back without expression. Well-used long-barreled pistols were strapped to every hip. These men would be tough to kill.

"Bueno. You are a man of your word," said the colonel. "Here is the gold I promised if you would come to Santa Fe and listen to my plan." He extracted a leather pouch from his pocket and tossed it to Kazian. "That is a quarter of the full price. Another quarter will be paid if you take the job. The last half will be yours when the task is finished."

"The price is still $1000 for each of my men and $2000 for me, all in gold."

"That is agreeable to me," said Archuleta.

"Good," said Kazian. "Let's find some shade and talk." He turned to a powerfully built American. "Murdock, you take care of the horses. The rest of you come with us."

Archuleta spoke to one of his men. "Muniz, water *los caballos* and then come join us."

"*Sí, patrón,*" responded Muniz and stalked off toward the animals.

Beneath a large cottonwood at the upstream end of the sandbar, the two groups found seats on the ground facing each other. The colonel removed his hat and tossed it aside. Kazian did likewise and mopped at his sweaty forehead with a dirty bandana.

"What's the deal?" asked the gringo leader leaning forward.

"I wish to steal many horses," said Archuleta.

"Here in Santa Fe?" said Kazian in surprise. "Hell, there's plenty of horse herds around here all right. But do you mean to say you have come three hundred miles to steal horses?"

"Exactly," responded Archuleta.

"And I suppose you plan to drive them all the way back to Mexico?" said the American, staring back with a small crooked smile at the Mexican horse thief.

"You are correct again."

"That's plumb foolish."

"Foolishness is when a game is not profitable or fails." The colonel felt his anger rising at the rudeness of the gringo.

Kazian straightened up, cast a doubting look around at his men and then faced back to the Mexican. "Best you tell me the whole plan so I can figure out whether or not I want a part of it."

You will never know all the scheme until it is too late, thought the colonel. He said, "You deserve to know the plan. I intend to take *aproximadamente* three hundred head of horses from the American Coldiron."

"Goddamn! You sure know who has the best horses and I can't fault you for wanting them. But his ranch is another seventy or eighty miles farther north. And he won't give his mustangs up easy."

"I know how far away his rancho is. I have been there."

"What job would be mine?"

"The first part would be to help me and my men round up *los caballos*. Then guard our back trail as we drive them south."

"From what I have heard about Coldiron, he'll have to be killed to be stopped," said Kazian.

"That is what I want. Him dead and not chasing after me into Mexico. I understand he is very good with a pistol, so I would expect you to lay your ambush carefully."

"Any man, regardless how tough or good with a gun, can be killed. It's just a matter of picking the right spot and time. How long will this job take?"

"From now until we are back in Mexico will take nine or ten days. Your task, if you have good fortune with Coldiron, could be over sooner. It depends on how good you are."

"You know half a hundred men will spot you driving such a large herd of horses that far. If Coldiron gets to the soldiers, they will catch you easy before you reach Mexico and you will lose everything."

"You will see that he does not reach the soldiers. And even if he should, I have a plan."

"I've heard it said in certain places that you are a cagey hombre, Archuleta. But this time you may be gambling on too much of a long shot."

"Let me worry about that," said the colonel.

Kazian rubbed his whiskered jaw and evaluated the Mexican.

"Well, now it's also my worry for my neck is stuck out right along with yours. But even so, we'll take the job. I've always wanted to meet up with this fellow Coldiron. I hear he's a real horse killer. I wonder if he's as good at killing something that can shoot back."

"*Excelente,*" said the colonel. "Now to pay you." He directed an order to Cuadrado. "Get the pouch of gold from my right saddle bag."

"*Sí,* Colonel," said Fabio.

Archuleta continued to speak to Kazian. "After you have disposed of Coldiron, meet me where the El Camino Real crosses into Texas. There is a large rock monument marking that spot. I will be waiting with the balance of your pay." As an afterthought he added, "If you kill him."

Kazian read the challenge and declared, "He's as good as dead right now."

"*Bueno.* Here is your gold," said Archuleta, taking it from Cuadrado and pitching it to the American.

Kazian stood up and poured part of the round gold coins from the bag into his hand. "American double eagles, damn good money." He spun on his four men, running his eye over the barrel-chested Murdock, Pollin, Dule and the old beaver trapper, Tashaw. "Get your mounts and let's get to Santa Fe."

Kazian looked back at Archuleta. "They'll keep their mouths shut about this deal, don't worry. Or I'll shut them up permanently."

The colonel nodded his understanding. If the bastard gringos only knew his full plan they would not be so pleased. He remained standing with his men and watched the Americans swing into their saddles and ride off.

"Muniz, climb that big tree until you can see over the brush and up to the road," said the colonel. "Watch the Americans and for any other danger. Someone will relieve you in a few minutes."

He pointed to the clear cold water of the Santa Fe River. "The rest of us will bathe and wash our clothes. We do not want to enter Santa Fe looking like bandits from Mexico." He laughed harshly. This land was once his and then he had ridden it as an important person. He jerked his sweat-stained shirt off and hurled it out into the water.

The youth who called herself Cris Penn sat in the rectangle of shade in front of Dunstock's General Store in Santa Fe and intently watched the sprinkling of people coming and going along sun-drenched San Francisco Street. She was dressed in a man's faded pants, oversized and cinched in with a frayed leather belt. Her shirt was even more baggy and sagged from thin shoulders, hiding the swell of her breast. She wore ancient boots that appeared to be older than she. The only item about her that looked relatively new was a six-gun, well oiled and buckled around her lean waist.

From her location she could see the entire main business district of the town. Firms, offices and establishments of many kinds lined the dusty street both to the north and south. The entrance of an imposing two-story adobe building with a tall sign declaring it to be the Bank of Santa Fe was across the street directly from her.

Miller Livery, a long rambling building, sprawled half a block south on her side of the street; Sanchez Blacksmithing adjoined the livery on the far end. The clank of metal being hammered sounded from its open door. At least a dozen cantinas were within sight, scattered among the other places of business.

Noon came and the young woman went into the store. A hundred tantalizing aromas teased her nose and she felt the sharp edge of her hunger. She wandered about the aisles between the shelves of food, ducking once to pass under a long line strung full of dried mutton, goat and venison, heavily seasoned with pepper to keep the flies off, and finally found the cracker barrel. She dipped up a handful of the round chips of bread, had the store keeper slice off a slab of cheese, selected an early season apple, paid for all and returned to the outside.

Without waste of time she retook her seat and, as she ate, scrutinized the faces of the men passing, measuring them against the one that had been described to her.

In the spring just passed, she had been told a story that turned her world upside down. The gentle people who had reared her, loved her, were not her parents. Her origin began when a strange trapper man came out of the New Mexico mountains with a handful of female humanity inside his shirt and paid a small fortune to a couple he chanced upon to raise the child. And he had told of killing the mother of the newborn infant.

Now she was on a long quest to find that man, to learn the reality of her beginnings and to kill the man if what he had said was the truth.

The blazing sun floated down on a long sliding trajectory from the high sky. It sank behind the tall crown of Redondo Peak and the shadow of the mountain hurried silently eastward, sweeping across the pine-cloaked Caja del Rio Plateau. Rapidly accelerating, the shade reached Santa Fe and threw its cooling dimness over the gathering of adobe buildings and its people. In the lessening heat, the wind that had swept the streets most of the day slowed to a gentle evening breeze.

A knot of five horsemen rode into sight at the distant south end of town and trotted their mounts along the street. An Indian came out of the General Store, walked past the youth and went to a long-legged dun tied at the hitching rail. As he untied the reins, he glanced up and down the street as if looking for someone.

The five riders, all Americans, halted at a large cantina near the youth and climbed down. Leading the dun, the Indian angled across the street toward the blacksmith shop.

"Well, I'll be Goddamned," exclaimed Murdock, catching sight of the bronze face of Two Suns beneath his white man's hat. "That's an Indian and right here in the center of Santa Fe."

Kazian and the other men glanced at the retreating back of Two Suns. "So what?" said Kazian. "Looks like he's friendly."

"Because I don't like Injuns," retorted Murdock. "I got a scar on my belly where one put a arrow once." He watched the Indian advancing toward the blacksmith shop. "I do believe this one is stealing a horse. See the silver bridle and the silver conchos on the saddle. No Injun ever had gear that good. He'll be in that alley by the smithy in a minute and be gone with that pony."

"Appears you are looking for a reason to start a fight," said Kazian. Before he could warn Murdock to let the matter drop and not draw attention to the presence of the gang in town, the man quickly stepped forward after Two Suns.

Murdock yelled out loudly. "Hey, you Injun, put that horse back where you found him."

Two Suns, not certain the shouted words were meant for him, merely slowed and looked over his shoulder. When he saw the white man's attention riveted upon him, he stopped and pivoted to face him.

Cris had seen the confrontation developing between the two men. She rose to her feet, not quite sure what she should do. Other people, hearing Murdock's strident cry, came out of the doorways onto the sidewalk to see what was happening.

"Damn thievin' Injun," snarled Murdock. "Where are you going with that horse?"

Two Suns warily watched the insulting white man and the four others close behind him. He felt the hot blood begin to pound in his veins, but he kept his face impassive. "I am taking him to the blacksmiths to have a shoe fixed."

"Like hell you are," countered Murdock, his voice sharp. "Once out of sight, you'll sneak off to the mountains like a coyote. Now, is that your pony?"

"No," said Two Suns. "He belongs to—"

"Just as I thought," interrupted Murdock. He cast a quick glance at Kazian. "We have us a horse stealin' Injun here just as I thought."

He faced back to Two Suns. "Do you know what happens to horse thieves?"

"They get hung," growled Tashaw from beside Kazian. "And I'll help you, Murdock."

"You two don't push this too far," cautioned Kazian.

"Why not?" retorted Tashaw. "He's a Ute and they once killed my pardner and took two hundred beaver pelts from me up in the Colorado Territory."

"That's right," agreed Murdock. "He's an Injun. Once he's dead, nobody is going to do anything to a white man."

Some of the curious onlookers moved closer. Cris stepped into the street. Before she could proceed further, a second Indian came through the door of Dunstock's store and with rapid strides hurried to stand beside the first.

Kazian sized up the two unarmed Indians, not large men, but their eyes were brave and set for trouble. They would fight and not run.

"Get the redskins, Tashaw!" shouted Murdock and lunged forward, bearing down on Two Suns.

The Indian danced to the side, escaping Murdock's clutching hands, and struck him a solid blow to the side of the head. The white man grunted at the sting of the hard fist, swerved his course and came again at Two Suns.

"Let's help him!" cried Tashaw. He sprang across the dusty street separating him from Lightning Blanket.

Lightning stood his ground and flat-footed met Tashaw head-on, hammering him to a dead stop with a flurry of blows. Tashaw backed up to reevaluate the Indian.

"Dumb bastards," Kazian cursed Murdock and Tashaw. Yet the cards had been dealt, and even if by a pair of fools, help had to be given. Kazian moved forward. The remaining two men fanned out and followed close behind to lend support.

The town residents crowded in close to better see the fight. A cavalcade of Mexican horsemen galloped up and sprang down to stand near the youth. She threw a quick, short look over them. Each one was dressed all in brown, with tight jackets decorated with needlework, silver studded trousers and big sombreros. They almost resembled soldiers in uniform.

Murdock, Kazian and Dule ganged up on Two Sons, slamming him with savage blows, staggering him, knocking him to his knees. Tashaw and Pollin went after Lightning Blanket. But the quick-muscled Indian fought clear, ducking and blocking the strikes of their fists.

"Let's get him at the same time!" yelled Tashaw.

Both white men bore down on Lightning Blanket, caught him between them and pummeled him with a storm of vicious blows.

Dust rose from under the scuffling boots of the struggling men and formed a thin cloud to hang in the air. The townsfolk ignored the dirt, tightening their ring around the fighters and craning their necks to watch the lopsided battle.

"Damnation. They sure are taking a beating," said a fat man to the blacksmith standing beside him.

"Very unfair fight," rejoined the smithy. "Old Horse Killer will be one mad son of a bitch when he finds out about his Indians."

CHAPTER 14

Coldiron rode down the grade of San Francisco Street toward the center of town. He felt good, relaxed with two tall drinks of the major's bourbon in his stomach and the weight of $1000 in gold in his pocket.

A woodcutter driving three donkeys, the diminutive animals invisible except for fuzzy ears and tiny hooves under towers of wood, came out of a side street. Luke pulled up and gave them the right-of-way.

Ahead he noticed the throng of people in front of the blacksmith shop and came up to peer over their heads and into the dust at a brawling mixture of men. He saw Two Suns on the ground, bloody, trying to rise to his knees.

Murdock rushed in and kicked the Indian savagely in the ribs.

"Out of the way," shouted Coldiron at the two men directly in front of him. Engrossed in the fight, they did not hear him.

With exploding anger Luke jabbed his mount with sharp spurs. The startled and hurt animal leaped ahead, knocking the men blocking his way sprawling on the ground.

Luke reined the big horse and ran him straight over Murdock, somersaulting the burly man. Then he spun the horse and jumped him at Kazian and Dule.

The two men scrambled clear just in time to avoid the iron-shod feet carrying a thousand pounds of excited horse.

Coldiron swung down from the back of his mount, caught Kazian by the shirt front before he could recover his footing and slugged him twice in the face. Dule drove in from Luke's right and with a looping right fist smashed him in the corner of the mouth.

Pain jolted Luke. He staggered, caught his balance. The taste of blood was suddenly salt and copper in his mouth. He charged upon Dule, broke through his defense and laid him flat on his back with a heart-jarring left and right.

Coldiron pivoted about to go to the aid of Lightning Blanket.

Murdock, rousing from the stunning blow of the horse, climbed to his feet and looked around. He saw Coldiron closing in on Tashaw and Pollin where they were beating on the second Indian. Murdock reached for his six-gun. Anyone who would ride his horse over a man needed to be killed.

Cris saw one of the Mexicans in the brown clothing pull his pistol. In a blur of movement he sprang close to Murdock, pointed the gun and fired twice into the dirt at the man's feet.

Murdock flinched and swept a startled look around at the Mexican.

"You are stupid!" hissed Archuleta, his long-barreled weapon pointing directly at the center of Murdock's chest. "Put your *pistola* back into your holster or I will kill you."

At the sound of the shots Coldiron whirled to the rear, and his hand flashed down and came up with his six-gun. He thrust it out, the round black eye of the barrel searching for the danger, for something to kill.

"Shoot them, Coldiron," shouted the blacksmith from the crowd.

Luke barely heard the call. His eyes darted to the Mexican standing with a pistol, threatening the gringo that had kicked Two Suns.

"Holster it, now!" commanded the colonel, his finger taut on the trigger of his pistol, as if wanting to blast lead into Murdock.

The gun hands of Archuleta's men hovered over the butts of their pistols as they waited for Murdock's next move.

Murdock's face was red with anger as he slid his six-gun into its holster.

Strange action for Mexicans, thought Coldiron, watching the confrontation. One gringo killing another usually made no difference to the recently conquered people. Still the intervention was welcome, for Luke's back had been unguarded.

Tashaw and Pollin had stopped their attack on Lightning Blanket as the pistol shots reverberated back and forth between the fronts of the buildings lining the streets. Now Coldiron aimed his six-gun at them.

"Get back from Lightning," Luke ordered.

The men backed away and their hands rose shoulder high.

"Can you get up, Lightning?" asked Luke.

Lightning Blanket staggered to his feet. "Appears I can," he said through battered lips.

"Then help Two Suns over to the well at the horse trough and you two clean some of the dirt and blood off."

Kazian and Dule worked their way up to their feet. With his head clearing rapidly, Kazian evaluated the situation. He saw Archuleta holding his pistol on Murdock and the rider who had charged into the fight threatening his other two men.

"Get out of here," ordered Archuleta, "all of you," and he motioned them away with his cocked pistol. His eyes locked with Kazian. "You, too, move it."

Murdock looked at Coldiron. "I'll see you later, and we'll settle this permanently."

"I would like that," said Coldiron, returning the baleful stare.

"Forget it, Murdock, and let's go," growled Kazian, half angry at Archuleta for his interference. But nevertheless satisfied to extract himself from the situation.

Murdock still eyed Coldiron. Kazian took him by the shoulders and roughly shoved him toward the door of the nearest cantina. "I'm buying drinks for all of you. The fight is over."

"Thanks for your help," Coldiron told Archuleta. "You kept this fight from getting bloody."

"*De nada* [It was nothing]," said Archuleta.

"You may have made some enemies out of that bunch."

"It does not bother me to have enemies of that caliber."

"Just the same, I would keep a sharp eye out for a few days."

"I am always watchful. *Hasta la vista.*" The colonel motioned to his men and mounted to lead them up the street.

Luke watched after the Mexicans, wondering what had prompted them to take a hand in the fight. The crowd faded away back into the buildings or off along the street. Lightning Blanket and Two Suns came up to Luke.

"You two need to see a doctor?" asked Coldiron.

"I don't think so," said Two Suns, "but every muscle in my body hurts."

"Some muscles hurt that I don't have," said Lightning Blanket and tried to smile, but cut it short with a wince.

"Good. Then finish your jobs. Afterwards better go out and set up camp near the army barracks. No one will bother you there."

They shuffled off, favoring various parts of their bodies.

"Mr. Coldiron," a soft voice intruded into Luke's thoughts.

"Yes," said Luke turning and looking down at a young man who had moved up close to talk.

"Mr. Coldiron, my name is Cris Penn. I have heard you have a large horse ranch up to the north. Could you use another hired hand?"

Luke examined the youth in the old baggy clothes. Certainly looked down-and-out and in need of employment. But he did not appear very strong.

"I can do a full day's work," said Cris. From the shadow of the brim of the battered hat, her brown eyes investigated Luke in turn. She saw the blood on his lips and the skinned places on his knuckles. He looked mean and there was a steely hardness about him that was almost frightening. "I really need a job for I'm flat broke. I'll work for my food and bed until you are satisfied I'm worth some cash money, too."

"Can you cook?"

"Yes. I'm a fair cook. I can ride, rope and shoot, too."

"There's always plenty of that to do. Right now my cook needs help. He's getting old and could use some young hands to help him prepare chow, tend the garden and all the other dozen chores around the ranch house."

"I'll do whatever needs to be done."

Luke studied the lightly chiseled features framed by ragged hair, appearing as if it had been cut with sheep shears. He was very young, his skin smooth with no sign of a beard, and his voice had not fully changed. There was something almost feminine about him. But his sincerity in wanting a job could not be doubted. "How old are you?" asked Luke.

"Fifteen."

"Where are you from?"

"San Francisco, California."

"Well, I'll be damned. That's a mighty long distance to travel, and there are many dangers on that rough trail. Did you come alone?"

"Most of the way. From time to time I would fall in with people going my way."

Luke noted the callous on the youth's thumb. A lot of practice would be required to do that. "You say you can ride and shoot. I would need to find out how well you do those things."

"I will show you soon," said Cris.

There was an odd tone to his voice that Luke could not identify. "Anybody that can make it from California can sure hold a job at my ranch. You are hired. I'll pay $20 a month and your keep." He reached into his pocket and extracted a coin. "Here's $10 in advance. Go tell those Indians, either Two Suns or Lightning Blanket, that I have hired you and ask what you can do to help them."

"Thank you, Mr. Coldiron."

"We'll be leaving at daybreak two days from now. Be ready."

"I'll be ready."

Out of sight of Coldiron, Archuleta stopped. *"Vengan aquí,"* he called his men near him. "Trujillo, Ochoa and you, Barrera, find the others that came ahead of us and tell them they are to leave Santa Fe at once. They must go north until they reach the place where the Santa Fe Trail crosses the canyon of the Rio Grande. Have them wait for me there. Go separately so the gringos will not have cause to wonder what we are doing."

The three left immediately, riding slowly, their routes diverging.

"Muniz, go to the cantina and tell Kazian to come out the back door and talk with me."

"*Sí*, Colonel, but they may be angry and want to fight."

"Then stand ready to help me."

"It would be a pleasure to kill one or two of them," said Muniz and trotted his mount up the street.

"Cuadrado, you come with me," said Archuleta and guided the way down an alley lined solidly with the walls of adobe houses and then along a street to the rear of the cantina.

As the two Mexicans arrived, Kazian and the members of his gang came warily out through the open door. The gringo leader scanned his sight both ways along the street before settling in on the unpredictable Mexican *jefe*.

"Archuleta, what was that play back there with Coldiron? You backed the very man you wanted dead. Why in hell did you do it?"

"Because I told you that I did not want him killed in town or his friend, the major, would send soldiers out to the ranch to take possession of all the horses. Then all would be lost. And I know about this man Coldiron. He is very good with a pistol. Unless your men are masters with handguns, there was an excellent chance several of you would be killed and Coldiron would still live."

"I don't think he is so good I should worry," said Kazian. "But, anyway, what you say about the army major may be correct."

"Coldiron and both of his wranglers are in town and that is fortunate for us," said the colonel. "We must ride quickly to his rancho and take his *caballos* before he returns."

"We haven't had our second drink yet," said Kazian. "But you are right about leaving now. We are ready."

"Good. Do you know where the ranch is?"

"I don't, but my man Tashaw does. One time he came through Coldiron's valley."

"Then meet me on the east side of the valley about mid length where the rimrock has fallen down and a horse trail comes up over it. Ride fast and be there soon as possible. You can probably be there near noon the second day from now."

"We'll be there waiting for you when you come," said Kazian. There was a challenge in his eyes.

"We shall see," said the colonel. "Do you know the shortest route, the one lying west of Mountain Cerro de la Olla?"

"Tashaw will know it."

"*Bueno.*"

Archuleta nodded at Cuadrado, who grinned with his teeth, and they stepped astride their swift *caballos*.

Coldiron led his crew of three down from the rimrock and north across the grassy bottom of his horse ranch valley. It was the second day since leaving Santa Fe. The evening shadows thrown by the mountains to the west overran the riders as they reached the base of a broad pine-topped hill.

Without slowing, the horses took to a well-used trail up the slope. They increased their pace without being urged, rattling the loose rocks as they climbed.

Luke glanced at Cris. "They are in a hurry, for they smell their stable and feed. The ranch headquarters is just up there."

The horses, breathing deeply, crested the top of the grade and came out onto a wide, level bench cut into the flank of the hill. Cris slowed her mount in surprise as she viewed the long ranch house of brown sandstone resting solidly in the center of the flat. The structure looked well built, to last a lifetime, maybe two.

The large building was roofed with thick pine shingles and two tall chimneys jutted up. Four windows with glass panes were evenly spaced along the front length. It was a rare sight to see glass in such a remote location. Heavy wooden shutters with gun ports bored through them flanked all the windows, ready to be jerked shut to ward off the arrows and bullets of enemies. Two doors opened into the front of the house.

To the right was a round corral constructed of pine logs set deeply on end in the ground. Above the corral was a fair-sized garden of hardy vegetables, cabbages, peppers, squash and other plants Cris could not make out because of the distance. A ditch carrying water to irrigate the garden slanted across the side of the hill from a walled up spring in the edge of the timber. Farther right a hundred yards was a stone and log barn big enough to shelter at least fifty horses.

The front door on the south end of the house popped open and an old white-haired man hurried down a short path to meet them. He lifted his hand high in greeting.

"Mr. Coldiron, welcome home," he called in a sonorous, pleasant voice.

"Hello, Cliff. Everything all right?" responded Luke.

"Yes. No visitors came within sight."

"Good. Cliff, I want you to meet a new hand for us. Cris Penn, this is Clifford Yerrington."

"Hello, Mr. Yerrington," said Cris. She judged his age at least seventy. He was immaculately groomed and dressed in clean white cotton shirt and trousers and low-heeled walking boots. A pearl-handled six-gun was strapped to his waist. And though the pistol was tied down with a strip of silk string to his leg, it was tied down like that of a gunfighter.

"Pleased to make your acquaintance, Cris," said Yerrington and smiled broadly.

"Cliff, you have first call on Cris's help. We'll have him work out on the range when he's not busy with a chore for you."

"Very good, Mr. Coldiron. And I suppose all of you are hungry, so in one hour supper will be ready. Before you go to the barn, unload the house goods from the packhorses and bring them inside. I'll get a fire started in the cooking stove to heat the oven. If you brought the apples like I asked, I will bake an apple pie."

"We didn't forget," said Two Suns.

"He's one fine cook," volunteered Lightning Blanket.

Yerrington acknowledged the compliment with even a wider smile. He looked at the new hand. "Cris, after you have tended to your horse, come to the house and help me."

Lightning Blanket spoke. "Cliff, do you need any kindling or wood?"

"Now that you mention it, I could use some fine wood to hurry the heating of the oven."

"Go ahead, Lightning, and help him," said Two Suns. "I'll take care of your cayuse."

Lightning Blanket slipped from his saddle and walked off toward the wood yard. The remaining crew unloaded the foodstuff and then turned their mounts in the direction of the barn.

They entered the stable end of the structure, heavy with the pungent odor of manure and hay and dimly lighted, with shadows of the falling dusk cloaking everything. Behind her, Cris heard the ring of Lightning Blanket's ax on a pine log.

Altogether it was somehow a pleasurable moment. And Coldiron's ranch was not supposed to be like that.

CHAPTER 15

Dust billowed up from inside the round rock corral where the Mexicans struggled to subdue the band of wild mustangs.

"Blind him," shouted Archuleta. "Blind him. Peña, use your lasso. Throw him."

The red stallion reared and struck out viciously with his front feet. He screamed savagely, the muscles of his throat swelling against the two ropes that stretched tautly in opposite directions from his neck. He stomped down, sending fresh dust boiling, and kicked backward, extending his long hind legs out level with his back.

Spinning the loop of his lasso, Peña spurred in close and sent it snaking out to ensnare both rear legs. He took a dally around the horn of his saddle, wheeled his horse and jerked the rope taut. The stallion crashed down on his stomach, rolled to his side.

"Ozuna! Now! Put the blindfold on him," yelled the colonel and swung his arm commandingly at the stud trying to tear free.

Ozuna snatched a black cloth hood from a half-dozen bundle of them at his feet and dashed forward, circling a little to come in behind the stallion. He jammed the blindfold over the beast's ears and halfway down over his head and tied it securely.

Peña released the tension on his lasso, flicked it twice to open the running noose, shook it once more to cause it to drop from the imprisoned feet and dragged it to him.

The red horse climbed to his feet. Never had he seen it so dark. Even in the blackest of nights, he had always been able to see forms, measure distance. He trembled and stood perfectly still. His big nostrils flared as he sucked in air and he began to listen closely to determine what his enemies were up to.

"Tie him in line just behind that big mare," ordered the colonel. "Then put another mare in back of him. They will help calm him down."

The men with the ropes led the unseeing stallion, now confused and

more tractable, up to the rear of a group of horses already tied nose to
tail in a line. Peña dismounted and hurried up to the mare, grabbed her
long unpruned tail, folded it up high over her back and tied the double
thickness of coarse hair tightly with several turns of rawhide. Then he
slipped a rope halter over the stallion's head and cast off the loops of the
two lassos. He ran the short lead rope through the mare's tail and
snubbed him up to within two feet of the mare's rump.

"Now one more mare and that bunch of mustangs is ready to go
south," said Archuleta. He turned to the horseman holding the rope of
the front animal of the string. "Deleon, it is your turn. Go swiftly. Stay
west of the Rio Grande. Stay far clear of any people, including those you
know. Go to water only once each day and even then spend only the
least possible time there. Do not use any roads."

"Sí, patrón," said Deleon. The instructions were not needed for he
had heard them several times already. And he was a good horse thief,
that was why he was here.

"The stallion may give you trouble for a few days, but he is un caballo
magnifico and is worth the extra work."

"He is one fine horse," agreed Deleon. He would take off the blindfold two days from now when the stallion had the edge worn off from a
hundred miles of hard travel.

"The last mare is tied on," said Peña.

Archuleta nodded to Deleon to be on his way. The man touched the
brim of his hat in salute and, towing the string of horses, guided his
mount toward the open end of the horse trap. He rode slowly, looking
back at seven colts standing two hundred feet off against the rock wall of
the enclosure.

One gray-colored youngster left the little knot of scared colts and on
long spindly legs moved haltingly after the departing mares and studs.
He recognized his dam, smelled her, and she was leaving. A second colt
separated from the pack of his peers and then yet a third, quite small,
pulled himself away, and all trotted to catch the departing horses.

Deleon let his mount feel the big metal spurs on his ribs and the line
of horses drew swiftly away from the trap and up a trail to a broken
section of the rimrock. The colts kept pace but hung back. They would
grow tired in a few miles and then Deleon, to keep them from being lost
along the trail, would rope and tie them to their mothers. However, he
did not expect the smallest colt to survive the long, fast trip to
Archuleta's rancho. Those little, tender hooves and young muscles would
wear out before that far place was reached.

As the colonel watched the formation of horses disappear up the trail,

he wiped sweat from his forehead with a bandana and retucked it into a
hip pocket. One damn hot day. On a flat stick, he cut a notch in one side
and three in the opposite. One hundred and ninety-nine mature horses
and thirty-four colts were moving to Mexico. Not bad for two days'
work. And the horses were in nineteen groups, spread over thousands of
square miles of desert, mountains and river bottoms. No one could stop
them from reaching Mexico, even if he knew what was happening. In
two weeks or less Archuleta would be much richer.

He surveyed the remaining two dozen or so horses and the men working to tie another eleven head in a line. The Steel Trap Brand showed
plainly on the hip of every animal. The colonel liked that.

A skittish bay mare dodged a rope thrown at her and darted for the
open side of the enclosure leading to the wings of the trap and freedom.
The rider guarding that escape route cut her off and stung her with the
end of his lasso, turning her back to rejoin the milling crowd of mustangs.

Archuleta was pleased at the skill of his men. But he knew a major
reason things had gone so smoothly was because of Coldiron's horse trap.
The structure was skillfully constructed astraddle a well-used horse trail
passing through small rolling hills, midway between the creek and the
rimrock. The area was moderately rocky and covered with a scattered
stand of small young pine. One-eighth mile wings of rock and chopped
brush that blended with the natural landscape had been built to funnel
into one of the open sides of a round rock corral. The corral itself had
been sited just below the brow of a ridge, so that any horse that came
racing to escape pursuing wranglers would not be able to detect the trap
until he had popped over the crest, and that would be too late to turn
back.

All Archuleta had to do to put the trap into operation was to wall up
the back side of the corral to close off the horse trail. And the mustangs,
used to moving along the trail unimpeded, had come, urged by his wranglers, one band after another.

Thinking of the tough hombre Coldiron, the colonel checked his lookout. Muniz still sat his horse at the tallest point of land around, a bare
hilltop a quarter of a mile south. He was a good man and Coldiron would
not arrive unseen.

Archuleta wanted to capture fifty more horses. Two bands had been
spotted to the west and the gringos were out after them now. He looked
at the red sun falling swiftly toward the horizon. With luck one of those
bands could still be driven in yet today. Then one band in the morning

and all would be finished, and the last of his men and he would leave for Chihuahua.

Except he would leave Kazian behind to kill Coldiron.

"*Patrón*, the gringos come with several mustangs," called Peña. "There, see the dust by the small round hill?"

The colonel easily spotted the running band of horses. "Get the men into position and hidden in the brush. Hurry."

The horse thieves scurried to mount and dash from the trap. All but one. He remained in the narrow neck where the funneling wings met the round enclosure. His duty was to keep those mustangs already captured from breaking away. He lay alongside the neck of his mount so the animals within could see him, but not those approaching.

The gringos urged their sweating mounts to close the gap between them and the wild ones. The honcho, Kazian, waved his arm to tell his men to close up even more. He knew the last few hundred yards were the most difficult, for the wily mustangs might notice something wrong and turn aside before they were into the wings of the trap. But push them hard, don't give them time to think or use those sharp eyes. He flogged his steed and yelled a loud, shrill call. His men took up the cry and spurred mercilessly.

The band of twenty-seven mustangs raced into the arms of the trap. The Mexicans sprang out of hiding behind the brush and joined the gringos, and the wall of men and their mounts charged down the channeling walls, closing the trap.

Cris left Coldiron and Two Suns doing chores at the barn and lugged her bedroll and saddlebags to the house. She had noticed when they arrived that the yard was grassy and she planned to sleep there. As she passed the kitchen door, she stopped to look in.

Two coal-oil lamps, one sitting on a large dining-room table and one on the reservoir of the stove, lit the room. Yerrington was working at some pans on the stove. He noticed Cris standing in the half darkness outside and motioned to her.

"Bring your possessions inside. There is a room here in this end of the house where you may sleep."

"You mean the hired hands live in the main house?" asked Cris in surprise.

"We have never hired men before, unless you would call Two Suns and Lightning Blanket hired. However, they are considerable more than that. They are nephews of the Ute chief, Big Tree, and are here as part of a treaty Mr. Coldiron has with them. Anyway they prefer to bunk outside unless it is the middle of winter and below zero."

"I would like to sleep outside, too," said Cris.

Yerrington smiled. "But it is more comfortable to use the house. The beds are very soft."

"Thank you for the invitation, but it is okay to just spread my blankets in the yard, isn't it?"

"Of course. But at least eat with us so I will have the opportunity to become acquainted with you."

Cris looked at the old man with the friendly smile. He was a pleasant sort, and besides it appeared the only food to be had was in the kitchen. "I would be pleased to do that."

"Excellent. Drop your bedroll there by the door and come inside and help me."

The food was delicious and in more than ample portions, the table laden with a wide variety of dishes—beef stew, slaw, green peppers, hot biscuits, sweet milk, cool from resting in the water of the spring, and an apple pie, thick, crusted and tasty.

Mr. Yerrington ate little and talked considerably. Most often he spoke to Cris, and as he did so he examined her fine young features.

His voice was deep and cultivated; obviously he was well educated. Strange to find such a person hidden away so far from civilization. It appeared Coldiron and the two Indians had learned from Yerrington for their English was also very good.

Yerrington said to Cris, "From what part of California do you come?"

"San Francisco."

"Ah yes, San Francisco. A city full of hustle and bustle. I was there in '50 and '51. I enjoyed it greatly, especially the waterfront. I always had a secret desire to go to sea. Be a pirate, you know."

Coldiron spoke. "Clifford Yerrington is a very well-traveled gent. Has seen both the Atlantic and Pacific oceans and the Gulf of Mexico. Been to every big city in the U.S. and its territories."

"Now, Mr. Coldiron, not every one," said Yerrington and smiled his broad smile.

"But, there is a dark side to our Mr. Well Educated and Traveled Gentleman. He was a ladies' man and fought many duels with husbands, boyfriends and brothers."

"That was many years ago," said Yerrington, "and I must confess my blood flowed hot then." He looked directly at Luke. "Now I would not trade this valley for all the plush hotels and restaurants in all the towns. But I surely would like to see a pretty face again."

He swept his eyes quickly to Cris. For just a moment she thought he knew her sex. Then he smiled innocently and returned his view to Luke.

"Well, I'm glad you plan to stay," said Coldiron. "Lightning, Two Suns and I could not survive without your apple pie."

All the men laughed and Cris found herself almost smiling with them before she caught herself.

In a grassy spot at the north end of the house, Cris unrolled her bedding and lay down. She rested quietly and reviewed the events of the days since she had found Coldiron. As she mulled her thoughts, a bright silver-dollar moon sailed up over the dark outline of the distant rimrock. The valley bottom cooled and a night wind began to fall down the slope of the hill. Somewhere beyond the yard there was a noise in the brush that disturbed the stillness once, then did not come again.

The close association with the Indians and Coldiron had exhausted Cris. It was not easy to play the role of a male, always remembering not to let go and act her natural self. It was even more difficult to hide her emotions about a man she had been told had killed her mother.

Coldiron had not turned out to be what she had expected. But then what had she expected? She knew he was fierce and unafraid, that was evident from the way he had attacked the men outnumbering him in Santa Fe. The Indians and Yerrington seemed to like him. But beyond that, all was unknown.

Was there something still to be learned tonight? She arose silently, buckled on her six-gun and slipped slowly around the rear of the house. Light spilled from a window and she crept up to peer in. Coldiron sat at a desk, his head tilted forward, making notations in a ledger. Behind him she saw a bed, chairs and clothes hanging on pegs in the wall.

It would be so easy to shoot him through the window, thought Cris. Had this man really killed her mother? Did he know where her grave was? Must I take deadly revenge? She rubbed the butt of her pistol with the palm of her hand as she thought about that.

From the darkness a form rushed upon her, grabbed her roughly about the shoulders to pinion her arms. A second figure sprang close and ripped the six-gun from its holster.

She fought fiercely to escape from the strong grip that held her, that clamped so mightily to compress her chest until she could not breathe. Her struggle did not budge the powerful hold.

Coldiron lifted his head and cocked it at an attentive, listening angle, as if sensing the silent struggle just outside the window.

"Quiet!" hissed Two Suns in Cris's ear. He lifted her bodily and backed away from the light and the window. Finally he stopped and lowered her feet to touch the ground.

"Let me go," said Cris in a harsh, savage whisper.

Lightning Blanket reached out his hand and caught her face in a vise-like hold. "Why were you about to pull a gun on Luke?"

"I wasn't going to pull it. Now turn me loose. Now! Damn it!"

"I do not believe you, for I saw your face. Now tell me why you want to harm Luke." Lightning Blanket's strong fingers hurt her face.

"I've told you all I intend to. Now get your damn hands off me." In the moonlight she saw Lightning Blanket put her gun in his belt.

Two Suns released his hold and stepped around to stand beside Lightning Blanket. He spoke to Cris. "It makes no difference whether or not you have told the truth. But hear me clearly. If you harm Luke in any way, we will track you down and kill you."

"Two Suns speaks for me, also," said Lightning Blanket. "You could never make it out of this valley before we would catch you."

"Why do you guard a white man so closely?" She tried to see their faces in the darkness, but only the outlines showed.

"Not a white man. Only Luke Coldiron," said Two Suns.

"He has a treaty with our tribe, with Big Tree who is our uncle. This land is the land of the Ute. The treaty says Coldiron can live in this valley and raise horses and our people will not drive him away. In payment Coldiron is to give us our choice each year of one hundred horses. Lightning Blanket and I came to stay with him to seal the bargain. We were only boys then and our time here was to be for a period of one year. As you can see, we have stayed to work for him.

"Go to your blanket and do not think of hurting our friend. We will give you back your pistol in the morning, after you think about what we have said."

Cris moved away from the Indians and into the gloom along the wall of the house. As she turned the corner to where her bed lay, a shudder shook her. She was positive they meant exactly what they said. She looked behind, searching the shadows of the night. Which dark form was an Indian watching her?

It was a dangerous world. She felt very much all alone.

Two Suns spoke to Lightning Blanket. "One of us must always be alert to protect Luke."

"Yes, I do not believe we changed the intention of that one. We have his pistol, but I saw a rifle in the scabbard of his saddle."

"We will take that also and put it back in the morning."

"We can watch him closely, but do you think we should tell Luke and Cliff about this?" asked Lightning Blanket.

"No. We can take care of this matter."

Cris awoke in the early dawn before the sun had crested the curve of the earth to find her pistol lying on the blanket beside her. Sometime during the night the Indians had crept to her very bed, had looked at her as she slept and had departed without violence.

She relaxed, listening to the stillness, and watched the stars vanish from the cloudless sky, washed away by the brightening light of the sun. As she rested, she reflected with some surprise upon the loyalty of the brothers in watching out for Coldiron's safety. Also, the white man's loyalty. He had come to the aid of Two Suns and Lightning Blanket in Santa Fe and had fought their enemies as if they were his own. An unexpected relationship. Yet she thought there would be something pleasing about such a situation for the men. To know there were strong men willing to risk their lives to give help without being asked.

When it was daylight enough to see, she circled the house and made her way to the spring. Below the place where the water poured forth from the earth, a pit five or six times the size of a washtub had been dug. It was waist deep with water and lined with stone, obviously a bathing place.

In the heat of the day the fifty degree water would have been pleasant on her skin, but now in the coolness of the morning Cris shivered as she hastily scrubbed herself clean. She hurried from the water, toweled briskly and donned fresh clothes. They were oversize, same as her other pants and shirt.

Cris returned to the house, and as she passed along the front she hesitated at the north door. All activity since their arrival had occurred in the end of the structure nearest the barn. Even Coldiron's study and bedroom were just off the kitchen. For what purpose was the north part of the house used? Curious, she lifted the wooden latch of the door and entered.

The room was a large parlor with a broad fireplace, heavy, overstuffed furniture and a tall china cabinet full of fine, delicate dishes. A thick wool carpet, spotlessly clean, covered the floor. There was a faint odor, like the stale air in a room long unused, pervading all.

She moved to a hallway leading off to the left. Four doors fronted it.

The first swung open soundlessly before the press of her hand. A wide bed with rich velvet cover and plump pillows dominated the room. Still, there was more than sufficient space for the dresser, two chairs and a wash stand topped with blue and white porcelain basin and pitcher.

Cris turned back to the hallway. She jumped, startled, for Clifford Yerrington stood watching her. His smile was missing.

"No one normally comes into this part of the house," said Yerrington. There was an edge of disapproval to his voice.

Cris wondered if the Indians had told him of her nighttime excursion to Coldiron's window. Then she decided they had not and he merely did not like her nosing about through these rooms. "The door was unlocked," she said.

"Doors are never locked here."

"What is this part of the house? Everything looks completely unused."

Yerrington studied her for a moment before he answered. "Mr. Coldiron furnished the house when he made his first big horse sale. That was perhaps fifteen years ago. He has never found the need to use any of the rooms except those near the kitchen."

"These furnishings are very expensive and must have been very difficult to bring here. Why did he build such a big house?"

"I suppose it was a laborious task to transport it. I understand most of it had to be disassembled, packed on many mules, then put back together once it arrived here. Some of the pieces, like that sofa there, had to be carried on stretchers tied between two animals. And I suppose he did all this because, like most young men, he thought he would marry some day."

"You have been with him a long time?"

"Ever since he kidnapped me in Santa Fe ten years ago."

"Kidnapped you! You mean you are a prisoner here?"

"In a manner of speaking, I am a prisoner. But not because of Mr. Coldiron. He told you part of my history last night. One part he did not tell you. I am overly fond of the spirits, the alcoholic kind. At one time I was practically destroyed by my uncontrollable vice. That was when he found me groveling in the dirt of the streets in Santa Fe, so intoxicated I could not stand. I was penniless and had just been thrown from the best hotel in the town for not paying my bill."

Yerrington rubbed the left side of his face. "A man leaned over me and slapped me here, very hard, and many times. Until I cursed and told him to stop or I would shoot him.

"The man asked me one question—could I cook? I told him I was the best of all cooks. So he hoisted me up on a horse, tied me so I would not fall off and in two days brought me here. That trip damn near killed me." He smiled for the first time since he had spoken to Cris. "I have not had a drink since. The house was furnished then as it is now."

"He has never married?"

"No. Plenty of women have displayed their charms for him. But for whatever his reasons, he has never taken one of them seriously."

"Maybe he doesn't like women."

Yerrington smiled for the first time. "From what I have observed, he is most fond of women."

Maybe not, thought Cris. I heard he killed one once. Her jaws were stiff with her emotion. She asked, "Have any women lived in the valley?"

"None that I know of."

Coldiron's voice calling loudly from the kitchen cut into their conversation. "Cliff, let's eat breakfast for there's a lot of work to do. Today's going to be a scorcher and I want to be done before the sun gets high enough to fry us."

"We must go," said Yerrington. "Better eat and get ready to ride. Mr. Coldiron is going to take you with him today to learn the lay of the ranch."

CHAPTER 16

Coldiron and his crew of three saddled and walked their horses up to the spring. They submerged their canteens in the cold water and then hung them dripping over the horns of their saddles.

"Lightning Blanket, you ride north and dig out any water holes that need it," said Coldiron. "Also, brand any colts we missed marking earlier and all new foals. Two Suns, you go south and do the same thing. Cris and I will work the center of the valley and on over to the west rim-rocks."

"Okay," said Lightning Blanket. "It will take three days to cover my end of the ranch. That brushy country east of the creek has a lot of mustangs and I'll work that part today." He rode away.

Two Suns hesitated, looking at Cris and Coldiron. Then without a word, he lifted his cayuse into a fast lope across the bench and disappeared over the edge and out of sight.

Coldiron spoke to Cris. "While we are still high enough to see most of the ranch, let me show you some landmarks." He swung his arm to point out over the land with its green mantle of grass and patches of pine. "That string of trees curving back and forth near the center of the valley marks the course of the creek. It enters up there to the north about fifteen miles. Comes in through a narrow, rocky gorge. I built a horse trail through there the first time I came here, but it has been washed out for many years. No horse can pass now. At its broadest point, the valley is about six miles wide. That is just about opposite us where we are right now. Then down at the south end, we have a rock fence to prevent the mustangs from drifting out."

Luke glanced at Cris. "You can't make out where the creek enters and leaves for it's too far away. In the next few days you will be at those places with either the Indians or me. Now let's ride out to the meadows along the creek and I'll show you how we prepare for winter."

With Luke leading, they dropped down the face of the bench. Cris pulled even with him at the bottom and they trotted their mounts toward the cottonwood- and willow-lined creek. Neither spoke. At one point Luke's dun, feeling frisky in the early morning, began to prance and the reins were loosened to let him run. Cris kept pace, enjoying the feel of speed and the wind on her face.

"Look, see the big buck deer drinking from the creek," said Luke.

"I see him. Just look at those large antlers."

The mule deer raised his head and pricked his big ears forward, investigating the intruders with intelligent eyes.

The riders did not slow, bearing down on the deer. "Let's see how close we can get," said Coldiron. "This time of year they're not very spooky."

At a hundred yards the buck tensed with mistrust and his muscles tightened, taut as the strings of a warrior's bow. The horsemen closed the distance by half. The buck snorted a harsh blast of air and stamped the ground with his sharp hooves. He exploded his breath a second time through his nose, and as he did so, hurled himself completely across the pool of water, struck the ground and bounded away with a series of long-legged leaps. He rounded the corner of a fenced pasture and was soon lost to sight in a low swale.

Coldiron chuckled. "Did you see how fat he was? This fall, after it starts freezing at night, we will come hunting the big fellow. Do you like to hunt, Cris?"

"Only when I am hungry," she responded.

"In this land, it's best not to wait until you are out of food to lay in a supply. A winter storm can come down on you and it can be days before you can get out to hunt.

"From here you can see something that is important to the ranch. We have about four hundred acres of our very best meadowland fenced off from the horses with barbed wire. It's in fields of thirty to forty acres scattered here and there along the creek. Nearly all of it is inside those bends of the creek where the ground is only a foot or so above the water level. The stream is dammed above the meadows we irrigate. You can see one of the dams, that brown ridge of rock and dirt. Part of the water is diverted out of the channel and brought in a ditch to the areas of good soil."

"Yes, I see where the water is taken out. I guess that strip of brush marks the location of the irrigation ditch that leads to a field. If all of that was done by hand, you have put in a great amount of work."

"It was all done by hand. The dams must be rebuilt each spring after the runoff from the snowmelt has passed. The horses are kept off the watered pastures until heavy snowfalls. Then we open the fences. To make good mounts, horses should be at least fourteen hands tall. That means they must have plenty of feed while they are growing."

They splashed through the creek and Luke opened a gap in the fence that surrounded a meadow. They rode inside and closed the fence.

"The grass is taller than my stirrup," said Cris. "I can understand how the horses could graze on it even if the snow got real deep."

"It gets deep alright. Much of our moisture comes as snow. Sometimes we still lose horses in the worst winters. They get bottled up by heavy snow back in the hills and trees and do not find the fields that have been opened up. Those are mostly yearlings. The older ones know to make their way to the creek when the snow comes. One of these years, when I can get a mower out here, we will start putting up hay. Then no mustangs should be lost."

Cris pulled the brim of her hat down to shade her cheek from the morning sun, rapidly growing hot, and ranged her sight to admire the high mountain valley ranch. She saw a large band of thirty horses watching from a low ridge to the west. Farther away near the rimrocks, small hills, some with dark green bonnets of pine, were randomly strewn about on both sides of the valley. The rimrocks themselves enclosed all of the land with brown vertical walls. Above the eastern rampart of stone, where the breeze was deflected upward, an eagle rode the updraft, its keen eyes watching the two humans and a thousand other living things.

The valley was very beautiful, she thought. Did the man deserve such a wonderful place? She turned to face Coldiron. "Are there any graves in the valley?"

"A few," said Luke, surprised at the strange question.

"Mostly horse thieves and Indians, I suppose?"

"Mostly."

Cris's eyes did not waver, "Any women buried here?"

"One," said Coldiron and thought there was a tinge of accusation in the question. He felt the stirring of his old, but not forgotten, memories of Morning Mist. He reined away from the young man, and the queries that were none of his business, and went through the field of grass and out through the fence on the far side.

During the hours of the morning, three unmarked colts were roped. Each time a fire was started and the hot branding iron pressed to the rump of the squealing, kicking youngster. Cris did the roping and was proud when every cast of her loop had sailed true, never once missing.

At a boggy seep in a gully on the west side of the valley, Luke untied a short-handled shovel from behind his saddle. He handed it to Cris. "Dig down and find where the water comes up clear from the ground. Horses like clean water same as humans."

Luke squatted down on his heels, rolled a cigarette and watched Cris wade out into the muck of the spring. He called to her. "Always start digging at the upper end of a wet spot. That's where the source of the water is."

Cris attacked the job. The mud was heavy and difficult to knock free from the blade of the shovel. The layer of rock she encountered was even harder to remove. But she did not look at the man lazily smoking. She did glance at the palms of her hands, fast becoming sore.

Coldiron made no offer to share in the excavation of the spring. It was good for a young man to wear some blisters the first day on the job. Except this young man had some feminine characteristics. Probably never would make a strong man.

Cris straightened up. "There it comes up, pure as melted snow. Sure a good-size flow now."

"Right. Small springs like this one, and those down in a low spot, can sometimes be almost stopped from running by horses stomping dirt into them. Now put those rocks you dug out back over it. That way animals will be kept off and it will continue to give water for a while without us having to rework it."

The rocks were heavy, rough to her sore hands, and she was soaked with sweat. Still she put her head down without a comment and began to lift and place the stones.

"Let me get that big one for you," said Coldiron. He stepped beside her, sucked in a deep breath and hoisted the heavy slab of stone to let it fall with a crunch on top of the mound.

"Where did all these rocks come from? There's none close to here."

Coldiron nodded his head at the rimrock two hundred yards distant. "I carried them from over there about sixteen or seventeen years ago." He grinned at her. "You're not the first to open up this spring. I guess it has been done at least a half dozen times. Horses are lazy critters and won't travel any further than they have to to feed. This water opens up about eight or ten square miles of range. The nearest other water is five miles away at the creek. If you got water and grass, you can make a living in this country."

"And the Indians?"

"Treat them fairly and pay for the use of the land and most times they'll leave you alone. After all, it is their land."

"And keep two of their people hostages."

Coldiron looked at her sharply. "Two Suns and Lightning Blanket can leave any time they want to." Luke was not sure he liked this quick-tongued kid.

Cris saw the half-angry expression on Luke's face. Better she not badger the man. If he had killed a woman, as she had been told, he could be dangerous. And she had not yet gotten answers to her questions.

But she now knew a woman was indeed buried here and the man Coldiron knew of it.

"It's getting mighty hot," said Luke. "Let's go to headquarters and take a siesta until it cools off this evening." He mounted and climbed the dun out of the gully. Immediately he spotted something moving out on the flat bottom. "Here comes Two Suns. I wonder why he came over to this side of the valley. I figured he would meet us at the house."

Cris looked in the same direction. Finally she located the tiny figure and was amazed at how quickly Coldiron had seen and identified such a distant speck.

"We'll go on," said Luke. "He can angle in toward our path and catch us."

Several minutes later Two Suns intercepted their course and fell in beside them. He measured Cris with a long look and then ignored her and began to talk to Coldiron.

The old grizzled mustang was at the very last gasp of extreme old age. He stood spraddle-legged to keep from falling. His neck was stretched and hung listlessly down, almost overbalancing the tottering body. The gray muzzle dragged the dirt. His bones were nearly through his stiffened skin, the backbone protruding sharp as a ridge pole.

On his back, three magpies hung on with taloned feet and tore at an old wound. One raised its head to swallow and saw the approaching riders.

"Is that Old Number One Stud?" asked Two Suns.

"Sure is," said Coldiron, pained at the sight of the shrunken, emaciated body. "He looks bad. And those damn magpies are eating him alive."

As if in defiance of the men, one of the black and white birds lowered its sharp beak, ripped loose a chunk of still-living flesh and greedily gulped it down.

As the men came closer, the magpies, with shrill calls of bother, launched themselves from the horse's back. They caught the hot air beneath their wings and flapped off a short ways to land on the ground.

"Looks like he's done for," said Two Suns. "Must have fallen and hurt himself. He can't even make it to water."

"He was getting plenty decrepit when I last saw him in the spring," responded Luke. "But I was still hoping he would live one more year."

Cris held back and followed the men in. As they drew near, the ancient animal tried to raise his head but was barely able to get one eye on the new arrivals.

Coldiron pulled his six-gun slowly, reluctantly. He stuck out his arm and aimed very carefully along the barrel at the skull-like head of the horse. He squeezed the trigger. The horse's head jerked to the side as the bullet crashed through the bone and brain. The frail, bony body sank to its knees and then toppled to the side.

Cris knew the killing of the horse was needed to end its misery; still she cried out in anger at Coldiron. "Why did you have to do that?"

He swung around to glance at her, then hastily away. But not before she saw the pain and sorrow on his face. He touched his mount with a heel and it moved away.

"Look here," Two Suns said to Cris and there was an edge to his voice. He poked a finger at the hip of the dead mustang. "See the Steel Trap Brand, and look here beside it. That is a number one. This old stud was the very first horse Luke ever branded in this valley, about twenty years ago. This old fellow must have sired at least a hundred colts. Every one turned out to be a damn fine horse, too."

Almost before Two Suns and Cris could leave and follow after Luke, the magpies came back in with a flutter of wings, landed on the carcass and began to eat again.

Coldiron heard the raucous call of the feeding birds and turned back. "Kill those Goddamn birds, Cris," he ordered harshly. "You said you could shoot. Show me. Kill them all."

She drew her pistol, sighted and fired. One of the birds was slammed from the body of the dead horse. The two remaining magpies sprang into the air and, pumping rapidly with their strong wings, fought for distance and altitude.

"Now, the other two," shouted Coldiron. "Quick before they are out of range."

"They are moving too fast to hit," Cris shouted back.

"Like hell!" exclaimed Coldiron and his pistol flashed from its holster with a whisper of metal on leather. He shot twice, the double crashes seeming to blend into one. The birds stopped their hurried flight and, trailing feathers, tumbled end over end to strike the ground with muffled thumps.

CHAPTER 17

The sun was at the peak of its flight and even the shade was hot. A lazy wind blew up the slope of the hill and found its way in under the porch on the east side of the ranch house. Luke sat cooling off, his chair reared back and propped against the wall. Two Suns and Cris rested near him.

Yerrington had brought cold water fresh from the spring and Luke drank slowly of the refreshing liquid from a tin cup. He felt relaxed in the companionship of the three and listened as Two Suns told Yerrington of the death of the old stud.

Cliff spoke to Coldiron. "I'm sorry about Number One dying. I know how much he meant to you. Do you think the big dun stallion you ride is one of his sons?"

"The old fellow was the harem stud of the band where I caught the dun. Also, they had almost the same color and markings."

"They had the same spirit, too," said Yerrington.

"You should have seen that old horse when he was in his prime," Luke said to Cris. "Nothing could catch him. He had a fighting heart, too. Captured his first harem of mares as a three year old. That's very unusual to do it so young. Only lost the mares a couple of years ago."

Two Suns had been sitting quietly, his ear tuned to the conversation of the others and gazing off across the valley. Now he let the front legs of his chair down onto the floor of the porch and stood up to sight steadily to the north.

His voice cut Yerrington off in mid sentence. "Lightning is coming. On foot. Fast."

Coldiron hastily climbed to his feet and went to stand beside Two Suns.

"Straight there, half a mile," said Two Suns pointing.

"Yes. I see him. Something is bad wrong," responded Luke.

"I'll take a horse to him," said Two Suns.

"No time for that. At the speed he is traveling, he'll be here before you could go to the barn and saddle one."

Cris arose and moved to the side of Yerrington to watch the dark figure of the running man, moving swiftly, his stride long and strong. He passed from sight beneath the protruding brow of the bench.

"I hope it isn't more gold prospectors," said Yerrington.

Luke waited, feeling his muscles growing tense. The temperature was at least a hundred degrees. Lightning would not run in such heat unless it was vitally important. If the problem were simply losing his horse, he would have laid up in the shade until sunset and walked home.

Lightning crested the upslope of the bench and came into view, his head down and legs driving hard. He was stripped down for running, wearing only his moccasins. A pistol was clutched in his hand.

"He's hurt. See the blood on his shoulder," exclaimed Yerrington and dashed into the house to get his medicine chest.

Lightning halted at the edge of the porch. His copper body glistened with sweat. It poured in rivulets down his face and chest and mixed with the blood on the side of his face and his shoulder.

His muscular legs quivered with the strain of his race. And his lungs pumped like bellows, sucking at the air to get breath to speak.

"Horse thieves," he whispered coarsely between breaths. "At the big horse trap in the rocks. Where the trail comes down through the rim-rock." He slumped onto a chair.

Two Suns handed him a tin of water just as Yerrington came hurrying out with a wooden box.

"Hold off, Cliff," said Lightning, motioning with the palm of his hand for Yerrington to stand back. "They just nicked my ear and it's not so bad but what it can't wait until I'm done talking."

He faced Luke. "I was working up the valley when I stopped seeing horses. Didn't see any at all. I thought something was wrong, so I slipped along slow, staying in the pine. Then I heard the voices of men working horses in the trap. Damn thieves, they were using our trap to catch our horses. I didn't see the lookout on the hill before he took a couple of shots at me. The first one killed my mustang. Second caught my ear. About ten or twelve riders came boiling out of that horse trap to finish me off. Almost did, too, but I got into the brush before they came close. After about a quarter hour chasing me around, they gave up."

Lightning Blanket wiped away the sweat flowing down from his brow and stinging his eyes. "There was both Mexicans and Americans. A tall Mex seemed to be the leader. There at the last, he was ordering them all to hurry and return to the trap and get the captured mustangs ready to go south. That's when I slipped away and came to warn you."

"How many horses do you think they took?" asked Coldiron.

"From the size of the country where I didn't see any, I would guess two hundred head, maybe a lot more. They have many men. It will be hard to get the mustangs back."

"Damn brave of them," said Yerrington. "No one has ever tried to take that many. They usually capture two or three and slip away."

"Maybe they knew we were in Santa Fe and thought they could capture a big herd and be long gone before we got back," said Two Suns.

"None of that matters," said Coldiron in a flinty voice. "Arm yourself with a rifle and pistol. Two Suns, saddle horses. Bring that big gray as a spare mount. Also my dun. He can rest up as we travel. Cris, fill canteens, the gallon ones, three of them. Get your bedrolls and rain slickers. Cliff, pack grub. Put it in three different bundles for we may have to split up and each one will need his own."

"I'm riding with you so bring me a horse and canteen, too," said Lightning.

Luke stooped to examine the wound. He straightened up and nodded his approval. "Okay, you can go. It'll need stitches, Cliff. I'll get ammunition and pass it out. Now move! All of you. They already have an hour head start on us." His tone was fierce.

"Sew it up, Cliff, and hurry or they will leave me behind," said Lightning.

Yerrington opened his medicine chest and stepped close to Lightning. "Shot about a quarter of the lobe of your ear away. Hold still now."

With deft fingers he pulled the raw edges of the damaged ear together and took quick, precise stitches with a threaded needle. He felt Lightning quiver under the stabs of the needle, but no utterance was made.

From a small tin of salve, Yerrington took a liberal measure and smeared it on the mutilated flesh. "That should prevent infection and help the healing."

"Good. I'll find pants and shirt and be ready when the rest of them are."

"Yes. And I must get the food ready at once."

Luke assembled cartridges for rifle and pistol. From a desk drawer he took a heavy bag of gold coins. This was going to be a tough trail and gold could buy many things with little delay in dickering.

Towing the horses by the bridle reins, Two Suns trotted up to the kitchen door. All but Cris had already gathered.

Yerrington handed out the rations of food. "Just hardtack, jerky, dried fruit and pine nuts."

"The lighter the better," said Coldiron as he stowed the bag of gold into his saddlebag. He saw Cris hurrying down from the spring with a dangle of canteens thumping and bumping together. "Hurry with that water," he called.

Luke passed a supply of cartridges to Two Suns and Lightning. A moment later he handed Cris her share as he took a canteen from her.

"Now get it all packed on and tied down tight," he ordered. "Cris, roll that canteen inside your blankets before you tie them behind your saddle. You can't ride fast with it just hanging over the horn. It will beat the horse to death."

In a flurry of activity, they packed their mounts. As Coldiron shoved shells into the loops of his gun belt, he evaluated the slight figure of Cris, saw the pistol, large and heavy in her hand as she buckled it on, and her eyes, large and shiny with excitement.

"Cris, you should stay here with Cliff," said Coldiron.

"Why do you say that? I can keep up and I'm not afraid." She had also been thinking of staying behind. This was not her affair. But the implication that she was not capable bothered her and stirred her desire to prove this man wrong.

"Have you ever shot a man or killed one?"

"No, but I can do it."

"Stay with me," said Yerrington.

"Thank you, Mr. Yerrington. I'm going." She grabbed the pommel of her saddle and hoisted herself astride.

"Mount up," called Luke in a loud voice and stepped aboard the black horse Two Suns had brought him. "Keep your eyes open, Cliff. The horse thieves may come down the valley and make a raid on the headquarters. Don't try to hold them off if they do. Go up to the woods, stay out of sight and play it safe."

"Sure, I'll do that," answered Yerrington and rested his blue-veined hands on the butt of his tied-down six-gun.

Coldiron saw the deep lines where the jaw was set in Yerrington's face and knew the man lied. Any horse thieves that came within rifle shot of the house would hear the whistle of lead.

"Let's ride." Coldiron spurred his mount. Cris fell in beside him. Two Suns tossed the lead rope of one of the spare horses to Lightning and the group of riders thundered out of the yard.

Yerrington watched for several minutes, tracing the plume of dust rising straight as a beeline north up the valley. He was worried for the safety of his friends, for Lightning had said the enemy were many. And Cris, what would that young person do when the thieves were overtaken and the fight started?

Yerrington went inside the house to fill his own cartridge belt and place his rifle handy.

The horse trap was empty. Within the round central corral the ground was trampled and pulverized into inches-deep dust. Manure, defecated by the stressed mustangs, lay scattered about in black piles on the tan soil. Here and there were imprints of the boots of the men who had left last.

Luke tested the air, breathing slow and deep. The finest of dust particles, too small to be seen, still floated in the dead-still air inside the tall walls of the trap. He smelled the minute specks of dirt, fresh churned and strong in his nose. He evaluated a dark splotch of soil where a horse had emptied itself, measuring with his eye the dampness and relating it to the temperature and angle of the sun. The horse thieves had left only four or five minutes ago, barely enough time to be out of sight.

Luke and his companions had ridden swiftly after leaving the headquarters, pushing their ponies until close to the location of the trap. From a concealed point on a pine-covered ridge they examined the rock structure, being able from their elevation to see most of the inside of the corral. Nothing stirred and all was quiet. Luke directed his followers to remain hidden while he rode in nearer to investigate.

Now he spun his mount and left the corral by a break in the wall of rock, where the wings of the trap intercepted the round central structure. A newly made, deeply worn trail passed through the narrow outlet and continued directly toward a notch in the rimrock half a mile distant to the east. A wild horse trail once had climbed up through that gap in the stone ledge until Luke had closed it with a fence of rock.

In the open, Coldiron faced to the south and jerked off his hat to wave it in a high arc over his head. Instantly from the ridge came the two Indians and Cris.

"What did you find?" Two Suns called to Luke as the three stopped by him.

"They've just left," said Coldiron. "Up that way."

"Well, what are we waiting for?" said Lightning Blanket. "Let's catch them for I want to collect some ears for what they did to me." He gingerly touched his mangled member.

Cris did not understand the men's anxiousness to meet with the thieves. She felt a tremble of fear deep inside at the thought of a dozen rifles firing upon her. Yet the expressions of the men were impatient and fierce. Even the horses pranced and tugged against the bits, straining to be on with the chase.

"Hold up a minute," said Luke. "If you had stolen horses and knew the owner would be on your trail close behind, what would you do?"

"I'd set an ambush for anyone following and shoot them all to hell," said Two Suns.

"Right. Can you think of a better place for that than where the trail goes through that crack in the rimrock?"

All four surveyed the smooth, bare terrain leading up the grade to the sandstone ledges. They raised their sight higher to the fringe of screening pine and boulders on the top.

"One man could kill several if he caught them on the slope or in the gap," said Two Suns.

"They know Lightning saw them so I think we had better figure someone is waiting there," said Luke. "The next way out of the valley is about five miles. Let us get to it before the thieves figure out what we are up to." The four kicked their ponies into a fast pace to the south, holding a course near the vertical face of the brown rimrock.

"Kazian had it figured exactly right," Murdock said to Pollin. "Coldiron and his crew checked out the trap and are now riding like all hell for the next trail up to the top. They looked up this way just once." He angrily slammed closed the telescope with which he had been stealthily observing the horse trap far below.

"I was hoping you and me would be the ones to put Horse Killer down," said Pollin. "Now it looks as if we will have to help the others do it."

"Appears so," said Murdock. "Let's be moving. I don't want to be late for this shoot-out. I owe that bastard a bullet."

They spurred their steeds without mercy. As the pine trees flashed past, Murdock grinned wolfishly. Soon he would have Coldiron in the sights of his rifle and pay him the promise he had made in Santa Fe.

The horses were blowing hard when Cris and the men stopped at the old mustang trail. They sat surveying the path that wound through a jumble of boulders that had collapsed down from the rimrock, some long ago time. The section of fallen rim had broken into scores of pieces, some waist tall. They lay dispersed at random, yet patterned roughly fan-shaped, the greatest width being farthest out from the bottom of the ledges. Small patches of brush grew among the rock and extended in fingers off to the south.

"No time to waste," said Coldiron. "It's a small trail and I will go first. Two Suns you come second. Lightning and Cris hold back and follow a couple hundred yards behind. This place may be guarded, too."

They moved ahead, following a path that the hard hooves of the wild mustangs had over the years beaten out through the boulders. The land lay quiet and empty above them as they crossed a steep-sided gully and began to climb.

Murdock's and Pollin's mounts came in under the tall trees with only a whisper of sound on the thick mat of pine needles. Kazian twisted away from watching Coldiron and motioned for the men to come to him.

"Good timing," Kazian whispered. "He's coming now. Find yourself a place to shoot from, but don't let him see you. I'll tell you when to fire. I want him another hundred yards closer."

Both men went off to the leader's left. Tashaw and Dule, already situated for the ambush, nodded a silent greeting.

Kazian's whispered voice drifted to all of them. "Remember, aim only at Coldiron, he's the biggest man and riding the black horse. He's the one that'll earn us our money. After he is dead, we can get the rest of them easy. We'll go to the ranch house later and see what valuables he's got there."

Luke scanned up to the top of the sandstone rim and probed his eyes in among the sprinkling of rounded boulders near the edge and the pine growing a few feet back where they had found soil. Nothing out of place. Still he hesitated. Already he was within range of a man with a rifle.

Luke's horse, tired of the tight rein and hard steel bit holding him in, danced sideways and tossed his head up.

Kazian misinterpreted the beast's movement. The thief thought Coldiron was wheeling around to retreat from the trap. "Fire!" he shouted. "Fire! Shoot the man in the lead." Kazian leveled his rifle and it roared down from the heights, striking out with deadly precision at Coldiron.

Luke heard the sharp crack of the gun. Felt the bullet hit his horse, smashing into the brute's head. In that fraction of time he understood that only the intervention of the horse's body had saved the bullet from striking him.

The fatally wounded animal started to fall half to the side and half backward. As Luke tried to kick free, more bullets whizzed past, two more struck the horse. Luke almost escaped from his mount but not entirely and was pulled down with the brute's body.

The big boulder came up at him with dizzying speed. He slammed into its unyielding bulk. Darkness caught him swift as a thunderclap.

Two Suns saw Luke tumble and recognized the sure death in the ambush unless he escaped instantly. He whirled his pony and jabbed it savagely with his spurs.

The rifles of all the horse thieves swung to come to bear on the Indian. A lead projectile sledgehammered him from the saddle. Other bullets caught his horse and it was driven off its feet, crying out in pain as it died.

"Back! Back!" Lightning Blanket cried in warning to Cris and pivoted his pony to flee.

Cris sat frozen, overwhelmed by the suddenness and violence of the volley of rifle fire that had struck down Coldiron and Two Suns. Lightning saw her befuddlement. He yanked off his hat, swerved his mount in front of her and swatted her horse hard across the nose. It whipped to the rear and leaped away.

Lightning sprang his pony after her. Then he gasped as a bullet punched through his chest. He almost lost his saddle. He dropped the lead ropes of the spare horses to keep from falling and clutched at the pommel. His hands were suddenly clumsy and weak and did not want to obey him.

Cris looked backward just in time to see the slug pierce Lightning, jerking his shirt as it tore out the front, a red stain appearing instantly. The shock of the grievous wound contorted the young Indian's face. Slowing to save her had caused him to be injured, maybe cost him his life.

"Stop there in that wash." Cris heard Lightning's voice come weakly.

She veered in the direction of the gully. At the verge of the steep bank her mount balked.

"Get your cayuse down in the bottom. Hurry! Spur him. Jump him down!"

She raked her mount, driving spurs into his flanks. A bullet plucked at her hat. Both horses plunged into the gully, rolling rocks, sliding, fighting to stay on their feet. Then they were under the lip of the ravine, protected from the terrible guns. The firing ceased.

On the bed of the dry wash, Cris hastily dismounted and hurried to help Lightning. He was leaning precariously from the saddle, his body growing limp. Before she could reach him, he fell with a bone-jarring thud to the cobbly floor of the stream channel.

She knelt down beside him and eased him over on his back. His brave eyes swept hers once then blanked out. Bright red blood bubbled up from his mouth and she knew he was shot through the lungs. He was dying and there was nothing she could do to help him. He would collect no ears from his enemies.

Cris sobbed a heart-tearing sob. "Damn you! Damn you all to hell!" she screamed up at the thieving bushwhackers hidden on the rimrock. She snatched her rifle from its scabbard and scurried to peer over the bank of the gully.

Three men had sprung out of concealment behind the boulders on top and were running along the edge toward the gap in the ledge and the horse trail leading down. They meant to be certain their bullets had slain their intended prey.

Let them come into that open space in the trail, she thought. But don't let them get into the rocks with Coldiron and Two Suns. It's going to be a long shot. How high should she hold the aim of her rifle—two feet? Take your time. Kill the bastards. Shoot the closest one first.

Draw a steady bead.

Cris's gun cracked.

She hit one of them. He stumbled and fell. Cris heard herself cackling with half-hysterical laughter.

They were trying to lift the wounded man to take back to cover. That will slow them. The big man on the right, he should be the easier target.

She fired again and again, emptying her rifle. The large man staggered, then steadied himself, not releasing his hold on the wounded man he helped support. The boulders and pine engulfed the thieves.

Cris lowered her weapon and watched the rim. They'll not come out in the open like that again. When it turns dark, though, they will try something.

She examined the rocks where Coldiron and Two Suns had fallen. There was absolutely no movement. Were they also dead? Or just badly hurt and unable to call out? But, oh, they had dropped so hard when the bullets struck them.

She rammed fresh cartridges into the loading slot of the rifle, then returned to hunker near Lightning. His chest did not move. She pressed her fingers into the side of the brown throat to feel for a pulse in the great artery. The young Ute warrior was dead.

Fearfully, yet determinedly, she took her rifle back to the bank of the ravine and scrutinized the place where her foes hid. When it grew dark so they could not see, she would go into the boulders and help her companions if they still lived.

She searched in her heart for the dislike she had once felt for Coldiron and the Indians. She could not find it.

CHAPTER 18

The yellow sun slid toward the horizon and shadows crept into the jumble of rocks beside the horse trail.

Coldiron came to consciousness a bit at a time with an ache gathering strength in his skull like a newborn storm. He tried to raise his head and he thought it would fall apart. He lowered it again into the dirt to wait for the slicing pain and the searing lightning inside his cranium to subside.

Flies buzzed and fed on the blood puddled beneath his head. He lifted a hand and weakly brushed at them. The insects only moved aside briefly and returned at once to continue gorging on the dark semicongealed mass.

He tested the other parts of his body. Gritty dust lay in his mouth. His nose was half clogged, for his face rested on the ground and had sucked dirt in with every breath. Something held him pinned down, heavy on his hips. But he could move his legs.

Luke remembered the fall and striking the rock. How long had he been knocked out? A minute? A day? Many things could have happened. Two Suns, Lightning and Cris could all be dead. He had to find out— help them if there was still time.

Were the horse thieves waiting for him to move, to show life, when they would then send another volley of lead at him? Or might they think him dead and have already ridden out. His dusty lips pulled back in a fierce grimace. They had almost finished that chore of killing him.

But he doubted they were gone from the top of the ledges. Anyone thorough enough to set up ambushes at two trails would not leave the job half done. A question bothered him—why hadn't the bushwhackers come down and completed the task before now?

He raised his head a second time and clinched his teeth at the pain. It was endurable, barely. Twisting partially around, he saw the hind quarters of the black horse bearing down on him. He shoved upward on the body and, halfway balanced over the boulder, it rose fairly easily. Hastily he ceased lifting for the movement of the horse might be seen.

Luke looked in the direction of the rimrock. Through a crack between two stones he checked the top of the rim. No sign of a human anywhere in the boulders or pine trees, sharply outlined in the slanting rays of the sun.

His enemies had to be driven from that cover on the high ground. There had to be a way to get them, to get up there without using the trail.

A tall angular block of stone obstructed his view to the north. The rock he had fallen upon prevented him from seeing to the west. Down the valley, the way was open and the string of brush and pine was visible for a long distance, to where it touched the stone ledges.

Slowly he dragged himself from under the dead horse. Then even more cautiously he slid a short way around the rock and reached up to ease the rifle out of its scabbard. He tugged at the tie that held his lariat and it dropped near him.

Luke crawled to the south, worming his way among the rocks. He came to a sagebrush and stopped in the shade that was large enough to give some scant shelter. He rested his head on his arm to ease the ache.

Dragging himself onward, he found more brush just as the concealing boulders gave out. Now most of the valley to the south was within his view. Standing off a quarter mile was his dun horse, watching intently. Luke saw two other horses much farther away, heads down and drifting off grazing. But the faithful dun would not readily leave without his master.

Good fellow, thought Coldiron, but don't come to me now or you will get me killed.

Closer to the ledges the brush gave way entirely to pine and broadened to a fairly wide strip. Luke moved swiftly, for there was little likelihood of being spotted in the trees by the outlaws.

He was sweating when the base of the rimrock was reached and he sank down to the ground to rest. When he started to wipe off the perspiration, the blood and dirt plastering the side of his face and top of his head were discovered. He did not try to dislodge the mass, afraid the bleeding would start again.

Coldiron came upon a big, dead pine leaning against the rock ledge. It was punky and looked ready to fall. Stubs of rotten limbs protruded out, spaced widely, yet close enough so a tall man could climb from one to the next. It would have to do for a ladder. However, fifteen feet of bare rock separated the top of the tree from the crest of the rimrock.

Luke tied the rifle across his shoulder by a length of cloth ripped from his shirttail. He went up the tree, ignoring the bark that peeled and fell from under his feet and hands. At the tip of the wooden column he angled his body into the rock and steadied himself. Gingerly he shook out the loop of his lariat and sighted up at a short rock overhang jutting out.

The distance was not great, but the straight up angle was a new and strange way to throw a rope. Still the sliding noose settled into place with the first cast. Luke jerked it tight. It held.

Hand over hand he hoisted himself up the lasso, his boots digging at the stone, trying to find purchase to help his straining arms. The side of his head where he had fallen felt as if it were bursting from the rest of his skull. The flashes of light started again and the dizziness returned.

The overhang came within reach and he clasped it tightly, hung there a moment to get his wind, then muscled his body upon the rock and dragged onto the flat top of the rim. He rolled to his back, cracking his head on the butt of the rifle, and dug his hands into the gravelly soil to hold onto the spinning world.

The sky settled to a stop and Coldiron sat up. Everything stayed in place. Slowly he rose to his feet.

He examined the working mechanism of his rifle and pistol closely. Then without sound he slipped forward through the shadows beneath the pines.

"Can somebody bring me a drink?" Dule's voice came plaintively.

"Pollin, put a canteen where he can reach it," said Kazian. He knew the man was badly wounded and would probably not last out the night.

It was Murdock's fault. Wanting to get Coldiron so badly, he had encouraged Pollin and Dule to break cover with him and charge down the trail toward the spot the mustang man had fallen. Someone in the wash was good with a rifle. Dule shot through the stomach and Murdock nicked in the leg. And there was no need for any of it. Dead now or dead later, Coldiron was pinned down and would soon be finished.

Pollin came back and retook his station. "Dule's really hurting. Not pretty to watch."

From off to the right, Tashaw laughed disdainfully. "You dumb bastards. Showing yourself like that. You all should've been killed. I don't know how you've lived as long as you have." He laughed again, dribbling it off into a disgusted chuckle.

"Coldiron hasn't stirred in two hours," said Murdock. "He's surely done for."

"That man in the wash with the rifle ain't," said Kazian. "It'll be dark in an hour or a little longer. Just hold your horses until then."

Coldiron stood behind the tree and sneaked a peek around it at the man laying on his back and sipping from a canteen with the corner of his mouth. A large bandage of bloody cloth was in the center of his stomach. Luke's memory flashed back and he recognized him as one of the five that had attacked Two Suns and Lightning in Santa Fe.

The man was gut shot. He would die. Now Luke knew why they had not come down from the rim and completed the ambush. But who had shot him? Whoever it was had saved Luke from being killed while unconscious and defenseless.

Coldiron circled wide of the man and crept toward a mumble of voices. A man laughed.

Laugh you son of a bitch, soon you will be dead, thought Coldiron. He moved ahead and Murdock's broad back came into view. The man sat easy, sighting down into the valley. To the right, Pollin hunkered and watched in the same direction.

Should he call out a warning and give the men a chance to draw their guns? Foolish damn question. There are two here and two hidden somewhere close. Coldiron's face grew hard and a merciless glitter washed over his eyes.

He raised his rifle and shattered Murdock's spine, then leaped around a short pine to get a clearer sight on Pollin and shot him between the startled eyes that had become scared just as the bullet struck.

Coldiron spun directly away from the face of the rimrock and dove into a thicker stand of trees. He turned immediately to the north, halting after a few swift strides in the deep shadow of a large pine, hugging in close to it, not moving.

"What in hell you firing at?" yelled Kazian.

"It's Coldiron!" screamed Dule. "I saw him. It's his ghost for he's all bloody and half his face is shot away."

Coldiron did not stir. The wounded man must have seen him when he jumped back after blasting those first two. But the man couldn't know where he was now.

"Murdock! Pollin! You all right?" shouted Kazian.

"They're dead," yelled Dule. "It's Coldiron, I tell you. He shot both of them."

"Shut up!" ordered Kazian in a ferocious voice. "Tashaw, you know what to do."

The old trapper did not answer. He already lay flat on his stomach, pressed to the ground near a log. His gun was cocked. He would not move until this fight was over or he had an easy, clear shot. Let Coldiron come to him. That way the odds were against Coldiron and for the man in hiding.

An object struck the ground off to Tashaw's left. He grinned. He had once used that trick to hoodwink an Indian buck into showing himself. Something landed nearer, bouncing twice on the blanket of pine needles before it stopped. Tashaw strained to determine the source of the thrown things.

A third object made a muffled racket on the ground near him. In sudden alarm Tashaw flung himself closer to the log. The trick was being used in reverse. He knew it. Coldiron was coming closer with the noise, utilizing the sound to hide his own footsteps.

Like a snake coiling to strike, Tashaw brought his rifle up in the direction of the last racket. Coldiron, his face a mess of blood, looked at him from not twenty feet away. Let's see if you are a ghost, thought Tashaw, and his finger tightened on the trigger.

Flame and smoke sprang at Tashaw from Coldiron's rifle. A heavy chunk of lead slammed the center of his chest.

"I got him, Kazian," sounded a gruff voice.

"Good," answered the chief of the horse thieves. He moved out of a clump of pine.

With the first footfall, Coldiron knew where his last enemy was and slipped forward and off at a slant to meet him. He remembered the leader from that day in Santa Fe, knew he was the only one remaining. The Mexican had called him by name, Kazian, and had ordered him to get away from the Indians.

The outlaw was in sight a bare rod away. "Kazian, over here," Luke called to him.

With unbelievable swiftness, the thief hurled himself to the side and his rifle jumped to his shoulder.

Damn fast, thought Coldiron. He shot the man through the heart. Saw the hammer blow cave him in. He fired the last bullet in his rifle into the body as it fell.

Luke stepped out into the open trail and yelled loudly into the basin. The effort made his head hurt, but he did not want to gamble his companions would recognize him at the distance and not start shooting.

Two Suns arose from the rocks. A moment later the slight figure of Cris climbed up over the bank of the wash. Luke waited for Lightning to show. No one else appeared.

Luke turned back and found the thieves' horses. He tightened the cinch of the saddle of one and rode down from the rim.

"You look like your head is all smashed," said Two Suns sighting doubtfully at the blood and dirt smeared on Luke's head. "How bad is it?"

"It's still holding together," responded Luke. "Where are you hit?"

"In the side. It's fairly well stopped bleeding now. I had time lying there to let it make a scab. If I travel slowly, I believe I can ride."

Cris trotted rapidly up. She halted, breathing hard, and locked her stare on Two Suns.

The Indian returned her look, seeing her strained and drawn face as she searched for words to speak. "Lightning Blanket is dead," he said in a low, yet certain voice.

"Yes." A sob burst from her. She cut it off and bit her lip. "Oh, I'm so sorry. He saved my life and they shot him."

Two Suns said nothing. His sight drifted up into the sky. Throughout his life he had never been separated from his brother. What a terrible empty place there was inside him now. He felt like half a person. For a long time he tracked a small white cloud floating up high without really seeing it. He lowered his view to Cris. "Then you are the one who stopped the horse thieves from coming down from the top?"

"Yes. But I only hit one to do much damage. They did run back though."

"We will take him back and bury him by the ranch house," said Luke.

"No," said Two Suns. "I will take him home to our village. It is time for both of us to return. I have been feeling this for many moons. You and I are friends and because of that I delayed leaving too long."

"Will you be back?"

"No. I have been thinking that one day something would give me a sign to return to being the Indian I am. This is the time. You and I know there will be a war between our people. Kit Carson is already marching on the Navajo. Soon the white man's army will fight my people. When that happens I will try to keep our warriors from harming you in this valley."

Coldiron remained silent, holding the eyes of the young Indian man who had been with him since a boy.

Cris stepped to be more in line with Luke's sight. "Are you just going to let him leave? Just like that?"

"Go round up the ponies," directed Coldiron in a flat voice. "And let's help him prepare for his trip."

Cris saw the sorrow in his face and said no more. She climbed upon the mount Luke had brought and headed it for the scattered horses.

Luke helped Two Suns build a travois. Two long, thin poles were cut, four cross pieces fastened between them and a blanket placed upon that. The travois was firmly attached to one of the ponies.

Two Suns insisted upon lifting and placing the body of Lightning Blanket upon the contraption. He secured it with leather ties. Blood was flowing freely from the wound in his side when he finished.

Two Suns climbed up on a second pony. He looked at Cris, almost spoke, but making some judgment turned to face Luke.

"Goodbye, Coldiron. May many years with peace be yours."

"I shall never make war upon the Ute people," said Luke.

"My people and I shall fight the white man for they will surely make war upon us," responded Two Suns.

"That will be a sad day."

"Yes, very sad." He looked deeply into the white man's blue eyes. "My people will be defeated for we are too few."

"I believe that also."

Two Suns lifted his hand in farewell and spoke to his pony to begin the trek. He must hurry, for his brother would be buried in the tall mountains to the north.

"He is hurt much worse than he is letting on," said Cris. "Did you see how badly he was bleeding?"

"I saw. But his mind was set on what he had to do. I could not have stopped him."

Luke removed the saddle and other gear from the carcass of the black horse and put it on the dun. Cris began to prepare her mount for travel.

"You should turn back," said Luke. "This is not your fight and already you have earned your pay."

"I'm going. You will have to sleep and then you will need a lookout. Do we take along any extra horses?"

"We'll take one, the best the horse thieves have, and the packhorse."

He mounted. "You lead the packhorse," he said to Cris. "We'll go up and pick a spare pony and be on our way."

"Is that the man I shot?" asked Cris, her face ashen as she viewed the wounded Dule.

The man lay breathing shallowly and rapidly and watching them from pain-filled eyes.

"Yep. Bad bullet through the stomach."

"We can't just leave him here to suffer and die."

"That's exactly what is going to happen."

"Can't you do something? Can't we take him to a doctor?"

"It's eighty miles to a doctor. And besides slowing us down considerably, he'd never live through the trip."

"Well, what do we do?"

"I can shoot him to put him out of his misery."

"I don't mean that!"

"I know you don't, Cris," said Luke in a gentle tone. "But he's a dead man regardless what we do." Luke went to the thief, extracted his six-gun and checked to be sure it was loaded.

"You are a bastard, Coldiron," Dule wheezed.

Luke ignored the profanity and laid the pistol on the thief's chest. "You may want to try your gun out after a while."

The man's eyes burned hatred up at Coldiron. His hand slipped toward the butt of the pistol.

Luke kicked him in the ribs with the pointed toe of his boot and pain overrode Dule's hate.

"Don't try to use the gun yet," said Luke. He walked off while the thief fought to recover from the onslaught of agony from the kick.

"Let's ride," Luke said to Cris. "There's still an hour of daylight left."

CHAPTER 19

Luke leaned on the horn of his saddle for a moment and examined the well-marked trail of freshly disturbed pine needles and duff slanting down the slope and into a forested canyon.

He spoke to Cris, sitting on her mount beside him. "We have crossed the tracks of several bunches of mustangs tied in strings of ten or so. They are of different ages, some as old as three days. Though the trails wind back and forth over each other, they are all heading south."

"This sign seems to be the youngest of all of them," said Cris.

"Yes, and we'll follow it. But I'm betting all of them end up at the same place."

The low land was already hidden from the sun and in shadow when Luke and Cris rode in under the tall pines in the bottom of the canyon. They urged their ponies into a fast lope along the easily discernible trail. Luke judged the man with the band of mustangs had a four-hour head start; that meant at least a twenty-mile lead. With luck he might be overhauled by tomorrow evening.

Dogging the trail, they went along the canyon for a ways, then climbed out and up and crested the top of the high pine-covered backbone of the San Juan mountains. The broad, almost level valley of the Rio Grande lay spread below them. The river itself, flowing in its deep lava gorge some thirty miles to the southeast, was hidden in the gray dusk, creeping in behind the retreating sun.

The tracks they pursued led straight toward the unseen stream. Without stopping to let the horses blow, Luke steered the route down the mountain side, riding the army of shadows among the trees.

Once striking the flat land, the direction of travel of the stolen mustangs was directly south down the valley, deviating only enough to detour around impassable obstacles. Luke sighted along the trail, marking the fact its probable course would be between a projecting shoulder of the San Juans and a tall round mountain rising up out of the flat bottomland.

The darkness thickened and congealed about the two horsemen. Luke could no longer see the trail and released all guidance with the reins, allowing the intelligent dun with its night-seeing eyes to continue on into the black gloom.

An hour later the high crown of the round mountain outlined itself against the sky by obscuring the stars. Coldiron halted and swung to the ground. "This is as far as we go tonight."

"Don't you think we have lost the trail?" asked Cris.

"Nope. This old horse knows what we are doing. Even if he doesn't, the tracks can't be more than two or three hundred yards left or right of us here in this narrow pass. Find a soft spot to spread your blankets and sleep, for it will be daylight in a very few hours."

"What about the horses? There's no water here."

"They'll have to do without. Hobble them and turn them loose. This will be one long trail and they must graze every chance we can give them."

They completed the necessary chores quickly and settled down in their bedrolls. The night sounds soon began again as the insects and animals grew accustomed to the presence of man and horses.

Cris did not fall asleep. Instead she lay looking up at the great black bowl of the sky, pitted and cracked in a million places and bright pinpoints of light leaking through. She reviewed the happenings of the day and shivered as the full realization struck her that she had shot a man, really had killed him, for surely he would die. It had seemed the proper thing to do at the time, yet she felt remorse. Upon reflection she still felt she had done the correct thing.

Coldiron groaned in his sleep. Cris rose up on an elbow to stare into the darkness in his direction. How badly was he injured? Not once had he complained. His blood-covered face was gruesome. He could be hurt very seriously. Yet there was nothing she could do.

The sun came up yellow and hot. Its bright rays melted the purple shadows from the land and illuminated the two riders hurrying along a trail that was slowly growing fresher.

An hour into the day, Luke and Cris found an exhausted colt by the side of the trail. They passed it without a word. The colt raised its head at the familiar sound of horses' hooves but could not see from its glazed eyes. Luke glanced at the small animal when it moved, saw it would soon be dead and pointed his face again along the sign of the horse thief.

By mid morning, horses and riders were bathed in sweat. With welcome relief they broke out of the sparse forest of pinion pine and found the channel of the Conejos River. Its sparkling water flowed in from the west, tumbling down through a deep pine-choked canyon from the high reaches of the San Juan Mountains. Just to the right of the horsemen, the rock walls of the canyon became broken and fell back from the river.

Coldiron ranged his sight in all directions, out through the openings in the woods and beyond that, across the brush and grassland along the Conejos toward the Rio Grande. He saw not one living thing.

He said to Cris, "The Rio Grande is east of us about ten miles," and he pointed. "Always watch carefully for landmarks so if you have to, you could find your way back by yourself."

Cris nodded at his advice and wiped the perspiration from her brow with her shirt sleeve.

"This fellow with my horses knows this country. He has followed no used trail, yet found this crossing, the first place the canyon of the Conejos can be gotten down into and be forded in more than twenty-five miles, coming from the west."

Luke roamed his eyes again over the land and then led the way down the bank and to the edge of the river. The horses began to drink, noisily swigging the cold water that riffled along in summer's low volume through round black rocks.

Man and woman stepped down from their saddles and lay down to slack their thirst with the horses.

"Cris, fill the canteens and climb back up on the bank and keep watch for a while. First, slip the bits of the ponies and let them graze there in that tall grass on the riverbank. I'm going to take a little time to wash the blood and dirt off my head."

"Okay," she said and picked up the reins of the horses.

The path of the thief held in the cover of the pine at the base of the San Juans and west of the open grass-covered plain of the Rio Grande. Several times during the day the trail crossed the older sign of groups of horses.

Luke recognized the correctness of his earlier evaluation of how the stolen animals were being taken away. He also realized the man whose trail he dogged would not be caught this day.

As the sun touched the horizon, he spoke to Cris. "This hombre is pushing hard. I bet he has covered more than fifty miles today."

Cris did not respond. She rode exhausted. Never had she traveled so far in a single day. And the heat was unbearable.

Coldiron measured the youth sagging in the saddle. Had Luke been alone, he would have changed mounts and made good another ten miles before stopping. Instead he called out, "We'll pull up soon as it gets dark and no one can see where we camp."

They made a dry bivouac on a point of land where a breeze floated by to fan them. Without conversation they ate lightly of their supply of food and lay down to rest on their bedrolls.

The sun dropped into the endless pit behind the mountains. A giant golden coin of a moon sailed up over the eastern horizon. Slowly, inexorably, it climbed its arc and, as it did, changed color to mystic silver and shrank to the size of a quarter.

Feeling a desire to talk with his young comrade, Luke almost called out to discuss the moon's altered appearance. But the slow even breathing coming out of the dark told him Cris was asleep. The young person was tough and did not grumble about a hard ride. Not a bad partner.

Coldiron's thoughts shifted to the horse thief. Tomorrow he would catch the first one and make him pay dearly. However, the man he really wanted to catch was the leader. Would it be the tall, thin Mexican who had pulled his pistol on the gringos in Santa Fe?

The day broke. The burning sun sprang up over the crown of the Sangre de Cristo Mountains and its rays sliced down full force to shred the last of the lingering darkness in the Rio Grande Valley.

Luke and Cris had been traveling for more than an hour. In the dim dusk, they had traced the tracks down a narrow rocky passageway through the three-hundred-foot-high walls of the river gorge, crossed the boulder-clogged bottom and climbed back up to the plain.

They passed under the towering southern point of Black Mesa and plunged into the forest clothing the top of Caja del Rio Plateau. Two hours later the woods ended and an open expanse of land, cut by scores of dry arroyos, was spread before them. They continued straight into the rough terrain.

"What's the country like farther ahead?" asked Cris.

"More mountains. Stretched along both sides of the Rio Grande between here and Mexico are a dozen or more mountain ranges. They are all smaller than the San Juans or the de Cristos. And they are shorter and have less forest on them. But it's all rough going."

"Where is Santa Fe from here?"

"East fifteen or sixteen miles."

"Why don't you go and try to get the Army to help get your horses back?"

"I've considered that, for the major is a friend of mine, but the horses are split up into many bunches and that makes it hard to catch them all.

Also, they've got enough lead to be in Mexico before the Army could catch up. With the bad feelings there are between us and the Mexicans, they would never allow our Army to chase the thieves south of the border. We are on our own."

"Too bad. We could use some help."

"You should part company with me and go to Santa Fe."

Cris gazed in the direction of the town. What did she really want? Surely not to find the horse thieves and fight a battle with them. Still she did not have the answers to her mother's death. And who was her father? Only this man knew those things. At the right moment he might tell her.

"I'll see this through," she said.

A half-mile distant the tiny dark form of a soaring buzzard was crisply silhouetted against the opal sky. As Coldiron watched, the vulture set its long wings stiffly and glided down to vanish behind the small hill.

"Something dead," said Luke. "Probably a mustang since it seems to be right on the trail."

"Our horses seem to be smelling it already," said Cris.

"We'll soon see it ourselves."

The score of startled buzzards snapped their featherless heads up from their feast on the dead to look as the riders popped over the peak of the hill. They craned their long red necks at the intruders, then scrambled away, flailing the hot air with thick wings. Their bloated stomachs, heavy with their gluttony, held them to the earth. The birds jostled each other as they ran awkwardly, trying to build speed. Pumping their wings fearfully, one after another became airborne, rising ponderously upward, struggling for distance and safety from the humans.

Two horses and a man sprawled on the ground. On the right hip of the horses the Steel Trap Brand showed. Luke swung down to examine the man. The buzzards had made no distinction in their food and the man's body also bore the rips and tears of the sharp beaks.

"A Mexican," said Coldiron rising up to survey the scene. "He's been scalped. Looks like he came upon some Indians last evening and they made short work of him. They took the rest of my horses, too."

"What tribe do you think?" asked Cris.

"Navajos would be my guess. They're out on the warpath now."

"What do we do now?"

"Pick up another trail and wear out our butts riding after it."

"It will be much older."

"Yep. Without some luck, it could take a long time to run it down.

We'll drive straight south for I've got a feeling it won't be long until we cross one."

They pushed ahead over the stony land. Their route gradually closed with the Rio Grande, and before they found a trail they came upon the well-used El Camino Real. It lay dusty and empty in the bright sunlight.

"We may as well take the road for a while for it'll be easier going," said Luke. "I've got a strong hunch it's going exactly in the direction we want."

On the more even surface of the road, the horses hit their full stride and moved swiftly on traveling legs. The sun blazed and tortured the air. Dust devils whirled in tiny brown spirals in the heated currents. Cris dozed, depending upon the man to guide and stay alert.

A well-beaten string of tracks crossed El Camino and went toward the Rio Grande. Coldiron did not turn aside to follow. Six miles later, that bunch of horses, or another of equal number, came back across the road and on in the direction of the rough country at the base of the Sandia Mountains three miles east. Luke grinned to himself with satisfaction. Someone had gone to water at the river then pulled back to ride country where no one would see them.

Now that Luke was certain of the strategy of the horse thieves, he could straighten his course and gain on them. I'm coming, you bastards. He laughed at his own gall.

"What's so funny?" questioned Cris, waking from her half sleep and feeling ornery under the scorching sun.

"You and me, Cris. A man and a kid chasing a whole gang of horse thieves with big plans to kill them and take back a herd of mustangs. That's downright funny."

"Such foolishness can get people killed," observed Cris in a tight voice.

They rode the heat of the afternoon hours and wore the evening into night. Just at dark the El Camino Real forded the Rio Grande. Coldiron steered away from the road and went along the edge of the water. At a hidden bend of the river, they unrolled their blankets and slept the night away to the rattle of the wind in the brittle desert brush.

"Time to wake up, pardner, and ride," Coldiron's voice penetrated the fuzziness in Cris's sleepy head.

She threw aside her blanket and said sharply, "I'm not your partner."

"Then why in hell are you sticking with me."

"I want to know about the dead woman in your valley," Cris cried out.

In shocked surprise Coldiron drew back. "That's none of your business."

"It is my business, damn it. I want to know because . . ." Cris caught herself just before blurting out that the woman might be her mother. But there was too much danger in telling all. She did not know what kind of a man she was dealing with. If he had murdered one woman, he might easily murder a second.

"Why is it so important to you?"

"I just want to know," said Cris lamely.

"Now what's the truth?" demanded Luke.

"None of your damn business, same as you told me," Cris said sharply, her head cocked defiantly to the side.

"Then it's a standoff," exclaimed Luke. What had he done to instill such hostility? He stomped off to begin swiftly saddling his mount. He called out over his shoulder as he worked, "I'll take the spare horse. You can have the packhorse. Santa Fe is north. Just stay on the main road and it'll take you directly there."

Cris jumped from her blankets and rolled them up hastily. She was saddled and ready to ride only a couple of minutes behind Luke. She trotted her mount to catch up and fell into her customary place to the rear of him. Coldiron looked back at her, shook his head in disbelief and kicked the pace to a canter.

The sun baked the earth as it had for the past week. The air began to tremble in the heat, distorting objects and distance. A mirage of some far-off landscape to the south started to quiver and fume and played tricks with the riders for more than an hour. A tall hill finally intervened and obliterated the false image.

At the junction of the muddy water of the Rio Puerco with the Rio Grande they came upon a caravan of eleven heavily laden wagons drawn up under a grove of cottonwoods. "Climb down and rest," said Luke, speaking for the first time since the morning. "This wagon train has come from the south and the drivers might have seen something that would be helpful to us."

Cris loosened the cinch of the saddles and slipped the bits from between the big teeth of the horses. The animals drank and started to feed on the sedges growing on the damp bank. She rested full length on the ground in the shade of a giant tree. She propped her head up to watch Luke talking with the teamsters.

A slight breeze, barely felt, came off the water. It helped to cool her and soon she felt the salt crystals hard and grainy forming on her forehead. She looked at the water slipping by a rod away and thought how wonderful a bath would be.

Luke walked up. "One of the men saw a string of horses at a long distance. Wasn't close enough to make out anything except they were going south. We already knew that. We'll rest a half hour and then take to the trail again." He lay down with a sigh and closed his eyes. In less than a minute he was asleep.

Coldiron came awake all at once. He opened his eyes and caught Cris watching him with a strange, unfathomable stare. She looked hurriedly away as their eyes met. Strange person, thought Luke.

"Let's be up and at it," he said and climbed to his feet.

In early afternoon the thunderheads began to build in the warm summer updrafts and scudded fast from the south. They grew swiftly, boiling up in twenty-thousand, thirty-thousand-foot white mounds of moisture, turning to dark gray as they thickened.

Within two hours some of the columns had matured to monsters reaching sixty thousand feet into the rarified zones of the sky. One of the mammoth thunderheads bore down on the two riders. As it neared the wind picked up, gusting erratically, whipping the limbs of the brush and stirring the dust.

Thin streamers of rain began to leak from the dark bottoms of the clouds. Lightning flashed orange and yellow, trapped within the towering cloud mass, lighting it internally with a smoldering, infernal glow.

Unmeasurable power created vertical lifts, hoisting moisture-laden air thousands of feet in a handful of seconds. Ice crystals formed, to plunge earthward in down drafts, passing through water that froze in shells about the crystals. The growing hailstone was thrown upward again and dropped, and the cycle was repeated over and over to add one concentric ice ring upon another.

The lightning broke free of the thunderhead and lashed out to strike the earth. The charge rebuilt quickly to uncontrollable level and slammed out a second time.

As the storm roared relentlessly upon Luke and Cris, the belly of the cloud split in a million tears and the rain poured down, driving hard, slapping their slickers and pounding down the brims of their hats. The horses pranced and turned to put their rumps to the onslaught. They humped their backs as the chilling rain fell upon their flanks.

Lightning flared all around, hissing and cracking like a thousand bullwhips. The explosions of the thunder deafened the riders, the lightning half blinded them.

Cris saw Luke spring from his horse and shout at her, but she could hear nothing above the uproar of the storm. However, she understood and jumped down, clinging firmly to the reins of her mount and the lead rope of the pack animal.

Luke hunkered beneath the neck of the stallion and backed in tightly against the broad chest. He dragged the spare horse in as close as possible. Cris started to press close to her mount but in the attempt lost hold of the packhorse. It dashed into the maelstrom and was lost to sight.

In the time span of a second the rain was replaced by hail, round balls of ice more than two inches in diameter crashing onto the earth and the living things like hammer strikes. They battered Cris to her knees. Her head rang with the blows and she felt the darkness of unconsciousness sweeping over her.

Strong hands grabbed her, snatching her up and carrying her bodily backward. She found herself pressed to Luke, clasped tightly by his arms. The beating of the hailstones ceased, for his body and the horse sheltered her. Her head cleared. She heard Luke shouting at the dun, exhorting it to stand against the storm.

The stalwart beast stood its ground. The bruising ice stones pummeled him, bouncing from his broad back. They left behind one massive welt of pain. The stallion whinnied loudly and bent its long neck to rest on top of Luke's head.

The tempest continued, eating away the warmth of their bodies. Cris shifted her stance to relieve the aching cramp from the crouched position.

Luke felt her press against his hands where he held her around the chest. Suddenly he became aware of the firm mounds of a woman's breasts in his wet, cold hands. Not believing his touch, he kneaded the soft flesh beneath the thin cotton shirt to be sure.

Cris cried out and tore free from his hold. The instant she was out of the shelter of his body the hailstones struck her to the ground. He stepped out, scooped her up and retreated back under the horse for as much protection as that poor beast could provide.

CHAPTER 20

Luke supported Cris's unconscious body and marveled at the amazing discovery. Why was a young woman working as a boy? More importantly, why play the role with him? What had she said? Yes, that was it —she wanted to know about the woman buried in his valley.

As he mulled the surprising situation, the tempest of the storm began to noticeably slacken. The pounding hail turned back to rain. The center of the storm rumbled off to the north. To the south the gray grew less dense.

Cris stirred and her muscles stiffened to carry her own weight. Her head came up. What had happened came flooding back with a rush. She twisted to look into Coldiron's face. "Let me go, please."

She stepped out into the rapidly diminishing rain and turned to look at Luke. The half-foot thickness of hail crunched beneath her boots as she spread her legs. The last flurry of raindrops pelted her and then marched on. She shoved the wet floppy brim of her hat back so she could see clearly.

Coldiron moved away from the horse and straightened his tired back. His eyes inspected Cris. In his new knowledge, he recognized the delicate features of the female face, the lack of dense muscle in the shoulders. Her slicker was open and under the soaked shirt her breast, made extra taut by the cold, jutted out. How could he have missed something so obvious?

Cris remained completely still, enduring the probing examination. She wiped a raindrop from the point of her nose. "Well, am I male or female?"

"Who are you?"

"My name is Cristine Tarpenning. Does that mean anything to you?"

"Tarpenning! My God!" Luke exclaimed in disbelief. Then he saw the likeness, the perfect oval of the face—like Morning Mist's—and the large eyes, a mixture of daring and steadfastness—Morning Mist again. However, the color of skin and hair was a lighter shade than that of the

Indian girl, a gift from George Tarpenning. She was also taller than Morning Mist, another characteristic of Tarpenning.

The inheritance from Morning Mist dominated. Luke shook his head in awe and wonderment.

Putting out his hand, he strode toward her through the slush of hail. Cris flinched at the sudden motion. Then she saw the tender expression on his face.

"Morning Mist's child," he whispered and touched the smoothness of her cheek with his fingertips. Tears gathered quickly and moistened his eyes. "George Tarpenning's child."

He lifted his face to the damp sky and laughed happily.

Cris watched the big man. The emotion on the strained countenance was real. This man had not harmed her mother.

"I carried you inside my shirt for two days looking for a full teat for you to nurse. Almost rode my horse to death searching. Then I found the Clarks. Just the right family to bring you up. Much better than one wild beaver trapper."

His features darkened. "They ran off with you. When I went to Independence to see you that first fall, they had already left. No word at all where they were going. The people in town told me they went west. I waited and waited for a letter or some word. Nothing ever came."

"We went to San Francisco," said Cris softly. "I grew up there. Father hauled freight along the coast road."

"You call Clark father? They never told you the truth? How did you know to come find me?"

"They told me this last spring. Described how you came up on their wagon train and gave them many furs and guns to look after me. You told them you had killed my mother."

Coldiron shook his head in the negative. But before he could speak, Cris continued. "Business was bad and they had been thinking of going to California. After what you said, they decided to go and just make me one of theirs."

"I wished they had told me. It has been a long time."

"Morning Mist. You called my mother Morning Mist. Was she Indian?"

"Yes, Arapaho. The most beautiful woman I have ever seen. A horse threw her. A mountain lion frightened it and it fell with her. She died a few hours after you were born." He looked penetratingly at her. "She is buried in the valley. I'll show you where."

Cris shivered, half at the cold, half at the flood of news.

Luke saw she was wet through, cold and exhausted. "We must find the stampeded horses and get a fire built to warm us up. They went with the storm. Nor far I would guess. We'll ride double."

He mounted the dun and pointed at the toe of his boot. Cris stepped up on the makeshift stirrup. He caught her by the hand and swung her in behind him. The horse headed to the north under Luke's pressure on the reins.

"I'm glad you are here, very glad," Luke said over his shoulder.

Cris thought she heard a break in his voice.

"Soon as we dry off, we'll beeline straight back for the ranch," he said.

The fire crackled and sparks rose vertically upward in the still air. They stood close to the flames, thawing out slowly. Both were silent, each thinking private thoughts.

The runaway animals had been found in less than a quarter hour. They seemed glad to see the humans and Luke easily caught them.

Knowing the patterns of such storms as had just occurred, Luke took a route at right angles to the drift of the thunderhead and down toward the Rio Grande. The area of rain and hail ended before the riders reached the river. A fire of dry driftwood was soon blazing on the bank of the stream.

Coldiron spread his hands to the warmth. Old memories came crowding back. He recalled the long journeys with George Tarpenning, this girl's father. They had trod some bad trails, some he could never brag about. That was many years ago. Yes, many years ago. A baby had grown into a woman since then.

He cast a glance at that young woman. Her face was tilted to the fire. A slight heat flush tinged her cheeks. She raised delicate fingers to her brow in a gesture of contemplation.

"Your father and I were partners for several years. That last year he was alive, we made a fair haul of furs. Also, I took the pelts of the men who killed him. I planned to use his share to pay for your care and schooling. Since I could not get that money to the Clarks, I invested it in the ranch. Therefore, you are part owner of the best horse ranch in all the New Mexico Territory. How does that feel to you?"

"That isn't necessary. You have spent most of your life building the ranch. I do not deserve such generosity."

"George would have done the same for me. We'll draw up the papers soon as we get to Santa Fe."

"I haven't done anything to give me the right to make a claim on my father's money."

"You do not have to make a claim, it is simply yours. I have no doubt you are his daughter. We can be in Santa Fe in three days."

"And let the horse thieves get away with the herd."

"They've set us back a year or so alright. But we'll make it up."

"What would my father have said about letting them escape."

"George Tarpenning was one of the bravest men I ever knew and no one took anything from him. He would say 'Damn it, pard, we got to make those horse-stealing bastards sorry they ever stepped foot on our ranch.' "

Cris stared directly into Luke's eyes and, lowering her voice to try to imitate his deep tones, said, "Damn it, pard, we got to make those horse-stealing bastards sorry they ever stepped foot on our ranch."

Luke smiled. "They surely should be made to pay."

"I mean what I just said. We'll go after them."

The smile faded from Luke's lips. "It's too dangerous."

"You were ready to take me two hours ago."

"Then I thought you were a young man, not a woman."

"Don't bullets kill young men just as dead as young women? And don't partners have equal say in what is to be done to keep the ranch safe? When the story gets out someone got away with a big part of your herd, won't that bring other thieves to try? I say we ride south after them."

Coldiron measured Cris, trying to determine how much of what she said was false bravado and how much solid courage. He made his judgment and said, "Then we ride south to Mexico. For that's really where they are heading."

Luke saw the shadow of a smile in the back of her eyes.

They rode the remainder of the day away along the El Camino Real in foot pursuit of the thieves. In the edge of the falling darkness, they climbed down stiff and weary from their horses and made camp.

Cris cast a wary eye at the cloud banks hanging over the mountains, both to east and west and threatening to bring their moisture into the valley. "Do you think it will rain?" she asked.

"I doubt it," said Luke.

"Well, I'm not going to worry about it." She placed her slicker near and stretched out on her blankets.

They slept through the dark night and were not bothered by the ill-tempered wind that gusted and whined and made the reeds of the grass whisper.

Morning found the clouds gone except for a high thin layer in the east. The sun exploded over the horizon and filled half the heavens with great swirls of purple and pink and flaming scarlet.

"Today we might catch us a horse thief," said Luke as they mounted and the big stallion set the pace.

Cris felt a chill run up her spine at what those words meant—a fight, maybe death for one or both of them. Where was the hot courage of yesterday? She did not respond to Luke's comment, afraid her voice would give away her true feeling.

Luke's eyes leaped the miles ahead. Somewhere there, two days' ride or less in the hazy distance, lay Mexico. Throughout the entire chase, mountains had been on every horizon. As the journey proceeded south, those high elevations had decreased and the forest cover worked its way up to the very topmost peaks and finally disappeared altogether. Now, to the full limit of vision in front of them, only short mountains and hills existed, barren and rocky, fading into the desert of Mexico.

They rode the heat, pushing hard for many hours with brush and cactus on all sides.

Francisco Campins woke and stretched. The bell calling the peons back to the fields after the siesta still sounded. He arose from the plush leather couch of his bedroom and went out onto the stone patio in front of the hacienda.

Reyes Campins also heard the bell tolling and climbed out of a net hammock in the shade under a giant cottonwood. He waved and smiled at his father. Without delay he tightened the cinch of the saddle on his horse and rode off down the slope toward the irrigated fields near the river.

"I would say he was a good son," spoke a voice behind Francisco.

Campins recognized the sonorous tones of his friend General Luis Padilla and turned to face the powerfully built man in the immaculate blue and red uniform. "Yes. A very fine son. Did you have a pleasant rest after your travel from Mexico City?"

The general had arrived shortly before noon. Leaving his escort of soldiers below in the town of Tuscora, he ascended to the top of the hill and Campins's hacienda. He arrived in time for a light lunch and then a nap in a shaded corner room where a cool breeze blew.

"Yes, a good rest. I always enjoy a few days at your beautiful home," answered the general.

"Thank you for the kind words."

"Francisco, you are a very fortunate man. Your sons make you proud, and you own one of the best ranchos in all the State of Chihuahua."

"I feel satisfied with my life," replied Campins. "My younger son, Reyes, cares for the crops and is attentive to the needs of the peons to keep them productive workers. My second son is equally industrious in tending the cattle and sheep."

"Ah, yes," smiled the general, "and you personally manage the silver mine. Isn't it off there in those quartz hills to the northeast?"

Francisco did not answer. Padilla knew exactly where the mine was. They stood together, relaxed in an old friendship of thirty years.

Campins gazed down into the valley with its lush green fields, orchards and the brown adobe village, then beyond the cultivated land to the rolling hills, turning yellow in the late-summer dry period. Even from this elevation he could not see the far-off boundaries of Rancho Tuscora.

Eighty years earlier his father had gained control of the widely flung holdings—a quarter million acres of excellent grassland and two thousand acres of rich bottomland. The dependable Rio Tuscora watered the flatland lavishly. Two hundred peons lived in the village of Tuscora. He owned all of this. He was a rich man.

He saw two horsemen coming along the main valley road that stretched from El Paso through Tuscora and continued all the way to Mexico City. The riders turned onto the private roadway leading up the slope and, with little puffs of dust trailing them, approached the house.

"*Buenos días*, Señor Campins," said Macrina Archuleta.

"Welcome, Señor Archuleta. Please dismount," Campins greeted him.

The tall one-time colonel of the Mexican Army stepped down.

"Señor Archuleta, please meet General Luis Padilla. General, Macrina Archuleta has a rancho twenty-five miles or so north of Rancho Tuscora."

The two men acknowledged the introduction.

"Come, both of you, and have a cool glass of wine with me," said Campins.

Archuleta tossed the reins of his mount to Muniz and stalked off beside Campins and Padilla into the shade of the large stone and adobe casa of the rancho. He quaffed his wine slowly and observed the rich Campins and the general. Campins had inherited a large rancho and through diligent effort had increased its value greatly. A very honest man. The general was a ruthless soldier and it was said he took more bribes than any other three generals in the Army.

"Are you ready to deliver the horses we discussed in the spring?" asked Campins.

"I will bring them to Tuscora in the morning two days from now," responded Archuleta.

"I would prefer you to bring them to my corrals in the bend of the Rio Tuscora five miles north of the village. We can use the cutting pens there to separate out the horses I will buy. I shall bring the gold to pay you at the same time. General Padilla will help me in the selection of the horses."

"That is very satisfactory," said Archuleta.

"I trust they will be equally good as the few you showed me when we first discussed this arrangement," said Campins.

"They will be even better," smiled Archuleta. "For a man as discriminating for quality as you, I have sorted through my herd very carefully and only the very best will be presented to you."

The general silently watched the bargaining. He knew the purpose of Campins's acquisition of the horses. They were to be given to him for his army. When he had first met Campins they had both been young lieutenants, their commissions bought by wealthy parents. Campins had served three years and then left to return and operate the family rancho, while he had continued on with the military. Now Francisco was securing army commissions for his two sons by a gift of two hundred horses, easily worth thirty thousand pesos in gold.

The general agreed with Campins plan. The military training, and better still the friends and contacts made in high places, made for a fuller and richer life.

Padilla spoke to Archuleta. "Your brand is a strange one. What is it called?"

"The Wolf Trap Brand."

"Have you used it long?"

"I designed it two years ago."

"Very unusual," said the general.

"Another glass, my friends," invited Campins. He poured the deliciously aged wine and raised his goblet. "To beautiful horses."

Luke and Cris rode the El Camino Real, following the well-used roadway where it skirted the base of the Sierra de Las Uvas Mountains and held west of the Rio Grande. At the extreme southern end of the mountains the road forded the river, to avoid the steep little chain of rocky peaks called the Robledos, and continued on its course to Mexico.

The Rio Grande, once free of the crowding flank of the Robledos, found a gentle grade and spread its flow into several braided channels to create a great marsh. Nourished by the abundant river water, the miles of luxuriant green growth of grass, sedges and phreatophyte brush and trees rested like a turquoise jewel among the brown desert mountains.

"It is beautiful, like another world," said Cris.

Luke barely nodded. He was worried as he measured the height of the sun already beginning its plummeting fall behind the horizon. He stopped and Cris pulled her mount up close to him.

"We are about twenty miles north of El Paso," said Coldiron. "We should have come up on one of the bands of stolen horses by now. Only one bunch has come to water at the Rio Grande since noon. I think now we should've taken after that one."

"Do you suppose they are all on the opposite side of the river?"

"No. From the sign we have seen, all, or at least most of the thieves are on this side. I think it means we are within a day's ride of where the animals are to end up."

"Then how do we get on to a trail that'll take us to that spot?"

Coldiron faced to the east. "We can strike off that direction and I bet we'll cut fresh tracks in an hour or two. Then we'll turn after it and follow it to the end."

"It'll be dark in a few minutes," said Cris.

"Let's find a spot to make camp."

The sun dipped the last remaining part of its great red body below the edge of the earth and the shadows of twilight began to form. And a million mosquitoes rose up from their day-long rest in the marsh. They swarmed upon the two riders.

"We can never sleep near the river," said Luke, fanning the small black insects from his face with his hand. "We'll have to get away from the water and find a high point where some wind will be blowing to keep them off us. First we'll water the ponies and then we'll be ready for a fifty- or sixty-mile ride tomorrow."

They traveled directly away from the river, working upward toward a shoulder of a small rocky mountain.

Coldiron suddenly jerked his mount to a halt. "Freeze!" he hissed. "Don't move. There's a man with a string of horses to the right down in that arroyo. Appears like he has just come up from the river."

CHAPTER 21

Cuadrado and Trujillo sat leaning against the head-high stone cairn that marked the boundary between the New Mexico Territory and Texas.

"I do not like to work with gringos," said Trujillo. "And to sit in the hot sun all day and wait for them is even worse." He rubbed his hands over his beard and spat on the ground. An itch developed on his back and he scratched the spot on a sharp, projecting rock of the border monument.

"Our *patrón* has ordered us to meet Kazian here and complete the payment for killing Coldiron," said Cuadrado.

"Do you think Kazian can beat Coldiron?"

"All five of them should be able to. I know five of us could."

"I believe we could do it easily, and with less than five men," said Trujillo. Restlessly he climbed to his feet and glanced both ways along the road that ran north and south past the marker. "El Camino Real is not busy. Not one wagon has passed the whole day."

"It is too hot for much travel. Business will increase in October. The days will be cooler then and people will be thinking of preparing for winter."

"There goes the last of the sun," said Trujillo, noting the shadows quickly gathering.

"Yes. We can leave now and go to that spring we found up in the hills. That place will make a good camp and we can take it easy until tomorrow morning."

"I am ready. I will go and get the horses." Trujillo climbed to his feet and walked to the brink of the bank above the broad, marshy valley of the Rio Grande. Both Cuadrado's and his mounts grazed below him in the edge of the green grass.

In an abandoned oxbow of the river, a gray crane stood vigilantly rigid on ramrod legs and watched the human. A flock of homing ducks, hurrying to beat the night, glided in on stiff wings to land on the deeper portion of the pond of water. A good feast on some of those would be very fine, thought Trujillo. He turned away from the river to ask Cuadrado if he should try to kill one or two of the birds.

Trujillo's eye caught movement on the hill to the northeast. He cried out. "Fabio, is that one of our amigos?"

"Where?"

"There on the side of the hill. About half a mile." He pointed. "He has several horses with him."

"Could be."

"*Madre de Dios!*" exclaimed Trujillo. "Two riders are behind him and catching up fast."

"Quick! Saddle the horses. We must go and help."

The man with the string of horses was not aware of the riders closing rapidly from the rear. Night was swiftly falling and he intently searched ahead for a suitable stopping place.

Coldiron judged the distance still separating him from his long-sought quarry. In another two or three minutes he would be near enough to send the big dun in a charge at the man. No one could escape the dun in this open land.

Luke cast a look back to see how Cris was keeping up and saw two horsemen racing up from the river bottom. Even as he spotted the men, they raised their rifles and began to fire from the backs of the running mounts.

The range was long and the light failing, but the men continued to shoot. The bullets struck here and there, spanging off the hard ground, kicking up dust and wailing away.

The man with the chain of horses spurred and whipped his mount to the top of its speed, dragging the others behind. The cavalcade disappeared into the gloom and could not be seen.

Luke snatched his rifle out, yanked the dun to a halt and leaped down for a steady base from which to shoot. He aimed into the murky shadows at the approaching horsemen, tracking the front rider with the sights of his gun. The two men, having accomplished the goal of aiding the horse thief to escape and their weapons empty, spun their steeds around to make for safety themselves.

At the exact moment when the lead rider was stopped and not yet turned, Coldiron fired. The speeding bullet crashed through Cuadrado's chest, tearing him from the saddle. His horse thundered on ahead. Coldiron shifted his aim to the second man.

Cris's rifle crashed and the man's horse fell, tumbling end over end.

Luke waited for the man to rise. Then he was up, running at a hobbling gait. Luke's shot slammed him forward on his face.

"Hold the horses," Luke directed Cris. "Don't let them get away in the dark."

Cris grabbed a tight grip on the lead rope of the packhorse and the reins of the mounts. Still spooked at the booming noise of the guns, the animals backed away, hauling and pulling at her hold.

Coldiron came up to the men lying in crumpled heaps on the ground. Both were dead. He searched them.

Cris arrived towing the horses. In the dim light she saw a strange thing. "Luke, look at the brand on that horse. It's your brand!"

Luke stripped a heavy money belt from Cuadrado's waist and went to kneel by the dead horse. "My mark, but this is not one of my cayuses."

"How can you tell that out of the hundreds of horses you have?"

"The color is wrong for one thing. And I have developed my own herd. They are longer, larger animals. This is not one of mine."

"Then how did it get your brand?"

Luke squatted there, tracing the outline of the burn on the skin and thinking the impossible. "Someone has copied my brand. Damn them."

"Then you will never be able to prove your ownership, even if we find them. All of this killing has been for nothing."

They ate leisurely, savoring the thick steak, the pinto beans in rich soup, buttered corn bread and fresh milk. A large slice of watermelon culminated the delicious feast.

Luke finished eating and shoved back his chair. He looked through the window of the restaurant and into the dusty street of El Paso. Cris and he had ridden in during the forenoon after camping not far from the site of the gun fight with the Mexican outlaws.

They needed supplies. Also, they must now design a new plan since the thieves were using his brand.

Above all he wanted to keep this young woman safe. However, he found that was proving to be a difficult task. She was determined to take some action not to allow the thieves to go free—some form of revenge to discourage others from trying the same thing. She was as tough and hard as her father.

Luke looked at her face, examining the lines of weariness etched in the skin, burned a deep brown by the hot sun. The long days of fast riding had taken their toll. Still she seemed strong and willing to go on. He was proud of her. There was another emotion stirring, one he could not yet decipher. He acknowledged to himself that he liked to look at her, baggy clothes, shaggy haircut and all.

He grinned at her. "Was the meal worth riding fifteen miles?" he asked.

With her stomach pleasingly full of the tasty food, Cris forgot the long, tiring ride of the past days and chuckled lightly.

Luke enjoyed the pleasant ripple of her laughter. His grin broadened. "For a pardner that has lost several thousand dollars worth of horse flesh, you seem in good spirits."

Her smile faded. Luke was sorry for his remark that saddened her.

"How much gold was in the money belt you took from that dead Mexican?" she asked.

"A little over three thousand dollars."

"Why do you suppose he was carrying so much gold?"

"I don't know. Let's ask around and see if we can find out who hereabouts is using the Steel Trap Brand."

"Alright."

They left the restaurant and, leaving their animals tied to the hitch rail, walked slowly along the dusty street.

"The stockyards should be the best place to find out about brands," said Coldiron. "I see it down at the end of the street near the river."

A man on horseback finished herding a small bunch of cattle into a holding corral and shut the gate on them. Coldiron called out to him and the man walked his horse in their direction. He ran his eye over the dusty, trail-worn appearance of the tall man and the young person in the oversized clothing. A strange pair.

"Howdy," said Luke.

"Hello." The man stopped his mount. "Something I can do for you?"

"Sure is. I'm trying to find out who runs a brand shaped like this." Luke squatted in the dirt and traced the pattern so familiar to him.

"Macrina Archuleta runs that brand on his horses. He calls it Wolf Trap Brand."

"Anybody else have stock with this mark?"

"Nope. But a big Mexican rancher named Campins living south of here will soon have horses with the brand. I hear he is getting ready to buy a sizable herd of horses from Archuleta."

"Do you know this Archuleta?"

"I know him," said the man shortly. "Do you plan to do business with him?"

"Maybe. Is there anything wrong about him?"

"You being American, I'm going to tell you something. He's a thief, horses, cattle. You just name it. If he can take it from a gringo, he has stolen it. Also without any doubt, he's the fastest man with a six-gun in these parts."

"And Campins?"

"I hear he's an honest hombre. But that is hearsay. I know he pays prompt and full for anything he buys in El Paso."

"How does he feel about gringos?"

"I can't say for sure. From his actions, I say he hates them less than most Mexicans do."

Coldiron was thinking swiftly. "How do I find the rancho of this man Campins?"

"Can't miss it. His land starts eighteen miles south of town and you're on it for the next fifteen. Just stay on the main-traveled road to the south. That'll be along the Rio Tuscora. His hacienda sits on the hill above the town of Tuscora. Big adobe and stone house painted white."

"Thanks," said Luke. A plan had jelled in his mind. Now to discuss it with Cris and see if she was game to try it.

Cris had to trot to keep up as they hurried back to their horses.

Coldiron and Cris speedily crossed the lands of Campins and rode down into the green, moist valley of the Rio Tuscora. The horses, lathered with sweat, stopped on their own volition at the first full irrigation ditch and began to pull at the water with noisy swigs. The riders stepped down to ease their seats.

Luke roamed his cautious sight over the scores of peons laboring in the fields. Some workers were chopping weeds with long-handled hoes. In other fields, needing to be irrigated, water from the main ditches was being diverted into corrugations to flood the thirsty soil.

The nearest workman straightened to get the ache out of his body and watch the two gringo horsemen. He saw the day was old and, laying his irrigating shovel over his shoulder, moved down from the field and into the road.

"The horses are hot so that's enough drink for them now," said Coldiron. He and Cris remounted and, pulling the reluctant heads of the ponies up from the water, continued along the roadway.

Other peons carrying their hoes and shovels in calloused hands came straggling out of the fields. They tagged to the rear of the Americans, gradually falling behind the faster pace of the horses.

"This must be Campins's peon town of Tuscora ahead," said Luke.

"Didn't that man in El Paso say Campins's casa was on the hill above the town. Well, I believe I can see a large white house up there," Cris pointed.

The street was of dirt and lined with the small flat-topped adobe homes of the workers. Tall cottonwoods grew on the banks of the irrigation ditches that watered the gardens present near most every house. Boisterous brown-skinned children played, wading the ditches with bare feet, running in and out of the open doors or gathering together in various games in the shade of the trees.

"Soldiers in front of the cantina," said Coldiron. "Damnation, that's bad luck."

"They see us already. Won't they be friendly?"

"Plenty unlikely. What are they doing in a little peon village like Tuscora? Usually the patrons of the hacienda appoint a constable to keep order."

"What can they do to us?"

"The Army has almost unlimited authority. The soldiers, especially the officers, are still angry at the Americans for whipping them and taking New Mexico and Texas. We could be in real trouble if they decide to take a little revenge."

"Shoot us?"

"More likely lock us up in one of their *calabosos* and forget us."

"They couldn't do that."

"They could and would. Just act like we belong here." Coldiron raised his hand in greeting as they drew close to the dozen soldiers lounging on a long wooden bench in the shade in front of the town cantina. *"Buenos días,"* Luke called.

A couple of soldiers halfheartedly nodded back at him. Most watched sullenly from black, hostile eyes. The one nearest the door of the cantina stuck his head inside and spoke to someone.

A lieutenant walked outside and, squinting into the slanting rays of the westering sun, looked the riders over. "Sergeant Charris, bring four men and come with me. Bring your rifles," he ordered and stalked out into the road to block the way. The soldiers fell into step behind him, their weapons at the ready.

The lieutenant called in Spanish, "Americans, what are you doing in Mexico? Why are you in Tuscora?"

Luke answered in the same language. "I wish to speak with Señor Campins."

"For what purpose?"

"It is personal. But he will want to see me." Luke doubted the last statement was fully true.

The lieutenant looked skeptical. He tugged at a short mustache. "Very well, but it is best that we escort you there to see that everything is as you say." He spoke to Charris. "Saddle six horses and we will ride up to the Casa de Campins."

"Yes, Lieutenant. At once," said the sergeant.

Campins and General Padilla sat talking in low tones in the coolness of the hacienda porch. At the sound of numerous iron-shod horses on the stone of the courtyard they stopped their conversation. They exchanged glances and the general arose to loosen his pistol in its holster.

The general had made many enemies and now he stood warily facing the direction the new arrivals would come. Almost immediately the lieutenant, accompanied by some of his military escort and two Americans, rode into view. With Campins following, Padilla strode out to meet the group of horsemen.

"What is the problem, Lieutenant Gonzalez?" questioned the general.

Gonzalez sat very erect in the saddle and saluted. "These *americanos* say they have come to Tuscora to see Señor Campins." His view rested briefly on Campins and then back to Padilla. "I thought we should come with them to insure the Señor's safety."

"You did correctly, Lieutenant," said the general. He stepped to the side, spread his legs and evaluated the dusty gringos.

Luke looked briefly at the square-built general and then at the slender man watching him questioningly. "You are Señor Campins?" Luke asked.

"Yes, Francisco Campins. This is General Padilla. What can I do for you?"

"My name is Luke Coldiron. I have a horse ranch north of Santa Fe. May I speak with you alone?"

Campins hesitated a moment to study the bewhiskered face of the American. Then he said, "Luis, would you have your soldiers move over to the shade of the trees? However, I wish you would remain and listen for I may need your advice."

"As you wish, *mi amigo*," said Padilla. "Lieutenant, please do as Señor Campins requested. Take the young Americano with you."

The soldiers watched Cris expectantly and waited. Luke did not like for Cris to be separated from him. That would make it difficult for him to protect her. However, if he wanted to talk to Campins, he had no choice.

Coldiron locked his eyes on the general. This man was the dangerous one. I will kill me a general if any harm comes to her, Coldiron promised himself. Padilla read the open threat and he blinked at the intensity of its force.

Luke nodded at Cris and she reined away. The soldiers trailed after her.

"Now, Señor Coldiron, what is it you have to say to me?" asked Campins.

"Señor Campins, I have heard you are an honest man. Therefore, I have come to ask for your help."

There was a flicker of surprise on Campins's face, then a measure of satisfaction.

Coldiron continued to speak. "A week or so ago, a band of men stole a herd of my horses. I have traced them to Mexico. I believe the horses are to be sold to you."

He is talking about Archuleta, thought Campins. It has to be the thief Archuleta. "That is a very serious charge. Who has taken your horses?"

"A man named Macrina Archuleta. I understand he has a ranch near here."

"The man does have a rancho near here. But how do you know he has stolen your animals?"

Luke pointed at the hip of the dun. "See the brand on my horse. Is that mark familiar to you?"

"That is the Wolf Trap Brand of Archuleta," said Campins examining the hairless burn scar with his eye.

"No. That's not correct. That is my Steel Trap Brand. I have been running it for twenty years. Anyone in Santa Fe can tell you that is the truth. How long has this man Archuleta been using his so called Wolf Trap Brand?"

"Only a couple of years," said Campins.

"Why would a man copy another's brand? Would it be to hide a theft?"

"Enough!" thundered the general. "*Madre de Dios*, what gall. You *americanos* are the greatest thieves in the world. In the last twenty years, you have stolen half of Mexico. You are our enemies. Now you come into Mexico without permission. Then accuse one of our people of stealing your horses. For proof you show the brand on one animal." He swung around to face Campins. "*Amigo* Campins, we must not be taken in by this gringo."

Campins looked from one man to the other. He believed the man Coldiron very likely spoke the truth. Luis is not stupid; he must also see the logic of the claim. Yet he is taking a strong stand to side with

Archuleta. The general in him would not let him aid the *americanos*. Lost battles were not soon forgiven, nor forgotten. Campins sighed. He wanted the officer commissions for his sons very badly.

The American's voice cut through his thoughts. "Señor Campins, I request your assistance in having my property returned to me."

General Padilla abruptly stepped toward Coldiron. His face was stiff with animosity. He spoke over his shoulder to Campins. "Francisco, let me attend to this gringo liar. I know how to deal with such as he."

"Luis, he may be telling the truth. Perhaps we should investigate the matter."

"I have no time to waste on such ridiculous tales," snorted the general. "Tomorrow I return to Mexico City."

Campins swiftly evaluated the possible solutions to this dilemma. If he forced the issue with the general, the commissions for his sons would go south with that hotheaded hombre. The solution lay with the *americano*. How brave are you Coldiron? Are you strong enough to take back what is yours?

"Señor Coldiron, tomorrow morning I am going to meet with Archuleta at the big bend of the river north of Tuscora. I have corrals there. I will buy two hundred horses and pay in gold. So you see I agree with General Padilla."

"The people who know you have made a very big mistake," said Coldiron in a hard tone. "They believe you to be a fair and just man. Today you have proved them wrong."

Campins flinched at the harsh words. "Think about my words and judge me after you have time to reflect," said Campins.

"No more insults to my friend Campins!" roared the general. He jerked his arm for the soldiers to come.

At the sudden motion, Coldiron's hand flashed down and touched the butt of his six-gun before he could halt his draw. Padilla had been looking at his soldiers and did not see the threatening action, but Campins had observed it. This *Americano* was brave, for he must know once his weapon came out a battle would begin. One against many to the death.

The general called an order. "Lieutenant, take these two gringos north off Señor Campins's rancho."

"Yes, Sir." The lieutenant saluted.

Padilla turned a hate-filled face to Coldiron. "I give you one warning, and that is only because of my friend Campins. You have made an accusation against a citizen of Mexico. A false claim, I am certain, to gain possession of his property. That is a serious crime. If you are ever found again in Mexico, I will hang you. Now get out of my country."

CHAPTER 22

In a small steep-sided canyon in the tall hills north of the Rio Tuscora, Cris and Luke rested near a small fire. Beyond the glow created by the leaping flames, deep darkness surrounded them. A light rain had fallen just at dusk, but now the sky was clear.

The soldiers had escorted them from the Rio Tuscora Valley and some five miles toward El Paso before turning back. During the ride Luke kept a guarded watch on the Mexicans, for he did not know what scheme they might have to do Cris and him harm. He saw Cris was also cautious and alert to the actions of the men.

By the time the courtyard was left behind, Coldiron had reasoned out the meaning and importance of Campins's departing statement. Once out of sight of Padilla's soldiers Luke called a halt.

"Since you are my partner, I should tell you what Campins told me. It's enough so we can make one last try at getting our mustangs back. If we want to take a big gamble."

"What did he tell you?"

"Campins is going to buy two hundred head of horses from Archuleta and pay in gold. They will meet on the river above Tuscora tomorrow."

"We can never take the horses back and drive them out of Mexico without getting caught," said Cris.

"You are right. But we might figure out a plan to maybe take the gold. We could haul that back with us. Do you want to talk about it?"

"We'll have to be careful the mad general doesn't catch us."

"It'll be very dangerous."

"I'm with you. Let's do it."

"Don't be so quick. We need to think this thing through. First we'll look over the land where Campins will meet Archuleta."

Before dark they had reached the top of the range of hills nearest the bend of the river. "I'm sure this is the place Campins meant," said Luke.

He surveyed the terrain spread below him. The river, lined with brush and trees, flowed north to south in the center of a two-mile-wide floodplain. The flat bottom grew a thick stand of grass. A few patches of dark green brush were randomly spotted about in the grass.

He could see the corrals, the road coming in from the northeast, the direction Archuleta should arrive, and from the opposite way the route of Campins. Until full dusk Luke studied the possibilities for ambush.

In the early night they retreated from the rim of the basin and found the hidden canyon.

In the ruddy illumination of the fire, they cleaned their rifles and pistols and argued the points of their plan for the morning. At one point, Cris's voice rose angrily, "I can do it and I will do it. Your part of the thing is just as dangerous as mine."

The voices fell back to a normal level. They talked into the night. As they finished discussing tactics, a tiniest puff of air, a mere whisper, came and went, so weak the flame of the fire did not flicker at all. They looked at each other to see if it had been heard or felt by someone else, to see if it had been real at all. And their eyes touching had a pleasant feel.

Finally the fire burned down for the last time and they went to their blankets. Cris slipped off into sleep; however, in that instant before it took her completely, she sensed a safe feeling knowing Luke was close there in the darkness. Her lips curved in a smile as she slept.

Cris lay on the top of a long low ridge flanking the floodplain of the Rio Tuscora and watched the road Macrina Archuleta would travel. The dawn was absolutely still and the grass glimmered with a silver film of dew from the moisture of the past evening's rainstorm.

Off to her right on the valley bottom, and miniaturized by a distance of almost two miles, sprawled the corrals of Campins. Traversing the valley from end to end, the road made its way straight across the open grass-covered land.

The morning was cool and Cris shivered, not all from the dampness of the grass beneath her. She was afraid and began to doubt her courage.

Guided by Luke's unerring sense of direction, they had ridden to the bend of the Rio Tuscora through the night gloom. He had taken her by the shoulders in the darkness and asked, "Are you still sure you want to go on with this?"

Her answer had come much stronger than she felt. "Yes. Let's do it."

Luke had vanished into the blackness, the sound of his horse's feet on the ground lasting but a few seconds. She had rested through the remainder of the night, waiting for the thief to come and the fight to start.

The sun struggled upward, wresting its orange sphere loose from the horizon. The dew began to disappear, whisked up by the warming day breeze. A herd of horses, like a cluster of tiny black ants, entered the valley on the upper end.

The drove of horses crossed the width of the valley. When they were opposite Cris, she heard the muffled rumble of the hundreds of hooves on the hard ground. The herd drifted onward and arrived at the corrals.

Cris waited. The sun turned hot. Luke's stallion, tied to a bush below the peak of the hill, pawed the stony ground fitfully.

Horsemen separated from the dark outline of the corrals and returned back the route to the north. They rode swiftly, galloping their mounts. Their voices calling in good humor reached Cris on the hilltop.

The group of riders drew near the center of the flat plain. Cris stood up, took a deep breath to steady her resolve and hastened to climb upon the back of the long-legged stallion. She pulled her rifle from its scabbard. The horse went willingly up over the crest of the hill and down the slope facing the valley. At the bottom, she touched the stallion gently with her spurs and he broke into a fast canter.

The Mexican horsemen saw her the moment she came over the ridge. They stopped and watched her. A small band of unridden horses, those not sold to Campins, wandered on ahead.

Cris approached the men rapidly. The distance closed to less than a quarter mile and she counted eight riders. Could two people take a large quantity of gold from eight gunmen? She thought not. There were too many for Luke and her to beat. But the play was started and she could not stop it.

Archuleta calmly sat his mount among his *pistoleros*. He expected no trouble from the lone rider and waited to see what was wanted. He cast his eye to check the heavy load of gold on the packhorse. From old caution he ranged his sight out over the grassy plain and the five or six patches of stunted brush, barely taller than the grass, and investigated the surrounding hills and the brush and trees of the riverbank. No enemy was in sight. Anyplace one could hide was at least a half mile away.

At a range of an extremely long rifle shot, Cris dragged the dun to a halt and leaped down with her weapon. She dropped to one knee for a steady position and sighted quickly at a rider in the center of the group. With the outlaws clustered close together like that she should be able to hit at least one. She squeezed the trigger.

The man tumbled from the saddle. Instantly she levered in another cartridge and fired. A horse crashed down, pinning its rider beneath. Cris shot again and again, emptying her gun, hardly aiming in her excitement and haste. She whirled to mount the stallion.

The brute, used mostly to Luke, shied away from this less well-known human rushing it. Cris made a dash and grabbed for the trailing reins, but the horse pivoted and trotted off a few feet.

Fear that she would not be able to catch the dun nearly panicked her. She heard the crack of rifles and bullets whizz past her, striking the ground and ricocheting onward with a deadly keening buzz.

Her hand closed on the leather reins just as the sound of shouting men and the thunder of racing horses reached her.

Cris dropped the rifle to free her hands. She rammed her foot into the almost too high stirrup and with the strength born of fright yanked herself into the saddle. She jerked the dun's head toward the hill and jammed her sharp spurs cruelly into his ribs, raking him savagely.

The large beast threw clods of dirt and in two strides was in a flat-out run. Cris almost lost her balance and grabbed the horn to keep from being thrown from her seat by the quickness of the stallion.

The wind began to swish past her face. She looked behind and found three pursuers. They were within two hundred yards, bent over the necks of their mounts, beating them with riding whips.

She thought the dun was at its fastest pace, yet she spurred him again. To her amazement the great animal lengthened his stride, his legs reaching for every possible inch of ground.

She had ridden swiftly before, but never like this. The speed was unbelievable. Now she knew why Luke had insisted she take the dun. "He can outrun any horse in Mexico. Point his head where you want to go. Watch behind and stay close enough to pull Archuleta's men after you for a ways. Then spur and run off and leave them in the dust."

Cris lay forward on the long muscular neck and fastened her sight on the beckoning hill.

She glanced backward as the edge of the plain was reached. The Mexicans were dropping behind. She must not get so far ahead that they would become discouraged and turn back. She tugged at the reins to slow the stallion.

They struck the upgrade of the slope and she allowed her pursuers to come closer, hoping that on the rough trail they could not hit with a rifle shot.

Even as that thought flashed in her mind, a hot bullet nicked her shoulder and she flinched at the stab of pain. A shout of satisfaction sounded and more shots zinged around her. She spurred the stallion to the full limit of his speed. He charged the rocky slope, climbing in rock-rattling lunges, drawing their pursuers behind him.

Coldiron lay pressed flat to the ground in the small patch of short greasewood beside the road. Hardly a hand width taller than his chest, the brush barely hid him. A man on horseback, if he was watchful, would be able to see him from a short distance. But then that man would be within range of Luke's rifle.

Luke had hidden in the trees of the riverbank until Archuleta had passed with the stolen horses. Then he had wormed his way through the brown grass to the cluster of a score or so of greasewood and crawled into the densest part of them. There would be no retreat from this ambush.

The dull thump of many horses coming along the roadway drifted over the floodplain. Luke heard the men talking and clasped his rifle close to him. The shooting would soon commence.

All sound ceased. Coldiron raised his head and peered through the top of a bush. Archuleta and his men were a hundred yards away, sitting on their mounts and looking to the northwest. Beyond them Cris was in sight on the open face of the hillside. She reached the plain and rode directly toward the outlaws.

Luke marveled at her courage. But he knew he was a fool to place her in such danger. Bullets could kill a young woman as easily as a man. If he could have called out to her at that moment, he would have sent her racing back into the hills and to the safety from the guns of the bandits.

He halted his thoughts. She was close to the thieves now. Too damn close! And still riding straight upon them.

Luke's mind yelled at her. Stop! Cris, Stop! You are within gun range. They will kill you.

She stopped, jumped down and began to shoot. When the first man fell, Luke realized Cris had intentionally come near enough to destroy part of their foes, to increase his chance of escaping from this fight alive. His heart jumped at the realization of her daring, maybe her sacrifice.

One of Archuleta's men shouted to the others, "He cannot catch his horse. Let's kill him."

"It is a trick. The man is a decoy," cried Archuleta. But his voice was drowned out by the thunder of horses as three of his gang sped toward Cris. Only his experienced *pistoleros,* Muniz, Ochoa and Barrera, stayed to guard the gold. Ochoa was trapped under his *caballo* and would be no help in a gunfight. Archuleta wished Cuadrado and Trujillo were here to help in the battle he knew was coming.

Coldiron saw the jeopardy Cris was in. He coiled upward on his knee from the brush and lifted his rifle. He would fire on the men and stop their charge on Cris.

Before he could shoot, Cris captured the reins of the stallion and
sprang astride. The horse stampeded away with her clinging to his back.

Coldiron lowered himself back into the brush. His hands were trembling at the nearness of Cris's being hurt and the whole scheme's falling
apart.

He waited two minutes, counting slowly, then once more rose up from
the brush and looked hastily. Cris and her pursuers had vanished over
the hilltop. One of the remaining thieves had stepped from his mount
and stood near the man pinned under his horse. The other two men
were scanning the hills to the west, the way Cris had gone.

Coldiron recognized one of the men still on horseback. It was the
Mexican who had aided him in Santa Fe. That would be Archuleta.

Muniz, the man on the ground, took hold of the dead horse's legs and
heaved powerfully to roll it off his trapped companion. As he strained
with the effort, his head came up and his sight spied Coldiron's head and
shoulders rising above the brush.

"*Un hombre!*" Muniz yelled a shrill warning. He released his grip on
the horse and grabbed for his six-gun.

The range was short for a rifle and Coldiron exploded Muniz's heart
with the first bullet. He pivoted on his knee to bring the gun to bear on
Archuleta.

The gang leader had hurled himself from the saddle. The second man
was half dismounted. Luke snapped a shot at the slower man. Saw him
jerk as the lead slug ripped into his chest, knocking him to the ground.

Two riderless horses plunged off across the plain. Only Archuleta's
mount—a big black—and a packhorse tied to it remained.

Coldiron flicked one short look to locate Archuleta but could not see
him, obscured behind his horse. Instantly Luke flung himself down into
the bushes and scrabbled left.

A rifle bullet plowed the brush where he had been a fraction of a
second before.

"Coldiron, is that you?" called Archuleta.

Luke did not answer. The horse thief had the protection of a horse's
thick body. Luke's shield was to remain hidden in the stand of brush—a
very flimsy screen of tiny green leaves.

Three shots, evenly spaced along the length of the brush patch, sliced
through, clipping leaves and shattering greasewood stems.

"Coldiron, it is you. I have known all the time we must meet."

Luke peeked between the minute leaves of the greasewood, seeking to
find some part of the Mexican's body not completely shielded. Here and
there he could detect a fragment of pants or boots as the man kept his

legs directly behind those of the horse. He could see nothing of the man caught beneath his pony.

It was a standoff. Luke would kill the horse if Archuleta tried to leave using it as cover. Yet he could not escape either. His only degree of safety was in the small clump of brush. The grass that surrounded him on all sides was too short to hide him. He waited.

The sun was a fireball burning down. Sweat trickled down Luke's face. Through the foliage he cautiously eyed the hilltop for the return of the other gang members.

He could wait no longer. This fight had to be finished now for Cris might need his help. He would shoot the legs off the Mexican's horse in hopes of disabling Archuleta's legs at the same time. Then he would kill the man when he was in the open.

First he would try one thing, for he needed that horse. To catch another of the distantly scattered mustangs would waste valuable time. He placed his hands around his mouth and, funneling his voice off to the side to confuse the Mexican as to his true location, shouted out, "Archuleta, come out in the open and let's settle this with pistols."

Archuleta laughed. "Why should I? My men will be back in a little while. Then you will be a dead man."

"You're a damn coward, Archuleta. And I'm not waiting for your men to get back. I'm going to shoot your horse and then you. I'll give you ten seconds to step out where I can see you. It'll be a fair fight. Just with pistols."

Archuleta did not respond. The only sound on the plain was the soft rustle of the grass under the slow wind. Luke cocked his rifle to kill the horse.

"Coldiron, I accept your challenge," called Archuleta. "I have never been beaten with pistols. Let us both step into the open at the same moment."

Coldiron loosened his six-gun in its holster. "Good enough by me. On the count of three."

He counted loudly. "One! Two! Three!" And stood up into plain view —exposed.

Every muscle in him was tensed to hurl himself back into the brush if the Mexican did not instantly appear.

Archuleta stepped from behind his horse and into the open. He smiled, a tight wrinkling of his thin dark face, and dropped his rifle to the ground.

Coldiron let his rifle fall. He started to walk toward the gang leader. Damn you to hell for stealing my mustangs.

Archuleta stepped purposefully forward.

The distance was closed to fifty yards. Forty.

The Mexican stopped smiling. He took three more long strides and began to smile again.

Archuleta's hand darted down for his pistol.

Coldiron fingered his six-gun from its holster. He fired as Archuleta's gun lined up on him.

The Mexican's pistol blossomed smoke as the punch of Luke's bullet spun him to the right. His bullet slammed the ground in front of Luke and whined between his legs.

With a pain-contorted face, Archuleta twisted back to the front and mightily fought to bring his pistol up. Coldiron raised his six-gun and with deadly aim shot the thief through the forehead.

Luke whirled to face the man pinned by his horse.

Through the agony from the pain of his shattered leg, Ochoa had watched the gunfight. Now he saw Coldiron running toward him. He gritted his teeth at the misery of the horse's half-ton weight upon him and lifted his hand gun, striving to fix the dancing sights on Coldiron.

At the appearance of the gun Luke zigged right, then halted abruptly and shattered Ochoa's gun hand with a shot.

Coldiron knelt beside the wounded man, grabbed him by the hair of his head and shook him. "My name is Coldiron. Can you hear me?"

Ochoa tried to nod, could not because of Luke's tight grip. "*Sí,*" he said hoarsely.

"Archuleta is dead. I killed him because he stole my horses. You tell the rest of your gang what happened here. Do you understand me?"

"*Sí. Yo comprendo.*"

Luke hastened to the packhorse and untied the flap on one of the oversized saddlebags. Plunging his hand in, he lifted out one of several heavy leather pouches and poured a mound of gold into his hand. He replaced the pouch and reached over the packhorse to heft the opposite saddlebag to test its weight. Satisfied with his find, he retied the flap.

Luke swung astride Archuleta's big black horse. Dragging the packhorse with its load of gold, he spurred for the hills.

CHAPTER 23

Coldiron raced recklessly across the steep hills, hounding the trail of Cris and the Mexican outlaws who chased her. Archuleta's steed and the packhorse were excellent brutes and Luke pushed them to their topmost speed. They rushed up one high ridge after another, to swoop down into the dry washes between them with a crunch and clatter of gravelly bottoms.

The pursuit stretched onward. With each passing minute he grew more angry at himself for placing Cris in such great peril. Only the strength and swiftness of the dun could keep her safe. Yet even that surefooted mustang could have a misstep, a fall, and the bandits would be upon her. Or a well-aimed or lucky bullet could knock her down and stop her flight.

Many hard miles fell behind. The black and the packhorse became frothed with sweat. Still Luke held the valiant animals to the heart-bursting pace.

On a steep upgrade the tracks of three horses showed their gait had slackened to a walk and veered off to go along the contour of the hill. One set of hoofprints continued on, the stride still long. That would be Cris heading for El Paso as they had planned. Coldiron reined the black down to a lope and followed the sign of the lone mustang.

Later on the top of a tall hill, he found where the dun had stopped and stood for a little while and then went on at a walk. There were drops of blood crusting on the ground.

Cris or the horse was injured. Luke hoped fervently it was not Cris. He sent the black into an all out streaking run down the far hillside.

The course struck the bottom of the hill and proceeded across a broad flat. Less than a mile later, Luke saw the stallion standing motionless and Cris sitting slumped on the ground at his feet. A large red smear stained her shoulder.

He dashed up, jumped to the ground and was running toward her before his mount could slide to a halt.

Cris's head snapped up, her eyes startled and wide with alarm. Her six-gun jerked up to aim point-blank at him.

"Oh Luke! You are safe! I was so afraid for you." She lowered her weapon.

"You were worried about me?"

"Oh, yes." Her eyes glistened with tears. She climbed to her feet and stood near him.

"Why are you here? I wanted you to go to El Paso."

"I had your wonderful stallion. He could outrun any horse in the world. And the horse thieves turned off way back. So I just rested here in the shade of the horse until you would come. I guess I dozed off for a moment."

"How bad are you hurt?"

"Nothing serious. Just a scratch. It bled some, but I bandaged it. Did you get the gold?"

"Yes. It's on the packhorse." His eyes examined her pretty face. How could he tell her she meant more to him than all the yellow metal in Mexico.

"Then we did it." She laughed and reached out and touched his arm. "We can go home now."

Luke caught her hand, felt the soft, trusting cling of her fingers. She laughed again, happily.

At the tone of her voice, his mind leaped backward twenty years and he recalled the music of Morning Mist's voice and the devilish chuckle of George Tarpenning. Old partner, Luke thought, I could not keep Morning Mist safe and she died. I am truly sorry about her. I loved her, too. Now your daughter has given me the opportunity to make up for the promise I failed to carry out. She is worthy in her own right of special care. I will protect and advise her as my own daughter. It will be a very pleasant task.

Luke said, "Yes, we can go home to the ranch."

Cris rested her hand on his arm. "There was a sad expression on your face for a moment. Was it something I said or did?"

"I was remembering two friends of many years ago."

"My parents?"

"Yes."

"I want you to tell me all about them. Everything, even the smallest detail."

"I will do that. And I'll show you the grave of a very brave and wonderful woman."

"Let's hurry." She climbed astride the stallion and reined it to the north.

Luke mounted and fell in behind her. He knew Morning Mist and Tarpenning would understand his plan and approve. Somewhere, perhaps, they were smiling about now.

About the Author

F. M. Parker has worked as a sheepherder, lumberman, sailor, factory worker, geologist, and a manager of wild horses, buffalo, and livestock grazing. He currently manages five million acres of rangeland in eastern Oregon. He is the author of two previous Double D Westerns, *Skinner* and *Nighthawk*.